THE COURAGE OF
MARGE O'DOONE

MORE WILDSIDE CLASSICS

Please see www.wildsidepress.com for a complete list!

THE COURAGE OF MARGE O'DOONE

JAMES OLIVER CURWOOD

WILDSIDE PRESS

THE COURAGE OF MARGE O'DOONE

This edition published in 2006 by Wildside Press, LLC.
www.wildsidepress.com

CHAPTER I

If you had stood there in the edge of the bleak spruce forest, with the wind moaning dismally through the twisting trees — midnight of deep December — the Transcontinental would have looked like a thing of fire; dull fire, glowing with a smouldering warmth, but of strange ghostliness and out of place. It was a weird shadow, helpless and without motion, and black as the half Arctic night save for the band of illumination that cut it in twain from the first coach to the last, with a space like an inky hyphen where the baggage car lay. Out of the North came armies of snow-laden clouds that scudded just above the earth, and with these clouds came now and then a shrieking mockery of wind to taunt this stricken creation of man and the creatures it sheltered — men and women who had begun to shiver, and whose tense white faces stared with increasing anxiety into the mysterious darkness of the night that hung like a sable curtain ten feet from the car windows.

For three hours those faces had peered out into the night. Many of the prisoners in the snowbound coaches had enjoyed the experience somewhat at first, for there is pleasing and indefinable thrill to unexpected adventure, and this, for a brief spell, had been adventure de luxe. There had been warmth and light, men's laughter, women's voices, and children's play. But the loudest jester among the men was now silent, huddled deep in his great coat; and the young woman who had clapped her hands in silly ecstasy when it was announced that the train was snowbound was weeping and shivering by turns. It was cold — so cold that the snow which came sweeping and swirling with the wind was like granite-dust; it *clicked*, *clicked*, *clicked* against the glass — a bombardment of untold billions of infinitesimal projectiles fighting to break in. In the edge of the forest it was probably forty degrees below zero. Within the coaches there still remained some little warmth. The burning lamps radiated it and the presence of many people added to it. But it was cold, and growing colder. A gray coating of congealed breath covered the car windows. A few men had given their outer coats to women and children. These men looked most frequently at their watches. The adventure de luxe was becoming serious.

For the twentieth time a passing train-man was asked the same question.

"The good Lord only knows," he growled down into the face of the young woman whose prettiness would have enticed the most chivalrous attention from him earlier in the evening.

"Engine and tender been gone three hours and the divisional point only twenty miles up the line. Should have been back with help long ago. Hell, ain't it?"

The young woman did not reply, but her round mouth formed a quick and silent approbation of his final remark.

"Three hours!" the train-man continued his growling as he went on with his lantern. "That's the hell o' railroading it along the edge of the Arctic. When you git snowed in you're *snowed in*, an' there ain't no two ways about it!"

He paused at the smoking compartment, thrust in his head for a moment, passed on and slammed the door of the car after him as he went into the next coach.

In that smoking compartment there were two men, facing each other across the narrow space between the two seats. They had not looked up when the train-man thrust in his head. They seemed, as one leaned over toward the other, wholly oblivious of the storm.

It was the older man who bent forward. He was about fifty. The hand that rested for a moment on David Raine's knee was red and knotted. It was the hand of a man who had lived his life in struggling with the wilderness. And the face, too, was of such a man; a face coloured and toughened by the tannin of wind and blizzard and hot northern sun, with eyes cobwebbed about by a myriad of fine lines that spoke of years spent under the strain of those things. He was not a large man. He was shorter than David Raine. There was a slight droop to his shoulders. Yet about him there was a strength, a suppressed energy ready to act, a zestful eagerness for life and its daily mysteries which the other and younger man did not possess. Throughout many thousands of square miles of the great northern wilderness this older man was known as Father Roland, the Missioner.

His companion was not more than thirty-eight. Perhaps he was a year or two younger. It may be that the wailing of the wind outside, the strange voices that were in it and the chilling gloom of their little compartment made of him a more striking contrast to Father Roland than he would have been under other conditions. His eyes were a clear and steady gray as they met Father Roland's. They were eyes that one could not easily forget. Except for his eyes he was like a man who had been sick, and was still sick. The Missioner had made his own guess. And now, with his hand on the other's knee, he said:

"And you say — that you are afraid — for this friend of yours?"

David Raine nodded his head. Lines deepened a little about his mouth.

"Yes, I am afraid." For a moment he turned to the night. A fiercer volley of the little snow demons beat against the window, as though his pale face just beyond their reach stirred them to greater fury. "I have a most disturbing inclination to worry about him," he added, and shrugged his shoulders slightly.

He faced Father Roland again.

"Did you ever hear of a man losing himself?" he asked. "I don't mean in the woods, or in a desert, or by going mad. I mean in the other way — heart, body, soul; losing one's grip, you might call it, until there was no earth to stand on. Did you?"

"Yes — many years ago — I knew of a man who lost himself in that way," replied the Missioner, straightening in his seat. "But he found himself again. And this friend of yours? I am interested. This is the first time in three years that I have been down to the edge of civilization, and what you have to tell will be different — vastly different from what I know. If you are betraying nothing would you mind telling me his story?"

"It is not a pleasant story," warned the younger man, "and on such a night as this — — "

"It may be that one can see more clearly into the depths of misfortune and tragedy," interrupted the Missioner quietly.

A faint flush rose into David Raine's pale face. There was something of nervous eagerness in the clasp of his fingers upon his knees.

"Of course, there is the woman," he said.

"Yes — of course — the woman."

"Sometimes I haven't been quite sure whether this man worshipped the woman or the woman's beauty," David went on, with a strange glow in his eyes. "He loved beauty. And this woman was beautiful, almost too beautiful for the good of one's soul, I guess. And he must have loved her, for when she went out of his life it was as if he had sunk into a black pit out of which he could never rise. I have asked myself often if he would have loved her if she had been less beautiful — even quite plain, and I have answered myself as he answered that question, in the affirmative. It was born in him to worship wherever he loved at all. Her beauty made a certain sort of completeness for him. He treasured that. He was proud of it. He counted himself the richest man in the world because he possessed it. But deep under his worship of her beauty he loved *her*. I am more and more sure of that, and I am equally sure that time will prove it — that he will never rise again with his old hope and faith out of that black pit into which he sank when he came face to face with the realization that there were forces in life — in nature perhaps, more potent than his love and his own strong will."

Father Roland nodded.

"I understand," he said, and he sank back farther in his corner by the window, so that his face was shrouded a little in shadow. "This other man loved a woman, too. And she was beautiful. He thought she was the most beautiful thing in the world. It is great love that makes beauty."

"But this woman — my friend's wife — was so beautiful that even the eyes of other women were fascinated by her. I have seen her when it seemed she must have come fresh from the hands of angels; and at first, when my friend was the happiest man in the world, he was fond of telling her that it must have been the angels who put the colour in her face and the wonderful golden fires in her shining hair. It wasn't his love for her that made her beautiful. She *was* beautiful."

"And her soul?" softly questioned the shadowed lips of the Missioner.

The other's hand tightened slowly.

"In making her the angels forgot a soul, I guess," he said.

"Then your friend did not love her." The Little Missioner's voice was quick and decisive. "There can be no love where there is no soul."

"That is impossible. He did love her. I know it."

"I still disagree with you. Without knowing your friend, I say that he worshipped her beauty. There were others who worshipped that same loveliness — others who did not possess her, and who would have bartered their souls for her had they possessed souls to barter. Is that not true?"

"Yes, there were others. But to understand you must have known my friend before he sank down into the pit — when he was still a man. He was a great student. His fortune was sufficient to give him both time and means for the pursuits he loved. He had his great library, and adjoining it a laboratory. He wrote books which few people read because they were filled with facts and odd theories. He believed that the world was very old, and that there was less profit for men in discovering new luxuries for an artificial civilization than in rediscovering a few of the great laws and miracles buried in the dust of the past. He believed that the nearer we get to the beginning of things, and not the farther we drift, the clearer comprehension can we have of earth and sky and God, and the meaning of it all. He did not consider it an argument for progress that Christ and His disciples knew nothing of the telephone, of giant engines run by steam, of electricity, or of instruments by which man could send messages for thousands of miles through space. His theory was that the patriarchs of old held a closer touch on the pulse of Life than progress in its present forms will ever bring to us. He was not a fanatic. He was not a crank. He was young, and filled with enthusiasm. He loved children. He wanted to fill his home with them. But his wife knew that she was too beautiful for that — and they had none."

He had leaned a little forward, and had pulled his hat a trifle over his eyes. There was a moment's lull in the storm, and it was so quiet that each could hear the ticking of Father Roland's big silver watch.

Then he said:

"I don't know why I tell you all this, Father, unless it is to relieve my own mind. There can be no hope that it will benefit my friend. And yet it cannot harm him. It seems very near to sacrilege to put into words what I am going to say about — his wife. Perhaps there were extenuating conditions for her. I have tried to convince myself of that, just as he tried to believe it. It may be that a man who is born into this age must consider himself a misfit unless he can tune himself in sympathy with its manner of life. He cannot be too critical, I guess. If he is to exist in a certain social order of our civilization unburdened by great doubts and deep glooms he must not shiver when his wife tinkles her champagne glass against another. He must learn to appreciate the sinuous beauties of the cabaret dancer, and must train himself to take no offence when he sees shimmering wines tilted down white throats. He must train himself to many things, just as he trains himself to classical music and grand opera. To do these things he must forget, as much as he can, the sweet melodies and the sweeter women who are sinking into oblivion together. He must accept life as a Grand Piano tuned by a new sort of Tuning Master, and unless he can dance to its music he is a misfit. That is what my friend said to extenuate *her*. She fitted into this kind of life splendidly. He was in the other groove. She loved light, laughter, wine, song, and excitement. He, the misfit, loved his books, his work, and his home. His greatest joy would have been to go with her, hand in hand, through some wonderful cathedral, pointing out its ancient glories and mysteries to her. He wanted aloneness — just they two. Such was his idea of love. And she — wanted other things. You understand, Father? . . . The thing grew, and at last he saw that she was getting away from him. Her passion for admiration and excitement became a madness. I know, because I saw it. My friend said that it was madness, even as he was going mad. And yet he did not suspect her. If another had told him that she was unclean I am sure he would have killed him. Slowly he came to experience the agony of knowing that the woman whom he worshipped did not love him. But this did not lead him to believe that she could love another — or others. Then, one day, he left the city. She went with him to the train — his wife. She saw him go. She waved her handkerchief at him. And as she stood there she was — glorious."

Through partly closed eyes the Little Missioner saw his shoulders tighten, and a hardness settle about his mouth. The voice, too, was changed when it went on. It was almost emotionless.

"It's sometimes curious how the Chief Arbiter of things plays His tricks on men — and women, isn't it, Father? There was trouble on the line ahead, and my friend came back. It was unexpected. It was late when he reached home, and with his night key he went in quietly, because he did not want to awaken *her.* It was very still in the house — until he came to the door of her room. There was a light. He heard voices — very low. He listened. He went in."

There was a terrible silence. The ticking of Father Roland's big silver watch seemed like the beating of a tiny drum.

"And what happened then, David?"

"My friend went in," repeated David. His eyes sought Father Roland's squarely, and he saw the question there. "No, he did not kill them," he said. "He doesn't know what kept him from killing — the man. He was a coward, that man. He crawled away like a worm. Perhaps that was why my friend spared him. The wonderful part of it was that the woman — his wife — was not afraid. She stood up in her ravishing dishevelment, with that mantle of gold he had worshipped streaming about her to her knees, *and she laughed*? Yes, she laughed — a mad sort of laugh; a laughter of fear, perhaps — but — *laughter.* So he did not kill them. Her laughter — the man's cowardice — saved them. He turned. He closed the door. He left them. He went out into the night."

He paused, as though his story was finished.

"And that is — the end?" asked Father Roland softly.

"Of his dreams, his hopes, his joy in life — yes, that was the end."

"But of your friend's story? What happened after that?"

"A miracle, I think," replied David hesitatingly, as though he could not quite understand what had happened after that. "You see, this friend of mine was not of the vacillating and irresolute sort. I had always given him credit for that — credit for being a man who would measure up to a situation. He was quite an athlete, and enjoyed boxing and fencing and swimming. If at any time in his life he could have conceived of a situation such as he encountered in his wife's room, he would have lived in a moral certainty of killing the man. And when the situation did come was it not a miracle that he should walk out into the night leaving them not only unharmed, but together? I ask you, Father — was it not a miracle?"

Father Roland's eyes were gleaming strangely under the shadow of his broad-brimmed black hat. He merely nodded.

"Of course," resumed David, "it may be that he was too stunned to act. I believe that the laughter — *her* laughter — acted upon him like a powerful drug. Instead of plunging him into the passion of a murderous desire for vengeance it curiously enough anesthetized his emotions. For hours he heard that laughter. I believe he will never forget it. He wandered the streets all that night. It was in New York, and of course he passed many people. But he did not see them. When morning came he was on Fifth Avenue many miles from his home. He wandered downtown in a constantly growing human stream whose noise and bustle and many-keyed voice acted on him as a tonic. For the first time he asked himself what he would do. Stronger and stronger grew the desire in him to return, to face again that situation in his home. I believe that he would have done this — I believe that the red blood in him would have meted out its own punishment had he not turned just in time, and at the right place. He found himself in front of The Little Church Around the Corner, nestling in its hiding place just off the Avenue. He remembered its restful quiet, the coolness of its aisles and alcoves. He was exhausted, and he went in. He sat down facing the chancel, and as his eyes became accustomed to the gloom he saw that the broad, low dais in front of the organ was banked with great masses of hydrangeas. There had been a wedding, probably the evening before. My friend told me of the thickening that came in his throat, of the strange, terrible throb in his heart as he sat there alone — the only soul in the church — and stared at those hydrangeas. Hydrangeas had been their own wedding flower, Father. And then — — "

For the first time there was something like a break in the younger man's voice.

"My friend thought he was alone," he went on. "But some one had come out like a shadow beyond the chancel railing, and of a sudden, beginning wonderfully low and sweet, the great organ began to fill the church with its melody. The organist, too, thought he was alone. He was a little, old man, his shoulders thin and drooped, his hair white. But in his soul there must have been a great love and a great peace. He played something low and sweet. When he had finished he rose and went away as quietly as he had come, and for a long time after that my friend sat there — alone. Something new was born in him, something which I hope will grow and comfort him in the years to come. When he went out into the city again the sun was shining. He did not go home. He did not see the woman — his wife — again. He has never seen her since that night when she stood up in her dishevelled beauty and *laughed* at him. Even the divorce proceedings did not bring them together. I believe that he treated her fairly. Through his attorneys he turned over to her a half of what he possessed. Then he went away. That was a year ago. In that year I know that he has fought desperately to bring himself back into his old health of mind and body, and I am quite sure that he has failed."

He paused, his story finished. He drew the brim of his hat lower over his eyes, and then he rose to his feet. His build was slim and clean-cut. He was perhaps five feet ten inches in height, which was four inches taller than the Little Missioner. His shoulders were of good breadth, his waist and hips of an athletic slimness. But his clothes hung with a certain looseness. His hands were unnaturally thin, and in his face still hovered the shadows of sickness and of mental suffering.

Father Roland stood beside him now with eyes that shone with a deep understanding. Under the sputter of the lamp above their heads the two men clasped hands, and the Little Missioner's grip was like the grip of iron.

"David, I've preached a strange code through the wilderness for many a long year," he said, and his voice was vibrant with a strong emotion. "I'm not Catholic and I'm not Church of England. I've got no religion that wears a name. I'm simply Father Roland, and all these years I've helped to bury the dead in the forest, an' nurse the sick, an' marry the living, an' it may be that I've learned one thing better than most of you who live down in civilization. And that's how to find yourself when you're down an' out. Boy, will you come with me?"

Their eyes met. A fiercer gust of the storm beat against the windows. They could hear the wind wailing in the trees outside.

"It was your story that you told me," said Father Roland, his voice barely above a whisper. "She was your wife, David?"

It was very still for a few moments. Then came the reply: "Yes, she was my wife. . . ."

Suddenly David freed his hand from the Little Missioner's clasp. He had stopped something that was almost like a cry on his lips. He pulled his hat still lower over his eyes and went through the door out into the main part of the coach.

Father Roland did not follow. Some of the ruddiness had gone from his cheeks, and as he stood facing the door through which David had disappeared a smouldering fire began to burn far back in his eyes. After a few moments this fire died out, and his face was gray and haggard as he sat down again in his corner. His hands unclenched. With a great sigh his head drooped forward on his chest, and for a long time he sat thus, his eyes and face lost in shadow. One would not have known that he was breathing.

CHAPTER II

Half a dozen times that night David had walked from end to end of the five snowbound coaches that made up the Transcontinental. He believed that for him it was an act of Providence that had delayed the train. Otherwise a sleeping car would have been picked up at the next divisional point, and he would not have unburdened himself to Father Roland. They would not have sat up until that late hour in the smoking compartment, and this strange little man of the forest would not have told him the story of a lonely cabin up on the edge of the Barrens — a story of strange pathos and human tragedy that had, in some mysterious way, unsealed his own lips. David had kept to himself the shame and heartbreak of his own affliction since the day he had been compelled to tell it, coldly and without visible emotion, to gain his own freedom. He had meant to keep it to himself always. And of a sudden it had all come out. He was not sorry. He was glad. He was amazed at the change in himself. That day had been a terrible day for him. He could not get *her* out of his mind. Now a depressing hand seemed to have lifted itself from his heart. He was quick to understand. His story had not fallen upon ears eager with sensual curiosity. He had met a *man*, and from the soul of that man there had reached out to him the spirit of a deep and comforting strength. He would have revolted at compassion, and words of pity would have shamed him. Father Roland had given voice to neither of these. But the grip of his hand had been like the grip of an iron man.

In the third coach David sat down in an empty seat. For the first time in many months there was a thrill of something in his blood which he could not analyze. What had the Little Missioner meant when, with that wonderful grip of his knotted hand, he had said, "I've learned how a man can find himself when he's down and out"? And what had he meant when he added, "Will you come with me"? Go with him? Where?

There came a sudden crash of the storm against the window, a shrieking blast of wind and snow, and David stared into the night. He could see nothing. It was a black chaos outside. But he could hear. He could hear the wailing and the moaning of the wind in the trees, and he almost fancied that it was not darkness alone that shut out his vision, but the thick walls of the forest.

Was that what Father Roland had meant? Had he asked him to go with him into *that*?

His face touched the cold glass. He stared harder. That

morning Father Roland had boarded the train at a wilderness station and had taken a seat beside him. They had become acquainted. And later the Little Missioner had told him how those vast forests reached without a break for hundreds of miles into the mysterious North. He loved them, even as they lay cold and white outside the windows. There was gladness in his voice when he had said that he was going back into them. They were a part of *his* world — a world of "mystery and savage glory" he had called it, stretching for a thousand miles to the edge of the Arctic, and fifteen hundred miles from Hudson's Bay to the western mountains. And tonight he had said, "Will you come with me?"

David's pulse quickened. A thousand little snow demons beat in his face to challenge his courage. The wind swept down, as if enraged at the thought in his mind, and scooped up volley after volley of drifting snow and hurled them at him. There was only the thin glass between. It was like the defiance of a living thing. It threatened him. It dared him. It invited him out like a great bully, with a brawling show of fists. He had always been more or less pusillanimous in the face of winter. He disliked cold. He hated snow. But this that beat and shrieked at him outside the window had set something stirring strangely within him. It was a desire, whimsical and undecided at first, to thrust his face out into that darkness and feel the sting of the wind and snow. It was Father Roland's world. And Father Roland had invited him to enter it. That was the curious part of the situation, as it was impressed upon him as he sat with his face flattened against the window. The Little Missioner had invited him, and the night was daring him. For a single moment the incongruity of it all made him forget himself, and he laughed — a chuckling, half broken, and out-of-tune sort of laugh. It was the first time in a year that he had forgotten himself anywhere near to a point resembling laughter, and in the sudden and inexplicable spontaneity of it he was startled. He turned quickly, as though some one at his side had laughed and he was about to demand an explanation. He looked across the aisle and his eyes met squarely the eyes of a woman.

He saw nothing but the eyes at first. They were big, dark, questing eyes — eyes that had in them a hunting look, as though they hoped to find in his face the answer to a great question. Never in his life had he seen eyes that were so haunted by a great unrest, or that held in their lustrous depths the smouldering glow of a deeper grief. Then the face added itself to the eyes. It was not a young face. The woman was past forty. But this age did not impress itself over a strange and appealing beauty in her countenance which was like the beauty of a flower whose petals are falling. Before David had seen more than this she turned her eyes from him slowly and doubtfully, as if not quite convinced that she had found what she sought, and faced the darkness beyond her own side of the car.

David was puzzled, and he looked at her with still deeper interest. Her seat was turned so that it was facing him across the aisle, three seats ahead, and he could look at her without conspicuous effort or rudeness. Her hood had slipped down and hung by its long scarf about her shoulders. She leaned toward the window, and as she stared out, her chin rested in the cup of her hand. He noticed that her hand was thin, and that there was a shadowy hollow in the white pallor of her cheek. Her hair was heavy and done in thick coils that glowed dully in the lamplight. It was a deep brown, almost black, shot through with little silvery threads of gray.

For a few moments David withdrew his gaze, subconsciously ashamed of the directness of his scrutiny. But after a little his eyes drifted back to her. Her head was sunk forward a little, he caught now a pathetic droop of her shoulders, and he fancied that he saw a little shiver run through her. Just as before he had felt the desire to thrust his face out into the night, he felt now an equally unaccountable impulse to speak to her and ask her if he could in any way be of service to her. But he could see no excuse for this presumptuousness in himself. If she was in distress it was not of a physical sort for which he might have suggested his services as a remedy. She was neither hungry nor cold, for there was a basket at her side in which he had a glimpse of broken bits of food; and at her back, draped over the seat, was a heavy beaver-skin coat.

He rose to his feet with the intention of returning to the smoking compartment in which he had left Father Roland. His movement seemed to rouse the woman. Again her dark eyes met his own. They looked straight up at him as he stood in the aisle, and he stopped. Her lips trembled.

"Are you . . . acquainted . . . between here and Lac Seul?" she asked.

Her voice had in it the same haunting mystery that he had seen in her eyes, the same apprehension, the same hope, as though some curious and indefinable instinct was telling her that in this stranger she was very near to the thing which she was seeking.

"I am a stranger," he said. "This is the first time I have ever been in this country."

She sank back, the look of hope in her face dying out like a passing flash.

"I thank you," she murmured. "I thought perhaps you might know of a man whom I am seeking — a man by the name of Michael O'Doone."

She did not expect him to speak again. She drew her heavy coat about her and turned her face toward the window. There was nothing that he could say, nothing that he could do, and he went back to Father Roland.

He was in the last coach when a sound came to him faintly. It was too sharp for the wailing of the storm. Others heard it and grew suddenly erect, with tense and listening faces. The young woman with the round mouth gave a little gasp. A man pacing back and forth in the aisle stopped as if at the point of a bayonet.

It came again.

The heavy-jowled man who had taken the adventure as a jest at first, and who had rolled himself in his great coat like a hibernating woodchuck, unloosed his voice in a rumble of joy.

"It's the whistle!" he announced. "The damned thing's coming at last!"

CHAPTER III

David came up quietly to the door of the smoking compartment where he had left Father Roland. The Little Missioner was
huddled in his corner near the window. His head hung heavily
forward and the shadows of his black Stetson concealed his face.
He was apparently asleep. His hands, with their strangely developed joints and fingers, lay loosely upon his knees. For fully half a
minute David looked at him without moving or making a sound,
and as he looked, something warm and living seemed to reach out
from the lonely figure of the wilderness preacher that filled him
with a strangely new feeling of companionship. Again he made no
effort to analyze the change in himself; he accepted it as one of the
two or three inexplicable phenomena this night and the storm had
produced for him, and was chiefly concerned in the fact that he
was no longer oppressed by that torment of aloneness which had
been a part of his nights and days for so many months. He was
about to speak when he made up his mind not to disturb the other.
So certain was he that Father Roland was asleep that he drew away
from the door on the tips of his toes and reëntered the coach.

He did not stop in the first or second car, though there were
plenty of empty seats and people were rousing themselves into
more cheerful activity. He passed through one and then the other
to the third coach, and sat down when he came to the seat he had
formerly occupied. He did not immediately look at the woman
across the aisle. He did not want her to suspect that he had come
back for that purpose. When his eyes did seek her in a casual sort
of way he was disappointed.

She was almost covered in her coat. He caught only the gleam
of her thick, dark hair, and the shape of one slim hand, white as
paper in the lampglow. He knew that she was not asleep, for he
saw her shoulders move, and the hand shifted its position to hold
the coat closer about her. The whistling of the approaching
engine, which could be heard distinctly now, had no apparent
effect on her. For ten minutes he sat staring at all he could see of
her — the dark glow of her hair and the one ghostly white hand.
He moved, he shuffled his feet, he coughed; he made sure she
knew he was there, but she did not look up. He was sorry that he
had not brought Father Roland with him in the first place, for he
was certain that if the Little Missioner had seen the grief and the
despair in her eyes — the hope almost burned out — he would
have gone to her and said things which he had found it impossible
to say when the opportunity had come to him. He rose again from

his seat as the powerful snow-engine and its consort coupled on to the train. The shock almost flung him off his feet. Even then she did not raise her head.

A second time he returned to the smoking compartment.

Father Roland was no longer huddled down in his corner. He was on his feet, his hands thrust deep down into his trousers pockets, and he was whistling softly as David came in. His hat lay on the seat. It was the first time David had seen his round, rugged, weather-reddened face without the big Stetson. He looked younger and yet older; his face, as David saw it there in the lampglow, had something in the ruddy glow and deeply lined strength of it that was almost youthful. But his thick, shaggy hair was very gray. The train had begun to move. He turned to the window for a moment, and then looked at David.

"We are under way," he said. "Very soon I will be getting off."

David sat down.

"It is some distance beyond the divisional point ahead — this cabin where you get off?" he asked.

"Yes, twenty or twenty-five miles. There is nothing but a cabin and two or three log outbuildings there — where Thoreau, the Frenchman, has his fox pens, as I told you. It is not a regular stop, but the train will slow down to throw off my dunnage and give me an easy jump. My dogs and Indian are with Thoreau."

"And from there — from Thoreau's — it is a long distance to the place you call home?"

The Little Missioner rubbed his hands in a queer rasping way. The movement of those rugged hands and the curious, chuckling laugh that accompanied it, radiated a sort of cheer. They were expressions of more than satisfaction. "It's a great many miles to my own cabin, but it's home — all home — after I get into the forests. My cabin is at the lower end of God's Lake, three hundred miles by dogs and sledge from Thoreau's — three hundred miles as straight north as a *niskuk* flies."

"A *niskuk*?" said David.

"Yes — a gray goose."

"Don't you have crows?"

"A few; but they're as crooked in flight as they are in morals. They're scavengers, and they hang down pretty close to the line of rail — close to civilization, where there's a lot of scavenging to be done, you know."

For the second time that night David found a laugh on his lips.

"Then — you don't like civilization?"

"My heart is in the Northland," replied Father Roland, and

David saw a sudden change in the other's face, a dying out of the light in his eyes, a tenseness that came and went like a flash at the corners of his mouth. In that same moment he saw the Missioner's hand tighten, and the fingers knot themselves curiously and then slowly relax.

One of these hands dropped on David's shoulder, and Father Roland became the questioner.

"You have been thinking, since you left me a little while ago?" he asked.

"Yes. I came back. But you were asleep."

"I haven't been asleep. I have been awake every minute. I thought once that I heard a movement at the door but when I looked up there was no one there. You told me today that you were going west — to the British Columbia mountains?"

David nodded. Father Roland sat down beside him.

"Of course you didn't tell me why you were going," he went on. "I have made my own guess since you told me about the woman, David. Probably you will never know just why your story has struck so deeply home with me and why it seemed to make you more a son to me than a stranger. I have guessed that in going west you are simply wandering. You are fighting in a vain and foolish sort of way to run away from something. Isn't that it? You are running away — trying to escape the one thing in the whole wide world that you cannot lose by flight — and that's memory. You can *think* just as hard in Japan or the South Sea Islands as you can on Fifth Avenue in New York, and sometimes the farther away you get the more maddening your thoughts become. It isn't travel you want, David. It's blood — *red* blood. And for putting blood into you, and courage, and joy of just living and breathing, there's nothing on the face of the earth like — *that*!"

He reached an arm past David and pointed to the night beyond the car window.

"You mean the storm, and the snow — — "

"Yes; storm, and snow, and sunshine, and forests — the tens of thousands of miles of our Northland that you've seen only the edges of. That's what I mean. But, first of all" — and again the Little Missioner rubbed his hands — "first of all, I'm thinking of the supper that's waiting for us at Thoreau's. Will you get off and have supper with me at the Frenchman's, David? After that, if you decide not to go up to God's Lake with me, Thoreau can bring you and your luggage back to the station with his dog team. Such a supper — or breakfast — it will be! I can smell it now, for I know Thoreau — his fish, his birds, the tenderest steaks in the forests! I can hear Thoreau cursing because the train hasn't come, and I'll wager he's got fish and caribou tenderloin and partridges just ready for a final turn in the roaster. What do you say? Will you get off with me?"

"It is a tempting offer to a hungry man, Father."

The Little Missioner chuckled elatedly.

"Hunger! — that's the real medicine of the gods, David, when the belt isn't drawn too tight. If I want to know the nature and quality of a man I ask about his stomach. Did you ever know a man who loved to eat who wasn't of a pretty decent sort? Did you ever know of a man who loved pie — who'd go out of his way to get pie — that didn't have a heart in him bigger than a pumpkin? I guess you didn't. If a man's got a good stomach he isn't a grouch, and he won't stick a knife into your back; but if he eats from habit — or necessity — he isn't a beautiful character in the eyes of nature, and there's pretty sure to be a cog loose somewhere in his makeup. I'm a grub-scientist, David. I warn you of that before we get off at Thoreau's. I love to eat, and the Frenchman knows it. That's why I can smell things in that cabin, forty miles away."

He was rubbing his hands briskly and his face radiated such joyous anticipation as he talked that David unconsciously felt the spirit of his enthusiasm. He had gripped one of Father Roland's hands and was pumping it up and down almost before he realized what he was doing.

"I'll get off with you at Thoreau's," he exclaimed, "and later, if I feel as I do now, and you still want my company, I'll go on with you into the north country!"

A slight flush rose into his thin cheeks and his eyes shone with a freshly lighted enthusiasm. As Father Roland saw the change in him his hands closed over David's.

"I knew you had a splendid stomach in you from the moment you finished telling me about the woman," he cried exultantly. "I knew it, David. And I do want your company — I want it as I never wanted the company of another man!"

"That is the strange part of it," replied David, a slight quiver in his voice. He drew away his hands suddenly and with a jerk brought himself to his feet. "Good God! look at me!" he cried. "I am a wreck, physically. It would be a lie if you told me I am not. See these hands — these arms! I'm down and out. I'm weak as a dog, and the stomach you speak of is a myth. I haven't eaten a square meal in a year. Why do you want me as a companion? Why do you think it would be a pleasure for you to drag a decrepit misfit like myself up into a country like yours? Is it because of your — your code of faith? Is it because you think you may save a soul?"

He was breathing deeply. As he excoriated himself and bared his weakness the hot blood crept slowly into his face.

"Why do you want me to go?" he demanded. "Why don't you ask some man with red blood in his veins and a heart that hasn't been burned out? Why have you asked me?"

Father Roland made as if to speak, and then caught himself. Again for a passing flash there came that mysterious change in him, a sudden dying out of the enthusiasm in his eyes, and a grayness in his face that came and went like a shadow of pain. In another moment he was saying:

"I'm not playing the part of the good Samaritan, David. I've got a personal and a selfish reason for wanting you with me. It may be possible — just possible, I say — that I need you even more than you will need me." He held out his hand. "Let me have your checks and I'll go ahead to the baggage car and arrange to have your dunnage thrown off with mine at the Frenchman's."

David gave him the checks, and sat down after he had gone. He began to realize that, for the first time in many months, he was taking a deep and growing interest in matters outside his own life. The night and its happenings had kindled a strange fire within him, and the warmth of this fire ran through his veins and set his body and his brain tingling curiously. New forces were beginning to fight his own malady. As he sat alone after Father Roland had gone, his mind had dragged itself away from the East; he thought of a woman, but it was the woman in the third coach back. Her wonderful eyes haunted him — their questing despair, the strange pain that seemed to burn like glowing coals in their depths. He had seen not only misery and hopelessness in them; he had seen tragedy; and they troubled him. He made up his mind to tell Father Roland about her when he returned from the baggage car, and take him to her.

And who was Father Roland? For the first time he asked himself the question. There was something of mystery about the Little Missioner that he found as strange and unanswerable as the thing he had seen in the eyes of the woman in the third car back. Father Roland had not been asleep when he looked in and saw him hunched down in his corner near the window, just as a little later he had seen the woman crumpled down in hers. It was as if the same oppressing hand had been upon them in those moments. And why had Father Roland asked him of all men to go with him as a comrade into the North? Following this he asked himself the still more puzzling question: Why had he accepted the invitation?

He stared out into the night, as if that night held an answer for him. He had not noticed until now that the storm had ceased its beating against the window. It was not so black outside. With his face close to the glass he could make out the dark wall of the forest. From the rumble of the trucks under him he knew that the two engines were making good time. He looked at his watch. It was a quarter of twelve. They had been travelling for half an hour and he figured that the divisional point ahead would be reached by midnight. It seemed a very short time after that when he heard the tiny bell in his watch tinkle off the hour of twelve. The last strokes were drowned in a shrill blast of the engine whistle, and a moment later he caught the dull glow of lights in the hollow of a wide curve the train was making.

Father Roland had told him the train would wait at this point fifteen minutes, and even now he heard the clanging of handbells announcing the fact that hot coffee, sandwiches, and ready-prepared suppers were awaiting the half starved passengers. The trucks grated harshly, the whirring groan of the air-brakes ran under him like a great sigh, and suddenly he was looking down into the face of a pop-eyed man who was clanging a bell, with all the strength of his right arm, under his window, and who, with this labour, was emitting a husky din of "Supper — supper 'ot an' ready at the Royal" in his vain effort to drown the competition of a still more raucous voice that was bellowing: "'Ot steaks *an'* liver'n onions at the Queen Alexandry!" As David made no movement the man under his window stretched up his neck and yelled a personal invitation, "W'y don't you come out and eat, old chap? You've got fifteen minutes an' mebby 'arf an 'our; supper — supper 'ot an' ready at the Royal!" Up and down the length of the dimly lighted platform David heard that clangor of bells, and as if determined to capture his stomach or die, the pop-eyed man never moved an inch from his window, while behind him there jostled and hurried an eager and steadily growing crowd of hungry people.

David thought again of the woman in the third coach back. Was she getting off here, he wondered? He went to the door of the smoking compartment and waited another half minute for Father Roland. It was quite evident that his delay was occasioned by some difficulty in the baggage car, a difficulty which perhaps his own presence might help to straighten out. He hesitated between the thought of joining the Missioner and the stronger impulse to go back into the third coach. He was conscious of a certain feeling of embarrassment as he returned for the third time to look at her.

He was not anxious for her to see him again unless Father Roland was with him. His hesitancy, if it was not altogether embarrassment, was caused by the fear that she might quite naturally regard his interest in a wrong light. He was especially sensitive upon that point, and had always been. The fact that she was not a young woman, and that he had seen her dark hair finely threaded with gray, made no difference with him in his peculiarly chivalric conception of man's attitude toward woman. He did not mean to impress himself upon her; this time he merely wanted to see whether she had roused herself, or had left the car. At least this was the trend of his mental argument as he entered the third coach.

The car was empty. The woman was gone. Even the old man who had hobbled in on crutches at the last station had hobbled out again in response to the clanging bells. When he came to the seat where the woman had been, David paused, and would have turned back had he not chanced to look out through the window. He was just in time to catch the quick upturn of a passing face. It was *her* face. She saw him and recognized him; she seemed for a moment to hesitate; her eyes were filled again with that haunting fire; her lips trembled as if about to speak; and then, like a mysterious shadow, she drifted out of his vision into darkness.

For a space he remained in his bent and staring attitude, trying to pierce the gloom into which she had disappeared. As he drew back from the window, wondering what she must think of him, his eyes fell to the seat where she had been sitting, and he saw that she had left something behind.

It was a very thin package, done up in a bit of newspaper and tied with a red string. He picked it up and turned it over in his hands. It was five or six inches in width and perhaps eight in length, and was not more than half an inch in thickness. The newspaper in which the object was wrapped was worn until the print was almost obliterated.

Again he looked out through the window. Was it a trick of his eyes, he wondered, or did he see once more that pale and haunting face in the gloom just beyond the lampglow? His fingers closed a little tighter upon the thin packet in his hand. At least he had found an excuse; if she was still there — if he could find her — he had an adequate apology for going to her. She had forgotten something; it was simply a matter of courtesy on his part to return it. As he alighted into the half foot of snow on the platform he could have given no other reason for his action. His mind could not clarify itself; it had no cohesiveness of purpose or of emotion at this particular juncture. It was as if a strange and magnetic undertow were drawing him after her. And he obeyed the impulse. He began seeking for her, with the thin packet in his hand.

CHAPTER IV

David followed where he fancied he had last seen the woman's face and caught himself just in time to keep from pitching over the edge of the platform. Beyond that there was a pit of blackness. Surely she had not gone there.

Two or three of the bells were still clanging, but with abated enthusiasm; from the dimly lighted platform, grayish-white in the ghostly flicker of the oil lamps, the crowd of hungry passengers was ebbing swiftly in its quest of food and drink; a last half-hearted bawling of the virtue to be found in the "hot steak *an'* liver'n onions at the Royal Alexandry" gave way to a comforting silence — a silence broken only by a growing clatter of dishes, the subdued wheezing of the engines, and the raucous voice of a train-man telling the baggage-man that the hump between his shoulders was not a head but a knot kindly tied there by his Creator to keep him from unravelling. Even the promise of a fight — at least of a blow or two delivered in the gray gloom of the baggage-man's door — did not turn David from his quest. When he returned, a few minutes later, two or three sympathetic friends were nursing the baggage-man back into consciousness. He was about to pass the group when some one gripped his arm, and a familiar and joyous chuckle sounded in his ear. Father Roland stood beside him.

"Dear Father in Heaven, but it was a *terrible* blow, David!" cried the Little Missioner, his face dancing in the flare of the baggage room lamps. "It was a tre*men*dous blow — straight out from his shoulders like a battering ram, and hard as rock! It put him to sleep like a baby. Did you see it?"

"I didn't," said David, staring at the other in amazement.

"He deserved it," explained Father Roland. "I love to see a good, clean blow when it's delivered in the right, David. I've seen the time when a hard fist was worth more than a preacher and his prayers." He was chuckling delightedly as they turned back to the train. "The baggage is arranged for," he added. "They'll put us off together at the Frenchman's."

David had slipped the thin packet into his pocket. He no longer felt so keenly the desire to tell Father Roland about the woman — at least not at the present time. His quest had been futile. The woman had disappeared as completely as though she had actually floated away into that pit of darkness beyond the far end of the platform. He had drawn but one conclusion. This place — Graham — was her home; undoubtedly friends had been at the station to meet her; even now she might be telling them, or a husband, or a grown-up son, of the strange fellow who had stared at her in such a curious fashion. Disappointment in not finding her had brought a reaction. He had an inward and uncomfortable feeling of having been very silly, and of having allowed his imagination to get the better of his common sense. He had persuaded himself to believe that she had been in very great distress. He had acted honestly and with chivalric intentions. And yet, after what had passed between him and Father Roland in the smoking compartment — and in view of his failure to establish a proof of his own convictions — he was determined to keep this particular event of the night to himself.

A loud voice began to announce that the moment of departure had arrived, and as the passengers began scrambling back into their coaches, Father Roland led the way to the baggage car.

"They're going to let us ride with the dunnage so there won't be any mistake or time lost when we get to Thoreau's," he said.

They climbed up into the warm and lighted car, and after the baggage-man in charge had given them a sour nod of recognition the first thing that David noticed was his own and Father Roland's property stacked up near the door. His own belongings were a steamer trunk and two black morocco bags, while Father Roland's share of the pile consisted mostly of boxes and bulging gunny sacks that must have weighed close to half a ton. Near the pile was a pair of scales, shoved back against the wall of the car. David laughed queerly as he nodded toward them. They gave him a rather satisfying inspiration. With them he could prove the incongruity of the partnership that had already begun to exist between him and the Missioner. He weighed himself, with Father Roland looking on. The scales balanced at 132.

"And I'm five feet nine in height," he said, disgustedly; "it should be 160. You see where I'm at!"

"I knew a 200-pound pig once that worried himself down to ninety because the man who kept him also kept skunks," replied Father Roland, with his odd chuckle. "Next to smallpox and a bullet through your heart, worry is about the blackest, man-killingest thing on earth, David. See that bag?"

He pointed to one of the bulging gunny sacks.

"That's the antidote," he said. "It's the best medicine I know of in the grub line for a man who's lost his grip. There's the making of three men in that sack."

"What is it?" asked David, curiously.

The Missioner bent over to examine a card attached to the

neck of the bag.

"To be perfectly accurate it contains 110 pounds of beans," he answered.

"Beans! Great Heavens! I loathe them!"

"So do most down-and-outs," affirmed Father Roland, cheerfully. "That's one reason for the peculiar psychological value of beans. They begin to tell you when you're getting weaned away from a lobster palate and a stuffed-crab stomach, and when you get to the point where you want 'em on your regular bill of fare you'll find more fun in chopping down a tree than in going to a grand opera. But the beans must be *cooked* right, David — browned like a nut, juicy to the heart of 'em, and seasoned alongside a broiling duck or partridge, or a tender rabbit. Ah!"

The Little Missioner rubbed his hands ecstatically.

David's rejoinder, if one was on his lips, was interrupted by a violent cursing. The train was well under way, and the baggageman had sat down to a small table with his back toward them. He had leaped to his feet now, his face furious, and with another demoniac curse he gave the coal skuttle a kick that sent it with a bang to the far end of the car. The table was littered with playing cards.

"Damn 'em — they beat me this time in ten plays!" he yelled. "They've got the devil in 'em! If they was alive I'd jump on 'em! I've played this game of solitaire for nineteen years — I've played a million games — an' damned if I ever got beat in my life as it's beat me since we left Halifax!"

"Dear Heaven!" gasped Father Roland. "Have you been playing all the way from Halifax?"

The solitaire fiend seemed not to hear, and resuming his seat with a low and ominous muttering, he dealt himself another hand. In less than a minute he was on his feet again, shaking the cards angrily under the Little Missioner's nose as though that individual were entirely accountable for his bad luck.

"Look at that accursed trey of hearts!" he demanded. "First card, ain't it? First card! — an' if it had been the third, 'r the sixth, 'r the ninth, 'r anything except that confounded Number One, I'd have slipped the game up my sleeve. Ain't it enough to wreck any honest man's soul? I ask you — ain't it?"

"Why don't you change the trey of hearts to the place that suits you?" asked David, innocently. "It seems to me it would be very easy to move it to third place in the deck if you want it there."

The baggage-man's bulging eyes seemed ready to pop as he stared at David, and when he saw that David really meant what he had said a look of unutterable disgust spread over his countenance. Then he grinned — a sickly and malicious sort of grin.

"Say, mister, you've never played solitaire, have you?" he asked.

"Never," confessed David.

Without another word the baggage-man hunched himself over his table, dealt himself another hand, and not until the train began slowing up for Thoreau's place did he rise from his seat or cease his low mutterings and grumblings. In response to the engineer's whistle he jumped to his feet and rolled back the car door.

"Now step lively!" he demanded. "We've got no orders to stop here and we'll have to dump this stuff out on the move!"

As he spoke he gave the hundred and ten pounds of beans a heave out into the night. Father Roland jumped to his assistance, and David saw his steamer trunk and his hand-bags follow the beans.

"The snow is soft and deep, an' there won't be any harm done," Father Roland assured him as he tossed out a 50-pound box of prunes.

David heard sounds now: a man's shout, a fiendish tonguing of dogs, and above that a steady chorus of yapping which he guessed came from the foxes. Suddenly a lantern gleamed, then a second and a third, and a dark, bearded face — a fierce and piratical-looking face — began running along outside the door. The last box and the last bag went off, and with a sudden movement the train-man hauled David to the door.

"Jump!" he cried.

The face and the lantern had fallen behind, and it was as black as an abyss outside. With a mute prayer David launched himself much as he had seen the bags and boxes sent out. He fell with a thud in a soft blanket of snow. He looked up in time to see the Little Missioner flying out like a curious gargoyle through the door; the baggage-man's lantern waved, the engineer's whistle gave a responding screech, and the train whirred past. Not until the tail-light of the last coach was receding like a great red firefly in the gloom did David get up. Father Roland was on his feet, and down the track came two of the three lanterns on the run.

It was all unusually weird and strangely interesting to David. He was breathing deeply. There was a warmth in his body which was new to him. It struck him all at once, as he heard Father Roland crunching through the snow, that he was experiencing an entirely new phase of life — a life he had read about at times and dreamed of at other times, but which he had never come physically in contact with. The yapping of the foxes, the crying of the dogs, those lanterns hurrying down the track, the blackness of the night, and the strong perfume of balsam in the cold air — an odour that he breathed deep into his lungs like the fumes of an exhilarating drink — quickened sharply a pulse that a few hours before he thought was almost lifeless. He had no time to ask himself whether he was enjoying these new sensations; he felt only the thrill of them as Thoreau and the Indian came up out of the night with their lanterns. In Thoreau himself, as he stood a moment later in the glow of the lanterns, was embodied the living, breathing spirit of this new world into which David's leap out of the baggage car had plunged him. He was picturesquely of the wild; his face was darkly bearded; his ivory-white teeth shining as he smiled a welcome; his tricoloured, Hudson's Bay coat of wool, with its frivolous red fringes, thrown open at the throat; the bushy tail of his fisher-skin cap hanging over a shoulder — and with these things his voice rattling forth, in French and half Indian, his joy that Father Roland was not dead but had arrived at last. Behind him stood the Indian — his face without expression, dark, shrouded — a bronze sphinx of mystery. But his eyes shone as the Little Missioner greeted him — shone so darkly and so full of fire that for a moment David was fascinated by them. Then David was introduced.

"I am happy to meet you, m'sieu," said the Frenchman. His race was softly polite, even in the forests, and Thoreau's voice, now mildly subdued, came strangely from the bearded wildness of his face. The grip of his hand was like Father Roland's — something David had never felt among his friends back in the city. He winced in the darkness, and for a long time afterward his fingers tingled.

It was then that David made his first break in the etiquette of the forests; a fortunate one, as time proved. He did not know that shaking hands with an Indian was a matter of some formality, and so when Father Roland said, "This is Mukoki, who has been with me for many years," David thrust out his hand. Mukoki looked him straight in the eye for a moment, and then his blanket-coat parted and his slim, dark hand reached out. Having received his lesson from both the Missioner and the Frenchman, David put into his grip all the strength that was in him — the warmest handshake Mukoki had ever received in his life from a white man, with the exception of his master, the Missioner.

The next thing David heard was Father Roland's voice inquiring eagerly about supper. Thoreau's reply was in French.

"He says the cabin is like the inside of a great, roast duck," chuckled the Missioner. "Come, David. We'll leave Mukoki to gather up our freight."

A short walk up the track and David saw the cabin. It was back in the shelter of the black spruce and balsam, its two windows that faced the railroad warmly illumined by the light inside. The foxes had ceased their yapping, but the snarling and howling of dogs became more bloodthirsty as they drew nearer, and David could hear an ominous clinking of chains and snapping of teeth. A few steps more and they were at the door. Thoreau himself opened it, and stood back.

"*Après vous, m'sieu,*" he said, his white teeth shining at David. "It would give me bad luck and possibly all my foxes would die, if I went into my house ahead of a stranger."

David went in. An Indian woman stood with her back to him, bending over a table. She was as slim as a reed, and had the longest and sleekest black hair he had ever seen, done in two heavy braids that hung down her back. In another moment she had turned her round, brown face, and her teeth and eyes were shining, but she spoke no word. Thoreau did not introduce his wild-flower wife. He had opened his cabin door, and had let David enter before him, which was accepting him as a friend in his home, and therefore, in his understanding of things, an introduction was unnecessary and out of place. Father Roland chuckled, rubbed his hands briskly, and said something to the woman in her own language that made her giggle shyly. It was contagious. David smiled. Father Roland's face was crinkled with little lines of joy. The Frenchman's teeth gleamed. In the big cook-stove the fire snapped and crackled and popped. Marie opened the stove door to put in more wood and her face shone rosy and her teeth were like milk in the fire-flash. Thoreau went to her and laid his big, heavy hand fondly on her sleek head, and said something in soft Cree that brought another giggle into Marie's throat, like the curious note of a bird.

In David there was a slow and wonderful awakening. Every fibre of him was stirred by the cheer of this cabin builded from logs rough-hewn out of the forest; his body, weakened by the months of mental and physical anguish which had been his burden, seemed filled with a new strength. Unconsciously he was smiling and his soul was rising out of its dark prison as he saw Thoreau's big hand stroking Marie's shining hair. He was watching Thoreau when, at a word from Marie, the Frenchman suddenly swung open the oven door and pulled forth a huge roasting pan.

At sight of the pan Father Roland gave a joyous cry, and he rubbed his hands raspingly together. The rich aroma of that pan! A delicious whiff of it had struck their nostrils even before the cabin door had opened — that and a perfume of coffee; but not until now did the fragrance of the oven and the pan smite them with all its potency.

"Mallards fattened on wild rice, and a rabbit — my favourite — a rabbit roasted with an onion where his heart was, and well peppered," gloated the Little Missioner. "Dear Heaven! was there ever such a mess to put strength into a man's gizzard, David? And coffee — this coffee of Marie's! It is more than ambrosia. It is an elixir which transforms a cup into a fountain of youth. Take off your coat, David; take off your coat and make yourself at home!"

As David stripped off his coat, and followed that with his collar and tie, he thought of his steamer trunk with its Tuxedo and dress-coat, its piqué shirts and poke collars, its suede gloves and kid-topped patent leathers, and he felt the tips of his ears beginning to burn. He was sorry now that he had given the Missioner the check to that trunk.

A minute later he was sousing his face in a big tin wash-basin, and then drying it on a towel that had once been a burlap bag. But he had noticed that it was clean — as clean as the pink-flushed face of Marie. And the Frenchman himself, with all his hair, and his beard, and his rough-worn clothing, was as clean as the burlap towelling. Being a stranger, suddenly plunged into a life entirely new to him, these things impressed David.

When they sat down to the table — Thoreau sitting for company, and Marie standing behind them — he was at a loss at first to know how to begin. His plate was of tin and a foot in diameter, and on it was a three-pound mallard duck, dripping with juice and as brown as a ripe hazel-nut. He made a business of arranging his sleeves and drinking a glass of water while he watched the famished Little Missioner. With a chuckle of delight Father Roland plunged the tines of his fork hilt deep into the breast of the duck, seized a leg in his fingers, and dismembered the luscious anatomy of his plate with a deft twist and a sudden pull. With his teeth buried in the leg he looked across at David. David had eaten duck before; that is, he had eaten of the family *anas boschas* disguised in thick gravies and highbrow sauces, but this duck that he ate at Thoreau's table was like no other duck that he had ever tasted in all his life. He began with misgivings at the three-pound carcass, and he ended with an entirely new feeling of stuffed satisfaction. He explored at will into its structure, and he found succulent morsels which he had never dreamed of as existing in this partic- ular bird, for his experience had never before gone beyond a leg of duck and thinly carved slices of breast of duck, at from eighty cents to a dollar and a quarter an order. He would have been ashamed of himself when he had finished had it not been that Father Roland seemed only at the beginning, and was turning the vigour of his attack from duck to rabbit and onion. From then on David kept him company by drinking a third cup of coffee.

When he had finished Father Roland settled back with a sigh of content, and drew a worn buckskin pouch from one of the voluminous pockets of his trousers. Out of this he produced a black pipe and tobacco. At the same time Thoreau was filling and lighting his own. In his studies and late-hour work at home David himself had been a pipe smoker, but of late his pipe had been dis- tasteful to him, and it had been many weeks since he had indulged in anything but cigars and an occasional cigarette. He looked at the placid satisfaction in the Little Missioner's face, and saw Thoreau's head wreathed in smoke, and he felt for the first time in those weeks the return of his old desire. While they were eating, Mukoki and another Indian had brought in his trunk and bags, and he went now to one of the bags, opened it, and got his own pipe and tobacco. As he stuffed the bowl of his English briar, and lighted the tobacco, Father Roland's glowing face beamed at him through the fragrant fumes of his Hudson's Bay Mixture.

Against the wall, a little in shadow, so that she would not be a part of their company or whatever conversation they might have, Marie had seated herself, her round chin in the cup of her brown hand, her dark eyes shining at this comfort and satisfaction of men. Such scenes as this amply repaid her for all her toil in life. She was happy. There was content in this cabin. David felt it. It impinged itself upon him, and through him, in a strange and mys- terious way. Within these log walls he felt the presence of that spirit — the joy of companionship and of life — which had so ter- ribly eluded and escaped him in his own home of wealth and luxury. He heard Marie speak only once that night — once, in a low, soft voice to Thoreau. She was silent with the silence of the Cree wife in the presence of a stranger, but he knew that her heart was throbbing with the soft pulse of happiness, and for some reason he was glad when Thoreau nodded proudly toward a closed door and let him know that she was a mother. Marie heard him, and in that moment David caught in her face a look that made his heart ache — a look that should have been a part of his own life, and which he had missed.

A little later Thoreau led the way into the room which David was to occupy for the night. It was a small room, with a sapling partition between it and the one in which the Missioner was to sleep. The fox breeder placed a lamp on the table near the bed, and bade David good-night.

It was past two o'clock, and yet David felt at the present moment no desire for sleep. After he had taken off his shoes and partially undressed, he sat on the edge of his bed and allowed his mind to sweep back over the events of the last few hours. Again he thought of the woman in the coach — the woman with those wonderful, dark eyes and haunting face — and he drew forth from his coat pocket the package which she had forgotten. He handled it curiously. He looked at the red string, noted how tightly the knot was tied, and turned it over and over in his hands before he snapped the string. He was a little ashamed at his eagerness to know what was within its worn newspaper wrapping. He felt the disgrace of his curiosity, even though he assured himself there was no reason why he should not investigate the package now when all ownership was lost. He knew that he would never see the woman again, and that she would always remain a mystery to him unless what he held in his hands revealed the secret of her identity.

A half minute more and he was leaning over in the full light of the lamp, his two hands clutching the thing which the paper had disclosed when it dropped to the floor, his eyes staring, his lips parted, and his heart seeming to stand still in the utter amazement of the moment!

CHAPTER V

David held in his hands a photograph — the picture of a girl. He had half guessed what he would find when he began to unfold the newspaper wrapping and saw the edge of gray cardboard. In the same breath had come his astonishment — a surprise that was almost a shock. The night had been filled with changes for him; forces which he had not yet begun to comprehend had drawn him into the beginning of a strange adventure; they had purged his thoughts of *himself*; they had forced upon him other things, other people, and a glimpse or two of another sort of life; he had seen tragedy, and happiness — a bit of something to laugh at; and he had felt the thrill of it all. A few hours had made him the bewildered and yet passive object of the unexpected. And now, as he sat alone on the edge of his bed, had come the climax of the unexpected.

The girl in the picture was not dead — not merely a lifeless shadow put there by the art of a camera. She was alive! That was his first thought — his first impression. It was as if he had come upon her suddenly, and by his presence had startled her — had made her face him squarely, tensely, a little frightened, and yet defiant, and ready for flight. In that first moment he would not have disbelieved his eyes if she had moved, if she had drawn away from him and disappeared out of the picture with the swiftness of a bird. For he — some one — had startled her; some one had frightened her; some one had made her afraid, and yet defiant; some one had roused in her that bird-like impulse of flight even as the camera had clicked.

He bent closer into the lampglow, and stared. The girl was standing on a flat slab of rock close to the edge of a pool. Behind her was a carpet of white sand, and beyond that a rock-cluttered gorge and the side of a mountain. She was barefooted. Her feet were white against the dark rock. Her arms were bare to the elbows, and shone with that same whiteness. He took these things in one by one, as if it were impossible for the picture to impress itself upon him all at once. She stood leaning a little forward on the rock slab, her dress only a little below her knees, and as she leaned thus, her eyes flashing and her lips parted, the wind had flung a wonderful disarray of curls over her shoulder and breast. He saw the sunlight in them; in the lampglow they seemed to move; the throb of her breast seemed to give them life; one hand seemed about to fling them back from her face; her lips quivered as if about to speak to him. Against the savage background of mountain and gorge she stood out clear-cut as a cameo, slender as a reed, wild, palpitating, beautiful. She was more than a picture. She was life. She was there — with David in his room — as surely as the woman had been with him in the coach.

He drew a deep breath and sat back on the edge of his bed. He heard Father Roland getting into his creaky bed in the adjoining room. Then came the Missioner's voice.

"Good-night, David."

"Good-night, Father."

For a space after that he sat staring blankly at the log of his room. Then he leaned over again and held the photograph a second time in the lampglow. The first strange spell of the picture was broken, and he looked at it more coolly, more critically, a little disgusted with himself for having allowed his imagination to play a trick on him. He turned it over in his hands, and on the back of the cardboard mount he saw there had been writing. He examined it closely, and made out faintly the words, "Firepan Creek, Stikine River, August. . . ." and the date was gone. That was all. There was no name, no word that might give him a clue as to the identity of the mysterious woman in the coach, or her relationship to the strange picture she had left in her seat when she disappeared at Graham.

Once more his puzzled eyes tried to find some solution to the mystery of this night in the picture of the girl herself, and as he looked, question after question pounded through his head. What had startled her? Who had frightened her? What had brought that hunted look — that half defiance — into her poise and eyes, just as he had seen the strange questing and suppressed fear in the eyes and face of the woman in the coach? He made no effort to answer, but accepted the visual facts as they came to him. She was young, the girl in the picture; almost a child as he regarded childhood. Perhaps seventeen, or a month or two older; he was curiously precise in adding that month or two. Something in the *woman* of her as she stood on the rock made it occur to him as necessary. He saw, now, that she had been wading in the pool, for she had dropped a stocking on the white sand, and near it lay an object that was a shoe or a moccasin, he could not make out which. It was while she had been wading — alone — that the interruption had come; she had turned; she had sprung to the flat rock, her hands a little clenched, her eyes flashing, her breast panting under the smother of her hair; and it was in this moment, as she stood ready to fight — or fly — that the camera had caught her.

Now, as he scanned this picture, as it lived before his eyes, a faint smile played over his lips, a smile in which there was a little humour and much irony. He had been a fool that day, twice a fool, perhaps three times a fool. Nothing but folly, a diseased conception of things, could have made him see tragedy in the face of the woman in the coach, or have induced him to follow her. Sleeplessness — a mental exhaustion to which his body had not responded in two days and two nights — had dulled his senses and his reason. He felt an unpleasant desire to laugh at himself. Tragedy! A woman in distress! He shrugged his shoulders, and his teeth gleamed in a cold smile at the girl in the picture. Surely there was no tragedy or mystery in her poise on that rock! She had been bathing, alone, hidden away as she thought; some one had crept up, had disturbed her, and the camera had clicked at the psychological moment of her bird-like poise when she was not yet decided whether to turn in flight or remain and punish the intruder with her anger. It was quite clear to him. Any girl caught in the same way might have betrayed the same emotions. But — Firepan Creek — Stikine River. . . . And she was wild. She was a creature of those mountains and that wild gorge, wherever they were — and beautiful — slender as a flower — lovelier than. . . .

David set his lips tight. They shut off a quick breath, a gasp, the sharp surge of a sudden pain. Swift as his thoughts there had come a transformation in the picture before his eyes — a drawing of a curtain over it, like a golden veil; and then *she* was standing there, and the gold had gathered about her in the wonderful mantle of her hair — shining, dishevelled hair — a bare, white arm thrust upward through its sheen, and *her* face — taunting, unafraid — *laughing at him*! Good God! could he never kill that memory? Was it upon him again tonight, clutching at his throat, stifling his heart, grinding him into the agony he could not fight — that vision of her — *his wife?* That girl on her rock, so like a slender flower! That woman in her room, so like a golden goddess! Both caught — unexpectedly! What devil-spirit had made him pick up this picture from the woman's seat? What. . . .

His fingers tightened upon the photograph, ready to tear it into bits. The cardboard ripped an inch — and he stopped suddenly his impulse to destroy. The girl was looking at him again from out of the picture — looking at him with clear, wide eyes, surprised at his weakness, startled by the fierceness of his assault upon her, wondering, amazed, questioning him! For the first time he saw what he had missed before — that *questioning* in her eyes. It was as if she were on the point of asking him something — as if her voice had just come from between her parted lips, or were about to come. And for *him*; that was it — for *him!*

His fingers relaxed. He smoothed down the torn edge of the cardboard, as if it had been a wound in his own flesh. After all, this inanimate thing was very much like himself. It was lost, a thing out of place, and out of home; a wanderer from now on depending largely, like himself, on the charity of fate. Almost gently he returned it to its newspaper wrapping. Deep within him there was a sentiment which made him cherish little things which had belonged to the past — a baby's shoe, a faded ribbon, a withered flower that *she* had worn on the night they were married; and memories — memories that he might better have let droop and die. Something of this spirit was in the touch of his fingers as he placed the photograph on the table.

He finished undressing quietly. Before he turned in he placed a hand on his head. It was hot, feverish. This was not unusual, and it did not alarm him. Quite often of late these hot and feverish spells had come upon him, nearly always at night. Usually they were followed the next day by a terrific headache. More and more frequently they had been warning him how nearly down and out he was, and he knew what to expect. He put out his light and stretched himself between the warm blankets of his bed, knowing that he was about to begin again the fight he dreaded — the struggle that always came at night with the demon that lived within him, the demon that was feeding on his life as a leech feeds on blood, the demon that was killing him inch by inch. Nerves altogether unstrung! Nerves frayed and broken until they were bleeding! Worry — emptiness of heart and soul — a world turned black! And all because of *her* — the golden goddess who had laughed at him in her room, whose laughter would never die out of his ears. He gritted his teeth; his hands clenched under his blankets; a surge of anger swept through him — for an instant it was almost hatred. Was it possible that she — that woman who had been his wife — could chain him now, enslave his thoughts, fill his mind, his brain, his body, *after what had happened?* Why was it that he could not rise up and laugh and shrug his shoulders, and thank God that, after all, there had been no children? Why couldn't he do that? *Why?* Why?

A long time afterward he seemed to be asking that question. He seemed to be crying it out aloud, over and over again, in a strange and mysterious wilderness; and at last he seemed to be very near to a girl who was standing on a rock waiting for him; a girl who bent toward him like a wonderful flower, her arms reaching out, her lips parted, her eyes shining through the glory of her windswept hair as she listened to his cry of "*Why? Why?*"

He slept. It was a deep, cool sleep; a slumber beside a shadowed pool, with the wind whispering gently in strange tree tops, and water rippling softly in a strange stream.

CHAPTER VI

Sunshine followed storm. The winter sun was cresting the tree tops when Thoreau got out of his bed to build a fire in the big stove. It was nine o'clock, and bitterly cold. The frost lay thick upon the windows, with the sun staining it like the silver and gold of old cathedral glass, and as the fox breeder opened the cabin door to look at his thermometer he heard the snap and crack of that cold in the trees outside, and in the timbers of the log walls. He always looked at the thermometer before he built his fire — a fixed habit in him; he wanted to know, first of all, whether it had been a good night for his foxes, and whether it had been too cold for the furred creatures of the forest to travel. Fifty degrees below zero was bad for fisher and marten and lynx; on such nights they preferred the warmth of snug holes and deep windfalls to full stomachs, and his traps were usually empty. This morning it was forty-seven degrees below zero. Cold enough! He turned, closed the door, shivered. Then he stopped halfway to the stove, and stared.

Last night, or rather in that black part of the early day when they had gone to bed, Father Roland had warned him to make no noise in the morning; that they would let David sleep until noon; that he was sick, worn out, and needed rest. And there he stood now in the doorway of his room, even before the fire was started — looking five years younger than he looked last night, nodding cheerfully.

Thoreau grinned.

"*Boo-jou, m'sieu,*" he said in his Cree-French. "My order was to make no noise and to let you sleep," and he nodded toward the Missioner's room.

"The sun woke me," said David. "Come here. I want you to see it!"

Thoreau went and stood beside him, and David pointed to the one window of his room, which faced the rising sun. The window was covered with frost, and the frost as they looked at it was like a golden fire.

"I think that was what woke me," he said. "At least my eyes were on it when I opened them. It is wonderful!"

"It is very cold, and the frost is thick," said Thoreau. "It will go quickly after I have built a fire, m'sieu. And then you will see the sun — the real sun."

David watched him as he built the fire. The first crackling of it sent a comfort through him. He had slept well, so soundly that not once had he roused himself during his six hours in bed. It was the first time he had slept like that in months. His blood tingled with a new warmth. He had no headache. There was not that dull pain behind his eyes. He breathed more easily — the air passed like a tonic into his lungs. It was as if those wonderful hours of sleep had wrested some deadly obstruction out of his veins. The fire crackled. It roared up the big chimney. The jack-pine knots, heavy with pitch, gave to the top of the stove a rosy glow. Thoreau stuffed more fuel into the blazing firepot, and the glow spread cheerfully, and with the warmth that was filling the cabin there mingled the sweet scent of the pine-pitch and burning balsam. David rubbed his hands. He was rubbing them when Marie came into the room, plaiting the second of her two great ropes of shining black hair. He nodded. Marie smiled, showing her white teeth, her dark eyes clear as a fawn's. He felt within him a strange rejoicing — for Thoreau. Thoreau was a lucky man. He could see proof of it in the Cree woman's face. Both were lucky. They were happy — a man and woman together, as things should be.

Thoreau had broken the ice in a pail and now he filled the wash-basin for him. Ice water for his morning ablution was a new thing for David. But he plunged his face into it recklessly. Little particles of ice pricked his skin, and the chill of the water seemed to sink into his vitals. It was a sudden change from water as hot as he could stand — to this. His teeth clicked as he wiped himself on the burlap towelling. Marie used the basin next, and then Thoreau. When Marie had dried her face he noted the old-rose flush in her cheeks, the fire of rich, red blood glowing under her dark skin. Thoreau himself blubbered and spouted in his ice-water bath like a joyous porpoise, and he rubbed himself on the burlap until the two apple-red spots above his beard shone like the glow that had spread over the top of the stove. David found himself noticing these things — very small things though they were; he discovered himself taking a sudden and curious interest in events and things of no importance at all, even in the quick, deft slash of the Frenchman's long knife as he cut up the huge whitefish that was to be their breakfast. He watched Marie as she wallowed the thick slices in yellow corn-meal, and listened to the first hissing sputter of them as they were dropped into the hot grease of the skillet. And the odour of the fish, taken only yesterday from the net which Thoreau kept in the frozen lake, made him hungry. This was unusual. It was unexpected as other things that had happened. It puzzled him.

He returned to his room, with a suspicion in his mind that he should put on a collar and tie, and his coat. He changed his mind when he saw the photograph in its newspaper wrapping on the table. In another moment it was in his hands. Now, with day in the room, the sun shining, he expected to see a change. But there was no change in her; she was there, as he had left her last night; the question was in her eyes, unspoken words still on her lips. Then, suddenly, it swept upon him where he had been in those first hours of peaceful slumber that had come to him — beside a quiet, dark pool — gently whispering forests about him — an angel standing close to him, on a rock, shrouded in her hair — watching over him. A thrill passed through him. Was it possible? . . . He did not finish the question. He could not bring himself to ask whether this picture — some strange spirit it might possess — had reached out to him, quieted him, made him sleep, brought him dreams that were like a healing medicine. And yet. . . .

He remembered that in one of his leather bags there was a magnifying glass, and he assured himself that he was merely curious — most casually curious — as he hunted it out from among his belongings and scanned the almost illegible writing on the back of the cardboard mount. He made out the date quite easily now, impressed in the cardboard by the point of a pencil. It was only a little more than a year old. It was unaccountable why this discovery should affect him as it did. He made no effort to measure or sound the satisfaction it gave him — this knowledge that the girl had stood so recently on that rock beside the pool. He was beginning to personalize her unconsciously, beginning to think of her mentally as the Girl. She was a bit friendly. With her looking at him like that he did not feel quite so alone with himself. And there could not be much of a change in her since that yesterday of a year ago, when some one had startled her there.

It was Father Roland's voice that made him wrap up the picture again, this time not in its old covering, but in a silk handkerchief which he had pawed out of his bag, and which he dropped back again, and locked in. Thoreau was telling the Missioner about David's early rising when the latter reappeared. They shook hands, and the Missioner, looking David keenly in the eyes, saw the change in him.

"No need to tell me you had a good night!" he exclaimed.

"Splendid," affirmed David.

The window was blazing with the golden sun now; it shot through where the frost was giving way, and a ray of it fell like a fiery shaft on Marie's glossy head as she bent over the table. Father Roland pointed to the window with one hand on David's arm.

"Wait until you get out into *that*," he said. "This is just a beginning, David — just a beginning!"

They sat down to breakfast, fish and coffee, bread and potatoes — and beans. It was almost finished when David split open his third piece of fish, white as snow under its crisp brown, and asked quite casually:

"Did you ever hear of the Stikine River, Father?"

Father Roland sat up, stopped his eating, and looked at David for a moment as though the question struck an unusual personal interest in him.

"I know a man who lived for a great many years along the Stikine," he replied then. "He knows every mile of it from where it empties into the sea at Point Rothshay to the Lost Country between Mount Finlay and the Sheep Mountains. It's in the northern part of British Columbia, with its upper waters reaching into the Yukon. A wild country. A country less known than it was sixty years ago, when there was a gold rush up over the old telegraph trail. Tavish has told me a lot about it. A queer man — this Tavish. We hit his cabin on our way to God's Lake."

"Did he ever tell you," said David, with an odd quiver in his throat — "Did he ever tell you of a stream, a tributary stream, called Firepan Creek?"

"Firepan Creek — Firepan Creek," mumbled the Little Missioner. "He has told me a great many things, this Tavish, but I can't remember that. *Firepan Creek*! Yes, he did! I remember, now. He had a cabin on it one year, the year he had small-pox. He almost died there. I want you to meet Tavish, David. We will stay overnight at his cabin. He is a strange character — a great object lesson." Suddenly he came back to David's question. "What do you want to know about Stikine River and Firepan Creek?" he asked.

"I was reading something about them that interested me," replied David. "A *very* wild country, I take it, from what Tavish has told you. Probably no white people."

"Always, everywhere, there are a few white people," said Father Roland. "Tavish is white, and he was there. Sixty years ago, in the gold rush, there must have been many. But I fancy there are very few now. Tavish can tell us. He came from there only a year ago this last September."

David asked no more questions. He turned his attention entirely to his fish. In that same moment there came an outburst from the foxes that made Thoreau grin. Their yapping rose until it was a clamorous demand. Then the dogs joined in. To David it seemed as though there must be a thousand foxes out in the Frenchman's pens, and at least a hundred dogs just beyond the cabin walls. The sound was blood-curdling in a way. He had heard nothing like it before in all his life; it almost made one shiver to think of going outside. The chorus kept up for fully a minute. Then it began to die out, and David could hear the chill clink of chains. Through it all Thoreau was grinning.

"It's two hours over feeding time for the foxes, and they know it, m'sieur," he explained to David. "Their outcry excites the huskies, and when the two go together — *Mon Dieu*! it is enough to raise the dead." He pushed himself back from the table and rose to his feet. "I am going to feed them now. Would you like to see it, m'sieu?"

Father Roland answered for him.

"Give us ten minutes and we shall be ready," he said, seizing David by the arm, and speaking to Thoreau. "Come with me, David. I have something waiting for you."

They went into the Little Missioner's room, and pointing to his tumbled bed, Father Roland said:

"Now, David, strip!"

David had noticed with some concern the garments worn that morning by Father Roland and the Frenchman — their thick woollen shirts, their strange-looking, heavy trousers that were met just below the knees by the tops of bulky German socks, turned over as he had worn his more fashionable hosiery in the college days when golf suits, bulldog pipes, and white terriers were the rage. He had stared furtively at Thoreau's great feet in their moose-hide moccasins, thinking of his own vici kids, the heaviest footwear he had brought with him. The problem of outfitting was solved for him now, as he looked at the bed, and as Father Roland withdrew, rubbing his hands until they cracked, David began undressing. In less than a quarter of an hour he was ready for the big outdoors. When the Missioner returned to give him a first lesson in properly "stringing up" his moccasins, he brought with him a fur cap very similar to that worn by Thoreau. He was amazed to find how perfectly it fitted.

"You see," said Father Roland, pleased at David's wonder, "I always take back a bale of this stuff with me, of different sizes; it comes in handy, you know. And the cap. . . ."

He chuckled as David surveyed as much as he could see of himself in a small mirror.

"The cap is Marie's work," he finished. "She got the size from your hat and made it while we were asleep. A fine fisher-coat that — Thoreau's best. And a good fit, eh?"

"Marie . . . did this . . . for me?" demanded David.

The Missioner nodded.

"And the pay, Father. . . ."

"Among friends of the forests, David, never speak of pay."

"But this skin! It is beautiful — valuable. . . ."

"And it is yours," said Father Roland. "I am glad you mentioned payment to me, and not to Thoreau or Marie. They might not have understood, and it would have hurt them. If there had been anything to pay, *they* would have mentioned it in the giving; *I* would have mentioned it. That is a fine point of etiquette, isn't it?"

Slowly there came a look into David's face which the other did not at first understand. After a moment he said, without looking at the Missioner, and in a voice that had a curious hard note in it:

"But for this . . . Marie will let me give her something in return — a little something I have no use for now? A little gift — my thanks — my friendship. . . ."

He did not wait for the Missioner to reply, but went to one of his two leather bags. He unlocked the one in which he had placed the photograph of the girl. Out of it he took a small plush box. It was so small that it lay in the palm of his hand as he held it out to Father Roland.

Deeper lines had gathered about his mouth.

"Give this to Marie — for me."

Father Roland took the box. He did not look at it. Steadily he gazed into David's eyes.

"What is it?" he asked.

"A locket," replied David. "It belonged to *her*. In it is a picture — her picture — the only one I have. Will you — please — destroy the picture before you give the locket to Marie?"

Father Roland saw the quick, sudden throb in David's throat. He gripped the little box in his hand until it seemed as though he would crush it, and his heart was beating with the triumph of a drum. He spoke but one word, his eyes meeting David's eyes, but that one word was a whisper from straight out of his soul, and the word was:

"Victory!"

CHAPTER VII

Father Roland slipped the little plush box into his pocket as he and David went out to join Thoreau. They left the cabin together, Marie lifting her eyes from her work in a furtive glance to see if the stranger was wearing her cap.

A wild outcry from the dogs greeted the three men as they appeared outside the door, and for the first time David saw with his eyes what he had only heard last night. Among the balsams and spruce close to the cabin there were fully a score of the wildest and most savage-looking dogs he had ever beheld. As he stood for a moment, gazing about him, three things impressed themselves upon him in a flash: it was a glorious day, it was so cold that he felt a curious sting in the air, and not one of those long-haired, white-fanged beasts straining at their leashes possessed a kennel, or even a brush shelter. It was this last fact that struck him most forcefully. Inherently he was a lover of animals, and he believed these four-footed creatures of Thoreau's must have suffered terribly during the night. He noticed that at the foot of each tree to which a dog was attached there was a round, smooth depression in the snow, where the animal had slept. The next few minutes added to his conviction that the Frenchman and the Missioner were heartless masters, though open-handed hosts. Mukoki and another Indian had come up with two gunny sacks, and from one of these a bushel of fish was emptied out upon the snow. They were frozen stiff, so that Mukoki had to separate them with his belt-axe; David fancied they must be hard as rock. Thoreau proceeded to toss these fish to the dogs, one at a time, and one to each dog. The watchful and apparently famished beasts caught the fish in mid-air, and there followed a snarling and grinding of teeth and smashing of bones and frozen flesh that made David shiver. He was half disgusted. Thoreau might at least have boiled the fish, or thawed them out. A fish weighing from one and a half to two pounds was each dog's allotment, and the work — if this feeding process could be called work — was done. Father Roland watched the dogs, rubbing his hands with satisfaction. Thoreau was showing his big, white teeth, as if proud of something.

"Not a bad tooth among them, *mon Père*," he said. "Not one!"

"Fine — fine — but a little too fat, Thoreau. You're feeding them too well for dogs out of the traces," replied Father Roland.

David gasped.

"Too *well*!" he exclaimed. "They're half starved, and almost frozen! Look at the poor devils swallow those fish, ice and all!

Why don't you cook the fish? Why don't you give them some sort of shelter to sleep in?"

Father Roland and the Frenchman stared at him as if they did not quite catch his meaning. Then a look of comprehension swept over the Missioner's face. He chuckled, the chuckle grew, it shook his body, and he laughed — laughed until the forest flung back the echoes of his merriment, and even the leathery faces of the Indians crinkled in sympathy. David could see no reason for his levity. He looked at Thoreau. His host was grinning broadly.

"God bless my soul!" said the Little Missioner at last. "Starved? Cold? *Boil* their fish? Give 'em *beds*!" He stopped himself as he saw a flush rising in David's face. "Forgive me, David," he begged, laying a hand on the other's arm. "You can't understand how funny that was — what you said. If you gave those fellows the warmest kennels in New York City, lined with bear skins, they wouldn't sleep in them, but would come outside and burrow those little round holes in the snow. That's their nature. I've felt sorry for them, like you — when the thermometer was down to sixty. But it's no use. As for the fish — they want 'em fresh or frozen. I suppose you might educate them to eat cooked meat, but it would be like making over a lynx or a fox or a wolf. They're mighty comfortable, those dogs, David. That bunch of eight over there is mine. They'll take us north. And I want to warn you, don't put yourself in reach of them until they get acquainted with you. They're not pets, you know; I guess they'd appreciate petting just about as much as they would boiled fish, or poison. There's nothing on earth like a husky or an Eskimo dog when it comes to lookin' you in the eye with a friendly and lovable look and snapping your hand off at the same time. But you'll like 'em, David. You can't help feeling they're pretty good comrades when you see what they do in the traces."

Thoreau had shouldered the second gunny sack and now led the way into the thicker spruce and balsam behind the cabin. David and Father Roland followed, the latter explaining more fully why it was necessary to keep the sledge dogs "hard as rocks," and how the trick was done. He was still talking, with the fingers of one hand closed about the little plush box in his pocket, when they came to the first of the fox pens. He was watching David closely, a little anxiously — thrilled by the touch of that box. He read men as he read books, seeing much that was not in print, and feeling by a wonderful intuitive power emotions not visible in a face, and he believed that in David there were strange and conflicting forces struggling now for mastery. It was not in the surrender of the box that he had felt David's triumph, but in the voluntary sacrifice of what that box contained. He wanted to rid himself of the picture, and quickly. He was filled with apprehension lest David should weaken again, and ask for its return. The locket meant nothing. It was a bauble — cold, emotionless, easily forgotten; but the other — the picture of the woman who had almost destroyed him — was a deadly menace, a poison to David's soul and body as long as it remained in his possession, and the Little Missioner's fingers itched to tear it from the velvet casket and destroy it.

He watched his opportunity. As Thoreau tossed three fish over the high wire netting of the first pen the Frenchman was explaining to David why there were two female foxes and one male in each of his nine pens, and why warm houses partly covered with earth were necessary for their comfort and health, while the sledge dogs required nothing more than a bed of snow. Father Roland seized this opportunity to drop back toward the cabin, calling in Cree to Mukoki. Five seconds after the cabin concealed him from David he had the plush box out of his pocket; another five and he had opened it and the locket itself was in his hand. And then, his breath coming in a sudden, hissing spurt between his teeth, he was looking upon the face of the woman. Again in Cree he spoke to Mukoki, asking him for his knife. The Indian drew it from his sheath and watched in silence while Father Roland accomplished his work of destruction. The Missioner's teeth were set tight. There was a strange gleam of fire in his eyes. An unspoken malediction rose out of his soul. The work was done! He wanted to hurl the yellow trinket, shaped so sacrilegiously in the image of a heart, as far as he could fling it into the forest. It seemed to burn his fingers, and he held for it a personal hatred. But it was for Marie! Marie would prize it, and Marie would purify it. Against her breast, where beat a heart of his beloved Northland, it would cease to be a polluted thing. This was his thought as he replaced it in the casket and retraced his steps to the fox pens.

Thoreau was tossing fish into the last pen when Father Roland came up. David was not with him. In answer to the Missioner's inquiry he nodded toward the thicker growth of the forest where as yet his axe had not scarred the trees.

"He said that he would walk a little distance into the timber."

Father Roland muttered something that Thoreau did not catch, and then, a sudden brightness lighting up his eyes:

"I am going to leave you today."

"Today, *mon Père!*" Thoreau made a muffled exclamation of astonishment. "Today? And it is fairly well along toward noon!"

"He cannot travel far." The Missioner nodded in the direction of the unthinned timber. "It will give us four hours, between noon and dark. He is soft. You understand? We will make as far as the old trapping shack you abandoned two winters ago over on Moose Creek. It is only eight miles, but it will be a bit of hardening for him. And, besides. . . ."

He was silent for a moment, as if turning a matter over again in his own mind.

"I want to get him away."

He turned a searching, quietly analytic gaze upon Thoreau to see whether the Frenchman would understand without further explanation.

The fox breeder picked up the empty gunny sack.

"We will begin to pack the sledge, *mon Père*. There must be a good hundred pounds to the dog."

As they turned back to the cabin Father Roland cast a look over his shoulder to see whether David was returning.

Three or four hundred yards in the forest David stood in a mute and increasing wonder. He was in a tiny open, and about him the spruce and balsam hung still as death under their heavy cloaks of freshly fallen snow. It was as if he had entered unexpectedly into a wonderland of amazing beauty, and that from its dark and hidden bowers, crusted with their glittering mantles of white, snow naiads must be peeping forth at him, holding their breath for fear of betraying themselves to his eyes. There was not the chirp of a bird nor the flutter of a wing — not the breath of a sound to disturb the wonderful silence. He was encompassed in a white, soft world that seemed tremendously unreal — that for some strange reason made him breathe very softly, that made him stand without a movement, and made him listen, as though he had come to the edge of the universe and that there were mysterious things to hear, and possibly to see, if he remained very quiet. It was the first sensation of its kind he had ever experienced; it was disquieting, and yet soothing; it filled him with an indefinable uneasiness, and yet with a strange yearning. He stood, in these moments, at the inscrutable threshold of the great North; he felt the enigmatical, voiceless spirit of it; it passed into his blood; it made his heart beat a little faster; it made him afraid, and yet daring. In his breast the spirit of adventure was waking — had awakened; he felt the call of the Northland, and it alarmed even as it thrilled him. He knew, now, that this was the beginning — the door opening to him — of a world that reached for hundreds of miles up there. Yes, there were thousands of miles of it, many thousands; white, as he saw it here; beautiful, terrible, and deathly still. And into this world Father Roland had asked him to go, and he had as good as pledged himself!

Before he could think, or stop himself, he had laughed. For an instant it struck him like mirth in a tomb, an unpleasant, soulless sort of mirth, for his laugh had in it a jarring incredulity, a mocking lack of faith in himself. What right had *he* to enter into a world like that? Why, even now, his legs ached because of his exertion in furrowing through a few hundred steps of foot-and-a-half snow!

But the laugh succeeded in bringing him back into the reality of things. He started at right angles, pushed into the maze of white-robed spruce and balsam, and turned back in the direction of the cabin over a new trail. He was not in a good humour. There possessed him an ingrowing and acute feeling of animosity toward himself. Since the day — or night — fate had drawn that great, black curtain over his life, shutting out his sun, he had been drifting; he had been floating along on currents of the least resistance, making no fight, and, in the completeness of his grief and despair, allowing himself to disintegrate physically as well as mentally. He had sorrowed with himself; he had told himself that everything worth having was gone; but now, for the first time, he cursed himself. Today — these few hundred yards out in the snow — had come as a test. They had proved his weakness. He had degenerated into less than a man! He was. . . .

He clenched his hands inside his thick mittens, and a rage burned within him like a fire. Go with Father Roland? Go up into that world where he knew that the one great law of life was the survival of the fittest? Yes, he *would go*! This body and brain of his needed their punishment — and they should have it! He would go. And his body would fight for it, or die. The thought gave him an atrocious satisfaction. He was filled with a sudden contempt for himself. If Father Roland had known, he would have uttered a paean of joy.

Out of the darkness of the humour into which he had fallen, David was suddenly flung by a low and ferocious growl. He had stepped around a young balsam that stood like a seven-foot ghost in his path, and found himself face to face with a beast that was cringing at the butt of a thick spruce. It was a dog. The animal was not more than four or five short paces from him, and was chained to the tree. David surveyed him with sudden interest, wondering first of all why he was larger than the other dogs. As he lay crouched there against his tree, his ivory fangs gleaming between half uplifted lips, he looked like a great wolf. In the other dogs David had witnessed an avaricious excitement at the approach of men, a hungry demand for food, a straining at leash ends, a whining and snarling comradeship. Here he saw none of those things. The big, wolf-like beast made no sound after that first growl, and made no movement. And yet every muscle in his body seemed gathered in a tense readiness to spring, and his gleaming fangs threatened. He was ferocious, and yet shrinking; ready to leap, and yet afraid. He was like a thing at bay — a hunted creature that had been prisoned. And then David noticed that he had but one good eye. It was bloodshot, balefully alert, and fixed on him like a round ball of fire. The lids had closed over his other eye; they were swollen; there was a big lump just over where the eye should have been. Then he saw that the beast's lips were cut and bleeding. There was blood on the snow; and suddenly the big brute covered his fangs to give a racking cough, as though he had swallowed a sharp fish-bone, and fresh blood dripped out of his mouth on the snow between his forepaws. One of these forepaws was twisted; it had been broken.

"You poor devil!" said David aloud.

He sat down on a birch log within six feet of the end of the chain, and looked steadily into the big husky's one bloodshot eye as he said again:

"You poor devil!"

Baree, the dog, did not understand. It puzzled him that this man did not carry a club. He was used to clubs. So far back as he could remember the club had been the one dominant thing in his life. It was a club that had closed his eye. It was a club that had broken one of his teeth and cut his lips, and it was a club that had beat against his ribs until — now — the blood came up into his throat and choked him, and dripped out of his mouth. But this man had no club, and he looked friendly.

"You poor devil!" said David for the third time.

Then he added, dark indignation in his voice:

"What, in God's name, has Thoreau been doing to you?"

There was something sickening in the spectacle — that battered, bleeding, broken creature huddling there against the tree, coughing up the red stuff that discoloured the snow. Loving dogs, he was not afraid of them, and forgetting Father Roland's warning he rose from the log and went nearer. From where he stood, looking down, Baree could have reached his throat. But he made no movement, unless it was that his thickly haired body was trembling a little. His one red eye looked steadily up at David.

For the fourth time David spoke;

"You poor, God-forsaken brute!"

There was friendliness, compassion, wonderment in his voice, and he held down a hand that he had drawn from one of the thick mittens. Another moment and he would have bent over, but a cry stopped him so sharply and suddenly that he jumped back.

Thoreau stood within ten feet of him, horrified. He clutched a rifle in one hand.

"Back — back, m'sieu!" he cried sharply. "For the love of God, jump back."

He swung his rifle into the crook of his arm. David did not move, and from Thoreau he looked down coolly at the dog. Baree was a changed beast. His one eye was fastened upon the fox breeder. His bared, bleeding lips revealed inch-long fangs between which there came now a low and menacing snarl. The tawny crest along his spine was like a brush; from a puzzled toleration of David his posture and look had changed into deadly hatred for Thoreau, and fear of him. For a moment after his first warning the Frenchman's voice seemed to stick in his throat as he saw what he believed to be David's fatal disregard of his peril. He did not speak to him again. His eyes were on the dog. Slowly he raised his rifle; David heard the click of the hammer — and Baree heard it. There was something in the sharp, metallic thrill of it that stirred his brute instinct. His lips fell over his fangs, he whined, and then, on his belly, he dragged himself slowly toward David!

It was a miracle that Thoreau the Frenchman looked upon then. He would have staked his very soul — wagered his hopes of paradise against a *babiche* thread — that what he saw could never have happened between Baree and man. In utter amazement he lowered his gun. David, looking down, was smiling into that one, wide-open, bloodshot eye of Baree's, his hand reaching out. Foot by foot Baree slunk to him on his belly, and when at last he was at David's feet he faced Thoreau again, his terrible teeth snarling, a low, rumbling growl in his throat. David reached down and touched him, even as he heard the fox breeder make an incoherent sound in his beard. At the caress of his hand a great shudder passed through Baree's body, as if he had been stung. That touch was the connecting link through which passed the electrifying thrill of a man's soul reaching out to a brute instinct.

Baree had found a man friend!

When David stepped away from him to Thoreau's side as

much of the Frenchman's face as was not hidden under his beard was of a curious ashen pallor. He seemed to make a struggle before he could get his voice.

And then: "M'sieu, I tell you it is incredible! I cannot believe what I have seen. It was a miracle!"

He shuddered. David was looking at him, a bit puzzled. He could not quite comprehend the fear that had possessed him. Thoreau saw this, and pointing to Baree — a gesture that brought a snarl from the beast — he said:

"He is bad, m'sieu, *bad*! He is the worst dog in all this country. He was born an outcast — among the wolves — and his heart is filled with murder. He is a quarter wolf, and you can't club it out of him. Half a dozen masters have owned him, and none of them has been able to club it out of him. I, myself, have beaten him until he lay as if dead, but it did no good. He has killed two of my dogs. He has leaped at my throat. I am afraid of him. I chained him to that tree a month ago to keep him away from the other dogs, and since then I have not been able to unleash him. He would tear me into pieces. Yesterday I beat him until he was almost dead, and still he was ready to go at my throat. So I am determined to kill him. He is no good. Step a little aside, m'sieu, while I put a bullet through his head!"

He raised his rifle again. David put a hand on it.

"I can unleash him," he said.

Before the other could speak, he had walked boldly to the tree. Baree did not turn his head — did not for an instant take his eye from Thoreau. There came the click of the snap that fastened the chain around the body of the spruce, and David stood with the loose end of the chain in his hand.

"There!"

He laughed a little proudly.

"And I didn't use a club," he added.

Thoreau gasped "*Mon Dieu!*" and sat down on the birch log as though the strength had gone from his legs.

David rattled the chain and then re-fastened it about the spruce. Baree was still watching Thoreau, who sat staring at him as if the beast had suddenly changed his shape and species.

In David's breast there was the thrill of a new triumph. He had done it unconsciously, without fear, and without feeling that there had been any great danger. In those few minutes something of his old self had returned into him; he felt a new excitement pumping the blood through his heart, and he felt the warm glow of it in his body. Baree had awakened something within him —

Baree and the *club*. He went to Thoreau, who had risen from the log. He laughed again, a bit exultantly.

"I am going north with Father Roland," he said. "Will you let me have the dog, Thoreau? It will save you the trouble of killing him."

Thoreau stared at him blankly for a moment before he answered.

"That dog? You? Into the North?" He shot a look full of hatred and disgust at Baree. "Would you risk it, m'sieu?"

"Yes. It is an adventure I would very much like to try. You may think it strange, Thoreau, but that dog — ugly and fierce as he is — has found a place with me. I like him. And I fancy he has begun to like me."

"But look at his eye, m'sieu — — "

"Which eye?" demanded David. "The one you have shut with a club?"

"He deserved it," muttered Thoreau. "He snapped at my hand. But I mean the other eye, m'sieu — the one that is glaring at us now like a red bloodstone with the heart of a devil in it! I tell you he is a quarter wolf. . . ."

"And the broken paw. I suppose that was done by a club, too?" interrupted David.

"It was broken like that when I traded for him a year ago, m'sieu. I have not maimed him. And . . . yes, you may have the beast! May the saints preserve you!"

"And his name?"

"The Indian who owned him as a puppy five years ago called him Baree, which among the Dog Ribs means Wild Blood. He should have been called The Devil."

Thoreau shrugged his shoulders, as though the matter and its consequences were now off his hands, and turned in the direction of the cabin. As he followed the Frenchman, David looked back at Baree. The big husky had risen from the snow. He was standing at the full length of his chain, and as David disappeared among the spruce a low whine that was filled with a strange yearning followed him. He did not hear the whine, but there came to him distinctly a moment later the dog's racking cough, and he shivered, and his eyes burned into Thoreau's broad back as he thought of the fresh blood-clots that were staining the white snow.

CHAPTER VIII

Much to Thoreau's amazement Father Roland made no objection to David's ownership of Baree, and when the Frenchman described with many gesticulations of wonder what had happened between that devil-dog and the man, he was still more puzzled by the look of satisfaction in the Little Missioner's face. In David there had come the sudden awakening of something which had for a long time been dormant within him, and Father Roland saw this change, and felt it, even before David said, when Thoreau had turned away with a darkly suggestive shrug of his shoulders:

"That poor devil of a beast is down and out, *mon Père*. I have never been so bad as that; never. Kill him? Bah! If this magical north country of yours will make a man out of a human derelict it will surely work some sort of a transformation in a dog that has been clubbed into imbecility. Will it not?"

It was not the David of yesterday or the day before that was speaking. There was a passion in his voice, a deep contempt, a half taunt, a tremble of anger. There was a flush in his cheeks, too, and a spark of fire in his eyes. In his heart Father Roland whispered to himself that this change in David was like a conflagration, and he rejoiced without speaking, fearing that words might quench the effect of it.

David was looking at him as if he expected an answer.

"What an accursed fool a man is to waste his soul and voice in lamentation — especially his voice," he went on harshly, his teeth gleaming for an instant in a bitter smile. "One ought to act and not whine. That beast back there is ready to act. He would tear Thoreau's jugular out if he had half a chance. And I . . . why, I sneaked off like a whipped cur. That's why Baree is better than I am, even though he is nothing more than a four-footed brute. In that room I should have had the moral courage that Baree has; I should have killed — killed them both!" He shrugged his shoulders. "I am quite convinced that it would have been justice, *mon Père*. What do you think?"

The Missioner smiled enigmatically.

"The soul of many a man has gone from behind steel bars to heaven or I vastly miss my guess," he said. "But — we don't like the thought of steel bars, do we, David? Man-made laws and justice don't always run tandem. But God evens things up in the final balance. You'll live to see that. He's back there now, meting out your vengeance to them. *Your* vengeance. Do you understand? And you won't be called to take a hand in the business." Suddenly he pointed toward the cabin, where Thoreau and Mukoki were already at work packing a sledge. "It's a glorious day. We start right after dinner. Let us get your things in a bundle."

David made no answer, but three minutes later he was on his knees unlocking his trunk, with Father Roland standing close beside him. Something of the humour of the situation possessed him as he flung out, one by one, the various articles of his worthless apparel, and when he had all but finished he looked up into the Missioner's face. Father Roland was staring into the trunk, an expression of great surprise in his countenance which slowly changed to one of eager joy. He made a sudden dive, and stood back with a pair of boxing gloves in his hands. From the gloves he looked at David, and then back at the gloves, fondling them as if they had been alive, his hands almost trembling at the smooth touch of them, his eyes glowing like the eyes of a child that had come into possession of a wonderful toy. David reached into the trunk and produced a second pair. The Missioner seized upon them.

"Dear Heaven, what a gift from the gods!" he chortled. "David, you will teach me to use them?" There was almost anxiety in his manner as he added, "You know how to use them well, David?"

"My chief pastime at home was boxing," assured David. There was a touch of pride in his voice. "It is a scientific recreation. I loved it — that, and swimming. Yes, I will teach you."

Father Roland went out of the room a moment later, chuckling mysteriously, with the four gloves hugged against the pit of his stomach.

David followed a little later, all his belongings in one of the leather bags. For some time he had hesitated over the portrait of the Girl; twice he had shut the lock on it; the third time he placed it in the big, breast pocket inside the coat Father Roland had provided for him, making a mental apology for that act by assuring himself that sooner or later he would show the picture to the Missioner, so would want it near at hand. Father Roland had disposed of the gloves, and introduced David to the rest of his equipment when he came from the cabin. It was very business-like, this accoutrement that was to be the final physical touch to his transition; it did not allow of skepticism; about it there was also a quiet and cold touch of romance. The rifle chilled David's bare fingers when he touched it. It was short-barrelled, but heavy in the breech, with an appearance of indubitable efficiency about it. It looked like an honest weapon to David, who was unaccustomed to firearms — and this was more than he could say for the heavy, 38-calibre automatic pistol which Father Roland thrust into his hand, and which looked and felt murderously mysterious. He frankly confessed his ignorance of these things, and the Missioner chuckled good-humouredly as he buckled the belt and holster about his waist and told him on which hip to keep the pistol, and where to carry the leather sheath that held a long and keen-edged hunting knife. Then he turned to the snow shoes. They were the long, narrow, bush-country shoe. He placed them side by side on the snow and showed David how to fasten his moccasined feet in them without using his hands. For three quarters of an hour after that, out in the soft, deep snow in the edge of the spruce, he gave him his first lesson in that slow, swinging, *out*-stepping stride of the north-man on the trail. At first it was embarrassing for David, with Thoreau and the Indians grinning openly, and Marie's face peering cautiously and joyously from the cabin door. Three times he entangled his feet hopelessly and floundered like a great fish in the snow; then he caught the "swing" of it and at the end of half an hour began to find a pleasurable exhilaration, even excitement, in his ability to skim over the feathery surface of this great white sea without so much as sinking to his ankle bones. When he slipped the shoes off and stood them up beside his rifle against the cabin, he was panting. His heart was pounding. His lungs drank in the cold, balsam-scented air like a suction pump and expelled each breath with the sibilancy of steam escaping from a valve.

"Winded!" he gasped. And then, gulping for breath as he looked at Father Roland, he demanded: "How the devil am I going to keep up with you fellows on the trail? I'll go bust inside of a mile!"

"And every time you go bust we'll load you on the sledge," comforted the Missioner, his round face glowing with enthusiastic approval. "You've done finely, David. Within a fortnight you'll be travelling twenty miles a day on snow shoes."

He suddenly seemed to think of something that he had forgotten and fidgeted with his mittens in his hesitation, as if there lay an unpleasant duty ahead of him. Then he said:

"If there are any letters to write, David . . . any business matters. . . ."

"There are no letters," cut in David quickly. "I attended to my affairs some weeks ago. I am ready."

With a frozen whitefish he returned to Baree. The dog scented him before the crunch of his footsteps could be heard in the snow, and when he came out from the thick spruce and balsam into the little open, Baree was stretched out flat on his belly, his gaunt gray muzzle resting on the snow between his forepaws. He made no movement as David drew near, except that curious shivers ran through his body, and his throat twitched. Thoreau would have analyzed that impassive posture as one of waiting and watchful treachery; David saw in it a strange yearning, a deep fear, a hope. Baree, outlawed by man, battered and bleeding as he lay there, felt for perhaps the first time in his life the thrilling presence of a friend — a man friend. David approached boldly, and stood over him. He had forgotten the Frenchman's warning. He was not afraid. He leaned over and one of his mittened hands touched Baree's neck. A tremor shot through the dog that was like an electric shock; a snarl gathered in his throat, broke down, and ended in a low whine. He lay as if dead under the weight of David's hand. Not until David had ceased talking to him, and had disappeared once more in the direction of the cabin, did Baree begin devouring the frozen whitefish.

Father Roland meditated in some perplexity when it came to the final question of Baree.

"We can't put him in with the team," he protested. "All my dogs would be dead before we reached God's Lake."

David had been thinking of that.

"He will follow me," he said confidently. "We'll simply turn him loose when we're ready to start."

The Missioner nodded indulgently. Thoreau, who had overheard, shrugged his shoulders contemptuously. He hated Baree, the beast that would not yield to a club, and he muttered gruffly:

"And tonight he will join the wolves, m'sieu, and prey like the very devil on my traps. There will be only one cure for that — a fox-bait! — poison!"

And the last hour seemed to prove that what Thoreau had said was true. After dinner the three of them went to Baree, and David unfastened the chain from the big husky's collar. For a few moments the dog did not seem to sense his freedom; then, like a shot — so unexpectedly that he almost took David off his feet — he leaped over the birch log and disappeared in the forest. The Frenchman was amused.

"The wolves," he reminded softly. "He will be with them tonight, m'sieu — that outlaw!"

Not until the crack of Mukoki's long, caribou-gut whip had set the Missioner's eight dogs tense and alert in their traces did Father Roland return for a moment into the cabin to give Marie the locket. He came back quickly, and at a signal from him Mukoki wound up the 9-foot lash of his whip and set out ahead of the dogs. They followed him slowly and steadily, keeping the broad runners of the sledge in the trail he made. The Missioner dropped in immediately behind the sledge, and David behind him. Thoreau spoke a last word to David, in a voice intended for his ears alone.

"It is a long way to God's Lake, m'sieu, and you are going with a strange man — a strange man. Some day, if you have not forgotten Pierre Thoreau, you may tell me what it has been a long time in my heart to know. The saints be with you, m'sieu!"

He dropped back. His voice rolled after them in a last farewell, in French, and in Cree, and as David followed close behind the Missioner he wondered what Thoreau's mysterious words had meant, and why he had not spoken them until that final moment of their departure. "A strange man! The saints be with you!" That last had seemed to him almost a warning. He looked at Father Roland's broad back; for the first time he noticed how heavy and powerful his shoulders were for his height. Then the forest swallowed them — a vast, white, engulfing world of silence and mystery. What did it hold for him? What did it portend? His blood was stirred by an unfamiliar and subdued excitement. An almost unconscious movement carried one of his mittened hands to his breast pocket. Through the thickness of his coat he could feel it — the picture. It did not seem like a dead thing. It beat with life. It made him strangely unafraid of what might be ahead of him.

Back at the door of the cabin Thoreau stood with one of his big arms encircling Marie's slim shoulders.

"I tell you it is like taking the life of a puppy, *ma cherie*," he was saying. "It is inconceivable. It is bloodthirsty. And yet. . . ."

He opened the door behind them.

"They are gone," he finished. "*Ka Sakhet* — they are gone — and they will not come back!"

CHAPTER IX

In spite of the portentous significance of this day in his life David could not help seeing and feeling in his suddenly changed environment, as he puffed along behind Father Roland, something that was neither adventure nor romance, but humour. A whimsical humour at first, but growing grimmer as his thoughts sped. All his life he had lived in a great city, he had been a part of its life — a discordant note in it, and yet a part of it for all that. He had been a fixture in a certain lap of luxury. That luxury had refined him. It had manicured him down to a fine point of civilization. A fine point! He wanted to laugh, but he had need of all his breath as he *clip-clip-clipped* on his snow shoes behind the Missioner. This was the last thing in the world he had dreamed of, all this snow, all this emptiness that loomed up ahead of him, a great world filled only with trees and winter. He disliked winter; he had always possessed a physical antipathy for snow; romance, for him, was environed in warm climes and sunny seas. He had made a mistake in telling Father Roland that he was going to British Columbia — a great mistake. Undoubtedly he would have kept on. Japan had been in his mind. And now here he was headed straight for the north pole — the Arctic Ocean. It was enough to make him want to laugh. Enough to make any sane person laugh. Even now, only half a mile from Thoreau's cabin, his knees were beginning to ache and his ankles were growing heavy. It was ridiculous. Inconceivable, as the Frenchman had said to Marie. He was soft. He was only half a man. How long would he last? How long before he would have to cry quits, like a whipped boy? How long before his legs would crumple up under him, and his lungs give out? How long before Father Roland, hiding his contempt, would have to send him back?

A sense of shame — shame and anger — swept through him, heating his brain, setting his teeth hard, filling him again with a grim determination. For the second time that day his fighting blood rose. It surged through his veins in a flood, beating down the old barriers, clearing away the obstructions of his doubts and his fears, and filling him with the *desire* to go on — the desire to fight it out, to punish himself as he deserved to be punished, and to win in the end. Father Roland, glancing back in benignant solicitude, saw the new glow in David's eyes. He saw, also, his parted lips and the quickness of his breath. With a sharp command he stopped Mukoki and the dogs.

"Half a mile at a time is enough for a beginner," he said to

David. "Back off your shoes and ride the next half mile."

David shook his head.

"Go on," he said, tersely, saving his wind. "I'm just finding myself."

Father Roland loaded and lighted his pipe. The aroma of the tobacco filled David's nostrils as they went on. Clouds of smoke wreathed the Little Missioner's shoulders as he followed the trail ahead of him. It was comforting, that smoke. It warmed David with a fresh desire. His exertion was clearing out his lungs. He was inhaling balsam and spruce, a mighty tonic of dry forest air, and he felt also the craving to smoke. But he knew that he could not afford the waste of breath. His snow shoes were growing heavier and heavier, and back of his knees the tendons seemed preparing to snap. He kept on, at last counting his steps. He was determined to make a mile. He was ready to groan when a sudden twist in the trail brought them out of the forest to the edge of a lake whose frozen surface stretched ahead of them for miles. Mukoki stopped the dogs. With a gasp David floundered to the sledge and sat down.

"Finding myself," he managed to say. "Just — finding myself!"

It was a triumph for him — the last half of that mile. He knew it. He felt it. Through the white haze of his breath he looked out over the lake. It was wonderfully clear, and the sun was shining. The surface of the lake was like an untracked carpet of white sprinkled thickly with tiny diamonds where the sunlight fell on its countless billions of snow crystals. Three or four miles away he could see the dark edge of the forest on the other side. Up and down the lake the distance was greater. He had never seen anything like it. It was marvellous — like a dream picture. And he was not cold as he looked at it. He was warm, even uncomfortably warm. The air he breathed was like a new kind of fuel. It gave him the peculiar sensation of feeling *larger* inside; he seemed to drink it in; it expanded his lungs; he could feel his heart pumping with an audible sound. There was nothing in the majesty and wonder of the scene about him to make him laugh, but he laughed. It was exultation, an involuntary outburst of the change that was working within him. He felt, suddenly, that a dark and purposeless world had slipped behind him. It was gone. It was as if he had come out of a dark and gloomy cavern, in which the air had been vitiated and in which he had been cramped for breath — a cavern which fluttered with the uneasy ghosts of things, poisonous things. Here was the sun. A sky blue as sapphire. A great expanse. A wonder-world. Into this he had escaped!

That was the thought in his mind as he looked at Father Roland. The Little Missioner was looking at him with an effulgent satisfaction in his face, a satisfaction that was half pride, as though he had achieved something that was to his own personal glory.

"You've beat me, David," he exulted. "The first time I had snow shoes on I didn't make one half that distance before I was tangled up like a fish in a net!" He turned to Mukoki. "*Mey-oo iss e chikao!*" he cried. "Remember?" and the Indian nodded, his leathery face breaking into a grin.

David felt a new pleasure at their approbation. He had evidently done well, exceedingly well. And he had been afraid of himself! Apprehension gave way to confidence. He was beginning to experience the exquisite thrill of fighting against odds.

He made no objection this time when Father Roland made a place for him on the sledge.

"We'll have four miles of this lake," the Missioner explained to him, "and the dogs will make it in an hour. Mukoki and I will both break trail."

As they set off David found his first opportunity to see the real Northland in action — the clean, sinuous movement of the men ahead of him, the splendid eagerness with which the long, wolfish line of beasts stretched forth in their traces and followed in the snow-shoe trail. There was something imposing about it all, something that struck deep within him and roused strange thoughts. This that he saw was not the mere labour of man and beast; it was not the humdrum toil of life, not the daily slaving of living creatures for existence — for food, and drink, and a sleeping place. It had risen above that. He had seen ships and castles rise up from heaps of steel and stone; achievements of science and the handiwork of genius had interested and sometimes amazed him, but never had he looked upon physical effort that thrilled him as did this that he was looking upon now. There was almost the spirit of the epic about it. They *were* the survival of the fittest — these men and dogs. They had gone through the great test of life in the raw, as the pyramids and the sphinx had outlived the ordeals of the centuries; they were different; they were proven; they were of another kind of flesh and blood than he had known — and they fascinated him. They stood for more than romance and adventure, for more than tragedy or possible joy; they were making no fight for riches — no fight for power, or fame, or great personal achievement. Their struggle in this great, white world — terrible in its emptiness, its vastness, and its mercilessness for the weak — was simply a struggle that they might *live*.

The thought staggered him. Could there be joy in that — in a mere existence without the thousand pleasures and luxuries and excitements that he had known? He drank deeply of the keen air as he asked himself the question. His eyes rested on the shaggy, undulating backs of the big huskies; he noted their half open jaws, the sharp alertness of their pointed ears, the almost joyous unction with which they entered into their task, their eagerness to keep their load close upon the heels of their masters. He heard Mukoki's short, sharp, and unnecessary commands, his *hi-yi's* and his *ki-yi's*, as though he were crying out for no other reason than from sheer physical exuberance. He saw Father Roland's face turned backward for a moment, and it was smiling. They were happy — now! Men and beasts were happy. And he could see no reason for their happiness except that their blood was pounding through their veins, even as it was pounding through his own. That was it — the blood. The heart. The lungs. The brain. All were clear — clear and unfettered in that marvellous air and sunlight, washed clean by the swift pulse of life. It was a wonderful world! A glorious world! He was almost on the point of crying aloud his discovery.

The thrill grew in him as he found time now to look about. Under him the broad, steel runners of the sledge made a cold, creaking sound as they slipped over the snow that lay on the ice of the lake; he heard the swift *tap, tap, tap* of the dogs' feet, their panting breath that was almost like laughter, low throat whines, and the steady swish of the snow shoes ahead. Beyond those sounds a vast silence encompassed him. He looked out into it, east and west to the dark rims of forest, north and south over the distance of that diamond-sprinkled *tundra* of unbroken white. He drew out his pipe, loaded it with tobacco, and began to smoke. The bitterness of the weed was gone. It was delicious. He puffed luxuriously. And then, suddenly, as he looked at the purplish bulwarks of the forest, his mind swept back. For the first time since that night many months ago he thought of the Woman — the Golden Goddess — without a red-hot fire in his brain. He thought of her coolly. This new world was already giving back to him a power of analysis, a perspective, a healthier conception of truths and measurements. What a horrible blot they had made in his life — that man and that woman! What a foul trick they had played him! What filth they had wallowed in! And he — he had thought her the most beautiful creature in the world, an angel, a thing to be worshipped. He laughed, almost without sound, his teeth biting hard on the stem of his pipe. And the world he was looking upon laughed; the snow diamonds, lying thickly as dust, laughed; there was laughter in the sun, the warmth of chuckling humour in those glowing walls of forest, laughter in the blue sky above.

His hands gripped hard.

In this world he knew there could not be another woman such as she. Here, in all this emptiness and glory, her shallow soul would have shrieked in agony; she would have shrivelled up and died. It was too clean. Too white. Too pure. It would have frightened her, tortured her. She could not have found the poison she required to give her life. Her unclean desires would have driven her mad. So he arraigned her, terribly, without malice, and without pity. And then, like the quieting touch of a gentle hand in his brain, came the thought of the other woman — the Girl — whose picture he carried in his pocket. This was *her* world that he was entering. She was up there — somewhere — and he looked over the barriers of the forest to the northwest. Hundreds of miles away. A thousand. It was a big world, so vast that he still could not comprehend it. But she was there, living, breathing, *alive*! A sudden impulse made him draw the picture from his pocket. He held it down behind a bale, so that Father Roland would not chance to see it if he looked back. He unwrapped the picture, and ceased to puff at his pipe. The Girl was wonderful today, under the sunlight and the blue halo of the skies, and she wanted to speak to him. That thought always came to him first of all when he looked at her. She wanted to speak. Her lips were trembling, her eyes were looking straight into his, the sun above him seemed to gleam in her hair. It was as if she knew of the thoughts that were in his mind, and of the fight he was making; as though through space she had seen him, and watched him, and wanted to cry out for him the way to come. There was a curious tremble in his fingers as he restored the picture to his pocket. He whispered something. His pipe had gone out. In the same moment a sharp cry from Father Roland startled him. The dogs halted suddenly. The creaking of the sledge runners ceased.

Father Roland had turned his face down the lake, and was pointing.

"Look!" he cried.

David jumped from the sledge and stared back over their trail. The scintillating gleams of the snow crystals were beginning to prick his eyes, and for a few moments he could see nothing new. He heard a muffled ejaculation of surprise from Mukoki. And then, far back — probably half a mile — he saw a dark object travelling slowly toward them. It stopped. It was motionless as a dark rock now. Close beside him the Little Missioner said:

"You've won again, David. Baree is following us!"

The dog came no nearer as they watched. After a moment David pursed his lips and sent back a curious, piercing whistle. In days to come Baree was to recognize that call, but he gave no attention to it now. For several minutes they stood gazing back at him. When they were ready to go on David for a third time that day put on his snow shoes. His task seemed less difficult. He was getting the "swing" of the shoes, and his breath came more easily. At the end of half an hour Father Roland halted the team again to give him a "winding" spell. Baree had come nearer. He was not more than a quarter of a mile behind. It was three o'clock when they struck off the lake into the edge of the forest to the northwest. The sun had grown cold and pale. The snow crystals no longer sparkled so furiously. In the forest there was gathering a gray, silent gloom. They halted again in the edge of that gloom. The Missioner slipped off his mittens and filled his pipe with fresh tobacco. The pipe fell from his fingers and buried itself in the soft snow at his feet. As he bent down for it Father Roland said quite audibly:

"Damn!"

He was smiling when he rose. David, also, was smiling.

"I was thinking," he said — as though the other had demanded an explanation of his thoughts — "what a curious man of God you are, *mon Père!*"

The Little Missioner chuckled, and then he muttered, half to himself as he lighted the tobacco, "True — very true." When the top of the bowl was glowing, he added: "How are your legs? It is still a good mile to the shack."

"I am going to make it or drop," declared David.

He wanted to ask a question. It had been in his mind for some time, and he burned with a strange eagerness to have it answered. He looked back, and saw Baree circling slowly over the surface of the lake toward the forest. Casually he inquired:

"How far is it to Tavish's, *mon Père?*"

"Four days," said the Missioner. "Four days, if we make good time, and another week from there to God's Lake. I have paid Tavish a visit in five days, and once Tavish made God's Lake in two days and a night with seven dogs. Two days and a night! Through darkness he came — darkness and a storm. That is what fear will do, David. Fear drove him. I have promised to tell you about it tonight. You must know, to understand him. He is a strange man — a very strange man!"

He spoke to Mukoki in Cree, and the Indian responded with a sharp command to the dogs. The huskies sprang from their bellies and strained forward in their traces. The Cree picked his way slowly ahead of them. Father Roland dropped in behind him. Again David followed the sledge. He was struck with wonder at the suddenness with which the sun had gone out. In the thick forest it was like the beginning of night. The deep shadows and darkly growing caverns of gloom seemed to give birth to new sounds. He heard the *whit, whit, whit,* of something close to him, and the next moment a great snow owl flitted like a ghostly apparition over his head; he heard the patter of snow as it fell from the bending limbs; from out of a patch of darkness two trees, rubbing slightly against each other, emitted a shivering wail that startled him — it had seemed so like the cry of a child. He was straining his ears so tensely to hear, and his eyes to see, that he forgot the soreness of his knees and ankles. Now and then the dogs stopped while Mukoki and the Missioner dragged a log or a bit of brushwood from their path. During one of these intervals there came to them, from a great distance, a long, mournful howl.

"A wolf!" said Father Roland, his face a gray shadow as he nodded at David. "Listen!"

From behind them came another cry. It was Baree.

They went on, circling around the edge of a great windfall. A low wind was beginning to move in the tops of the spruce and cedar, and soft splashes of snow fell on their heads and shoulders, as if unseen and playful hands were pelting them from above. Again and again David caught the swift, ghostly flutter of the snow owls; three times he heard the wolf-howl; once again Baree's dismal, homeless cry; and then they came suddenly out of the thick gloom of the forest into the twilight gray of a clearing. Twenty paces from them was a cabin. The dogs stopped. Father Roland fumbled at his big silver watch, and held it close up to his eyes.

"Half past four," he said. "Fairly good time for a beginner, David!"

He broke into a cheerful whistle. The dogs were whining and snapping like joyous puppies as Mukoki unfastened them. The Cree himself was voluble in a chuckling and meaningless way. There was a great contentment in the air, an indefinable inspiration that seemed to lift the gloom. David could not understand it, though in an elusive sort of way he felt it. He did not understand until Father Roland said, across the sledge, which he had begun to unpack:

"Seems good to be on the trail again, David."

That was it — the trail! This was the end of a day's achievement. He looked at the cabin, dark and unlighted in the open, with its big white cap of snow. It looked friendly for all its darkness. He was filled with the desire to become a partner in the activities of Mukoki and the Missioner. He wanted to help, not because he placed any value on his assistance, but simply because his blood and his brain were imposing new desires upon him. He kicked off his snow shoes, and went with Mukoki to the door of the cabin, which was fastened with a wooden bolt. When they entered he could make out things indistinctly — a stove at first, a stool, a box, a small table, and a bunk against the wall. Mukoki was rattling the lids of the stove when Father Roland entered with his arms filled. He dropped his load on the floor, and David went back to the sledge with him. By the time they had brought its burden into the cabin a fire was roaring in the stove, and Mukoki had hung a lighted lantern over the table. Then Father Roland seized an axe, tested its keen edge with his thumb, and said to David: "Let's go cut our beds before it's too dark." Cut their beds! But the Missioner's broad back was disappearing through the door in a very purposeful way, and David caught up a second axe and followed. Young balsams twice as tall as a man were growing about the cabin, and from these Father Roland began stripping the branches. They carried armfuls into the cabin until the one bunk was heaped high, and meanwhile Mukoki had half a dozen pots and kettles and pans on the glowing top of the sheet-iron stove, and thick caribou steaks were sizzling in a homelike and comforting way. A little later David ate as though he had gone hungry all day. Ordinarily he wanted his meat well done; tonight he devoured an inch-and-a quarter sirloin steak that floated in its own gravy, and was red to the heart of it. When they had finished they lighted their pipes and went out to feed the dogs a frozen fish apiece.

An immense satisfaction possessed David. It was like something soft and purring inside of him. He made no effort to explain things. He was accepting facts, and changes. He felt bigger tonight, as though his lungs were stretching themselves, and his chest expanding. His fears were gone. He no longer saw anything to dread in the white wilderness. He was eager to go on, eager to reach Tavish's. Ever since Father Roland had spoken of Tavish that desire had been growing within him. Tavish had not only come from the Stikine River; he had lived on Firepan Creek. It was incredible that he should not know of the Girl: who she was; just where she lived; why she was there. White people were few in that far country. Tavish would surely know of her. He had made up his mind that he would show Tavish the picture, keeping to himself the manner in which he had come into possession of it. The daughter of a friend, he would tell them — both Father Roland and Tavish. Or of an acquaintance. That, at least, was half truth.

A dozen things Father Roland spoke about that night before he alluded to Tavish. David waited. He did not want to appear too deeply interested. He desired to have the thing work itself out in a fortuitous sort of way, governed, as he was, by a strong feeling that he could not explain his position, or his strange and growing interest in the Girl, if the Missioner should by any chance discover the part he had played in the haunting though incidental encounter with the woman on the train.

"Fear — a great fear — his life is haunted by it," said Father Roland, when at last he began talking about Tavish. He was seated on a pile of balsams, his legs stretched out flat on the floor, his back to the wall, and he smoked thoughtfully as he looked at David. "A coward? I don't know. I have seen him jump at the snap of a twig. I have seen him tremble at nothing at all. I have seen him shrink at darkness, and then, again, he came through a terrible darkness to reach my cabin that night. Mad? Perhaps. It is hard to believe he is a coward. Would a coward live alone, as he does? That seems impossible, too. And yet he is afraid. That fear is always close at his heels, especially at night. It follows him like a hungry dog. There are times when I would swear it is not fear of a living thing. That is what makes it — disturbing. It is weird — distressing. It makes one shiver."

The Missioner was silent for some moments, as if lost in a reverie. Then he said, reflectively:

"I have seen strange things. I have had many penitents. My ears have heard much that you would not believe. It has all come in my long day's work in the wilderness. But never, never have I seen a fight like this that is being made by Tavish — a fight against that mysterious fear, of which he will not speak. I would give a year of my life — yes, even more — to help him. There is something about him that is lovable, that makes you want to cling to him, be near him. But he will have none of that. He wants to be alone with his fear. Is it not strange? I have pieced little things together, and that night — when terror drove him to my cabin — he betrayed himself, and I learned one thing. He is afraid of a *woman*!"

"A woman!" gasped David.

"Yes, a woman — a woman who lives — or lived — up in the Stikine River country you mentioned today."

David's heart stirred strangely.

"The Stikine River, or — or — Firepan Creek?" he asked.

It seemed a long time to him before Father Roland answered. He was thinking deeply, with his eyes half closed, as though striving to recall things that he had forgotten.

"Yes — it was on the Firepan. I am sure of it," he said slowly. "He was sick — small-pox, as I told you — and it was on the Firepan. I remember that. And whoever the woman was, she was there. A woman! And he — afraid! Afraid, even *now*, with her a thousand miles away, if she lives. Can you account for it? I would give a great deal to know. But he will say nothing. And — it is not my business to intrude. Yet I have guessed. I have my own conviction. It is terrible."

He spoke in a low voice, looking straight at David.

"And that conviction, Father?" David barely whispered.

"Tavish is afraid of some one who is *dead*."

"Dead!"

"Yes, a woman — or a girl — who is dead; dead in the flesh, but living in the spirit to haunt him. It is that. I know it. And he will not bare his soul to me."

"A girl . . . who is dead . . . on Firepan Creek. Her spirit. . . ."

A cold, invisible hand was clutching at David's throat. Shadows hid his face, or Father Roland would have seen. His voice was strained. He forced it between his lips.

"Yes, her spirit," came the Missioner's answer, and David heard the scrape of his knife as he cleaned out the bowl of his pipe. "It haunts Tavish. It is with him always. *And he is afraid of it!*"

David rose slowly to his feet and went toward the door, slipping on his coat and cap. "I'm going to whistle for Baree," he said, and went out. The white world was brilliant under the glow of a full moon and a billion stars. It was the most wonderful night he had ever seen, and yet for a few moments he was as oblivious of its amazing beauty, its almost startling vividness, as though he had passed out into darkness.

"A girl . . . Firepan . . . dead . . . haunting Tavish. . . ."

He did not hear the whining of the dogs. He was again piecing together in his mind that picture — the barefooted girl standing on the rock, disturbed, startled, terrified, poised as if about to fly from a great danger. What had happened after the taking of that picture? Was it Tavish who had taken it? Was it Tavish who had surprised her there? Was it Tavish — Tavish — Tavish. . . .?

His mind could not go on. He steadied himself, one hand clutching at the breast of his coat, where the picture lay.

The cabin door opened behind him. The Missioner came out. He coughed, and looked up at the sky.

"A splendid night, David," he said softly. "A splendid night!"

He spoke in a strange, quiet voice that made David turn. The Little Missioner was facing the moon. He was gazing off into that wonder-world of forests and snow and stars and moonlight in a fixed and steady gaze, and it seemed to David that he aged, and shrank into smaller form, and that his shoulders drooped as if under a weight. And all at once David saw in his face what he had seen before when in the coach — a forgetfulness of all things but one, the lifting of a strange curtain, the baring of a soul; and for a few moments Father Roland stood with his face turned to the light of the skies, as if preoccupied by an all-pervading and hopeless grief.

CHAPTER X

It was Baree who disturbed the silent tableau in the moonlight. David was staring at the Missioner, held by the look of anguish that had settled so quickly and so strangely in his face, as if this bright night with its moon and stars had recalled to him a great sorrow, when they heard again the wolf-dog's howl out in the forest. It was quite near. David, with his eyes still on the other, saw Father Roland start, as if for an instant he had forgotten where he was. The Missioner looked his way, and straightened his shoulders slowly, with a smile on his lips that was strained and wan as the smile of one worn out by an arduous toil.

"A splendid night," he repeated, and he raised a naked hand to his head, as if slowly brushing away something from before his eyes. "It was a night like this — this — fifteen years ago. . . ."

He stopped. In the moonlight he brought himself together with a jerk. He came and laid a hand on David's shoulder.

"That was Baree," he said. "The dog has followed us."

"He is not very far in the forest," answered David.

"No. He smells us. He is waiting out there for you."

There was a moment's silence between them as they listened.

"I will take him a fish," said David, then. "I am sure he will come to me."

Mukoki had hoisted the gunny sack full of fish well up against the roof of the cabin to keep it from chance marauders of the night, and Father Roland stood by while David lowered it and made a choice for Baree's supper. Then he reëntered the cabin.

It was not Baree who drew David slowly into the forest. He wanted to be alone, away from Father Roland and the quiet, insistent scrutiny of the Cree. He wanted to think, ask himself questions, find answers for them if he could. His mind was just beginning to rouse itself to the significance of the events of the past day and night, and he was like one bewildered by a great mystery, and startled by visions of a possible tragedy. Fate had played with him strangely. It had linked him with happenings that were inexplicable and unusual, and he believed that they were not without their meaning for him. More or less of a fatalist, he was inspired by the sudden and disturbing thought that they had happened by inevitable necessity.

Vividly he saw again the dark, haunting eyes of the woman in the coach, and heard again the few low, tense words with which she had revealed to him her quest of a man — a man by the name of Michael O'Doone. In her presence he had felt the nearness of tragedy. It had stirred him deeply, almost as deeply as the picture she had left in her seat — the picture hidden now against his breast — like a thing which must not be betrayed, and which a strange and compelling instinct had made him associate in such a startling way with Tavish. He could not get Tavish out of his mind; Tavish, the haunted man; Tavish the man who had fled from the Firepan Creek country at just about the time the girl in the picture had stood on the rock beside the pool; Tavish, terror-driven by a spirit of the dead! He did not attempt to reason the matter, or bare the folly of his alarm. He did not ask himself about the improbability of it all, but accepted without equivocation that strong impression as it had come to him — the conviction that the girl on the rock and the woman in the coach were in some way identified with the flight of Tavish, the man he had never seen, from that far valley in the northwest mountains.

The questions he asked himself now were not to establish in his own mind either the truth or the absurdity of this conviction. He was determining with himself whether or not to confide in Father Roland. It was more than delicacy that made him hesitate; it was almost a personal shame. For a long time he had kept within his breast the secret of his own tragedy and dishonour. That it was *his* dishonour, almost as much as the woman's, had been his own conviction; and how, at last, he had come to reveal that corroding sickness in his soul to a man who was almost a stranger was more than he could understand. But he had done just that. Father Roland had seen him stripped down to the naked truth in an hour of great need, and he had put out a hand in time to save him. He no longer doubted this last immeasurable fact. Twenty times since then, coldly and critically, he had thought of the woman who had been his wife, and slowly and terribly the enormity of her crime had swept further and further away from him the anguish of her loss. He was like a man risen from a sick bed, breathing freely again, tasting once more the flavour of the air that filled his lungs. All this he owed to Father Roland, and because of this — and his confession of only two nights ago — he felt a burning humiliation at the thought of telling the Missioner that another face had come to fill his thoughts, and stir his anxieties. And what less could he tell, if he confided in him at all?

He had gone a hundred yards or more into the forest, and in a little open space, lighted up like a tiny amphitheatre in the glow of the moon, he stopped. Suddenly there came to him, thrilling in its promise, a key to the situation. He would wait until they reached Tavish's. And then, in the presence of the Missioner, he would suddenly show Tavish the picture. His heart throbbed uneasily as he anticipated the possible tragedy — the sudden betrayal — of that moment, for Father Roland had said, like one who had glimpsed beyond the ken of human eyes, that Tavish was haunted by a vision of the dead. The dead! Could it be that she, the girl in the picture. . . .? He shook himself, set his lips tight to get the thought away from him. And the woman — the woman in the coach, the woman who had left in her seat this picture that was growing in his heart like a living thing — who was she? Was her quest one of vengeance — of retribution? Was Tavish the man she was seeking? Up in that mountain valley — where the girl had stood on that rock — had his name been Michael O'Doone?

He was trembling when he went on, deeper into the forest. But of his determination there was no longer a doubt. He would say nothing to Father Roland until Tavish had seen the picture.

Until now he had forgotten Baree. In the disquieting fear with which his thoughts were weighted he had lost hold of the fact that in his hand he still carried the slightly curved and solidly frozen substance of a fish. The movement of a body near him, so unexpected and alarmingly close that a cry broke from his lips as he leaped to one side, roused him with a sudden mental shock. The beast, whatever it was, had passed within six feet of him, and now, twice that distance away, stood like a statue hewn out of stone levelling at him the fiery gleam of a solitary eye. Until he saw that one eye, and not two, David did not breathe. Then he gasped. The fish had fallen from his fingers. He stooped, picked it up, and called softly:

"Baree!"

The dog was waiting for his voice. His one eye shifted, slanting like a searchlight in the direction of the cabin, and turned swiftly back to David. He whined, and David spoke to him again, calling his name, and holding out the fish. For several moments Baree did not move, but eyed him with the immobility of a half blinded sphinx. Then, suddenly, he dropped on his belly and began crawling toward him.

A spatter of moonlight fell upon them as David, crouching on his heels, gave Baree the fish, holding for a moment to the tail of it while the hungry beast seized its head between his powerful jaws with a grinding crunch. The power of those jaws sent a little shiver through the man so close to them. They were terrible — and splendid. A man's leg-bone would have cracked between them like a pipe stem. And Baree, with that power of death in his jaws, had a second time crept to him on his belly — not fearingly, in the shadow of a club, but like a thing tamed into slavery by a yearning adoration. It was a fact that seized upon David with a peculiar hold. It built up between them — between this down-and-out beast and a man fighting to find himself — a comradeship which perhaps only the man and the beast could understand. Even as he devoured the fish Baree kept his one eye on David, as though fearing he might lose him again if he allowed his gaze to falter for an instant. The truculency and the menace of that eye were gone. It was still bloodshot, still burned with a reddish fire, and a great pity swept through David, as he thought of the blows the club must have given. He noticed, then, that Baree was making efforts to open the other eye; he saw the swollen lid flutter, the muscle twitch. Impulsively he put out a hand. It fell unflinchingly on Baree's head, and in an instant the crunching of the dog's jaw had ceased, and he lay as if dead. David bent nearer. With the thumb and forefinger of his other hand he gently lifted the swollen lid. It caused a hurt. Baree whined softly. His great body trembled. His ivory fangs clicked like the teeth of a man with ague. To his wolfish soul, trembling in a body that had been condemned, beaten, clubbed almost to the door of death, that hurt caused by David's fingers was a caress. He understood. He saw with a vision that was keener than sight. Faith was born in him, and burned like a con-flagration. His head dropped to the snow; a great, gasping sigh ran through him, and his trembling ceased. His good eye closed slowly as David gently and persistently massaged the muscles of the other with his thumb and forefinger. When at last he rose to his feet and returned to the cabin, Baree followed him to the edge of the clearing.

Mukoki and the Missioner had made their beds of balsam boughs, two on the floor and one in the bunk, and the Cree had already rolled himself in his blanket when David entered the shack. Father Roland was wiping David's gun.

"We'll give you a little practice with this tomorrow," he prom-ised. "Do you suppose you can hit a moose?"

"I have my doubts, *mon Père*."

Father Roland gave vent to his curious chuckle.

"I have promised to make a marksman of you in exchange for your — your trouble in teaching me how to use the gloves," he said, polishing furiously. There was a twinkle in his eyes, as if a moment before he had been laughing to himself. The gloves were on the table. He had been examining them again, and David found himself smiling at the childlike and eager interest he had taken in them. Suddenly Father Roland rubbed still a little faster, and said:

"If you can't hit a moose with a bullet you surely can hit me with these gloves — eh?"

"Yes, quite positively. But I shall be merciful if you, in turn, show some charity in teaching me how to shoot."

The Little Missioner finished his polishing, set the rifle against the wall, and took the gloves in his hands.

"It is bright — almost like day — outside," he said a little yearningly. "Are you — tired?"

His hint was obvious, even to Mukoki, who stared at him from under his blanket. And David was not tired. If his afternoon's work had fatigued him his exhaustion was forgotten in the mental excitement that had followed the Missioner's story of Tavish. He took a pair of the gloves in his hands, and nodded toward the door.

"You mean. . . ."

Father Roland was on his feet.

"If you are not tired. It would give us a better stomach for sleep."

Mukoki rolled from his blanket, a grin on his leathery face. He tied the wrist laces for them, and followed them out into the moonlit night, his face a copper-coloured gargoyle illuminated by that fixed and joyous grin. David saw the look and wondered if it would change when he sent the Little Missioner bowling over in the snow, which he was quite sure to do, even if he was careful. He was a splendid boxer. In the days of his practice he had struck a terrific blow for his weight. At the Athletic Club he had been noted for a subtle strategy and a cleverness of defence that were his own. But he felt that he had grown rusty during the past year and a half. This thought was in his mind when he tapped the Missioner on the end of his ruddy nose. They squared away in the moonlight, eight inches deep in the snow, and there was a joyous and eager light in Father Roland's eyes. The tap on his nose did not dim it. His teeth gleamed, even as David's gloves went *plunk, plunk,* against his nose again. Mukoki, still grinning like a carven thing, chuckled audibly. David pranced carelessly about the Little Missioner, poking him beautifully as he offered suggestions and criticism.

"You should protect your nose, *mon Père*" — *plunk!* "And the pit of your stomach" — *plunk!* "And also your ears" — *plunk, plunk!* "But especially your nose, *mon Père*" — *plunk, plunk!*

"And sometimes the tip of your jaw, David," gurgled Father Roland, and for a few moments night closed in darkly about

David.

When he came fully into his senses again he was sitting in the snow, with the Little Missioner bending over him anxiously, and Mukoki grinning down at him like a fiend.

"Dear Heaven, forgive me!" he heard Father Roland saying. "I didn't mean it so hard, David — I didn't! But oh, man, it was such a chance — such a beautiful chance! And now I've spoiled it. I've spoiled our fun."

"Not unless you're — tired," said David, getting up on his feet. "You took me at a disadvantage, *mon Père*. I thought you were green."

"And you were pulverizing my nose," apologized Father Roland.

They went at it again, and this time David spared none of his caution, and offered no advice, and the Missioner no longer posed, but became suddenly as elusive and as agile as a cat. David was amazed, but he wasted no breath to demand an explanation. Father Roland was parrying his straight blows like an adept. Three times in as many minutes he felt the sting of the Missioner's glove in his face. In straight-away boxing, without the finer tricks and artifice of the game, he was soon convinced that the forest man was almost his match. Little by little he began to exert the cleverness of his training. At the end of ten minutes Father Roland was sitting dazedly in the snow, and the grin had gone from Mukoki's face. He had succumbed to a trick — a swift side step, a feint that had held in it an ambush, and the seat of the Little Missioner's faculties had rocked. But he was gurgling joyously when he rose to his feet, and with one arm he hugged David as they returned to the cabin.

"Only one other man has given me a jolt like that in many a year," he boasted, a bit proudly. "And that was Tavish. Tavish is good. He must have lived long among fighting men. Perhaps that is why I think so kindly of him. I love a fighting man if he fights honourably with either brain or brawn, even more than I despise a coward."

"And yet this Tavish, you say, is pursued by a great fear. Can he be so much of a fighting man, in the way you mean, and still live in terror of. . . ."

"What?"

That single word broke from the Missioner like the sharp crack of a whip.

"Of *what* is he afraid?" he repeated. "Can you tell me? Can you guess more than I have guessed? Is one a coward because he fears whispers that tremble in the air and sees a face in the darkness of night that is neither living nor dead? Is he?"

For a long time after he had gone to bed David lay wide awake in the darkness, his mind working until it seemed to him that it was prisoned in an iron chamber from which it was making futile efforts to escape. He could hear the steady breathing of Father Roland and Mukoki, who were asleep. His own eyes he could close only by forced efforts to bring upon himself the unconsciousness of rest. Tavish filled his mind — Tavish and the girl — and along with them the mysterious woman in the coach. He struggled with himself. He told himself how absurd it all was, how grotesquely his imagination was employing itself with him — how incredible it was that Tavish and the girl in the picture should be associated in that terrible way that had occurred to him. But he failed to convince himself. He fell asleep at last, and his slumber was filled with fleeting visions. When he awoke the cabin was filled with the glow of the lantern. Father Roland and Mukoki were up, and a fire was crackling in the stove.

The four days that followed broke the last link in the chain that held David Raine to the life from which he was fleeing when the forest Missioner met him in the Transcontinental. They were four wonderful days, in which they travelled steadily northward; days of splendid sunshine, of intense cold, of brilliant stars and a full moon at night. The first of these four days David travelled fifteen miles on his snow shoes, and that night he slept in a balsam shelter close to the face of a great rock which they heated with a fire of logs, so that all through the cold hours between darkness and gray dawn the boulder was like a huge warming-stone. The second day marked also the second great stride in his education in the life of the wild. Fang and hoof and padded claw were at large again in the forests after the blizzard, and Father Roland stopped at each broken path that crossed the trail, pointing out to him the stories that were written in the snow. He showed him where a fox had followed silently after a snow-shoe rabbit; where a band of wolves had ploughed through the snow in the trail of a deer that was doomed, and in a dense run of timber where both moose and caribou had sought refuge from the storm he explained carefully the slight difference between the hoofprints of the two. That night Baree came into camp while they were sleeping, and in the morning they found where he had burrowed his round bed in the snow not a dozen yards from their shelter. The third morning David shot his moose. And that night he lured Baree almost to the side of their campfire, and tossed him chunks of raw flesh from where he sat smoking his pipe.

He was changed. Three days on the trail and three nights in camp under the stars had begun their promised miracle-working. His face was darkened by a stubble of beard, his ears and cheek bones were reddened by exposure to cold and wind; he felt that in those three days and nights his muscles had hardened, and his weakness had left him. "It was in your mind — your sickness," Father Roland had told him, and he believed it now. He began to find a pleasure in that physical achievement which he had wondered at in Mukoki and the Missioner. Each noon when they stopped to boil their tea and cook their dinner, and each night when they made camp, he had chopped down a tree. Tonight it had been an 8-inch jack pine, tough with pitch. The exertion had sent his blood pounding through him furiously. He was still breathing deeply as he sat near the fire, tossing bits of meat out to Baree. They were sixty miles from Thoreau's cabin, straight north, and for the twentieth time Father Roland was telling him how well he had done.

"And tomorrow," he added, "we'll reach Tavish's."

It had grown upon David that to see Tavish had become his one great mission in the North. What adventure lay beyond that meeting he did not surmise. All his thoughts had centred in the single desire to let Tavish look upon the picture. Tonight, after the Missioner had joined Mukoki in the silk tent buried warmly under the mass of cut balsam, he sat a little longer beside the fire, and asked himself questions which he had not thought of before. He would see Tavish. He would show him the picture. And — what then? Would that be the end of it? He felt, for a moment, uncomfortable. Beyond Tavish there was a disturbing and unanswerable problem. The Girl, if she still lived, was a thousand miles from where he was sitting at this moment; to reach her, with that distance of mountain and forest between them, would be like travelling to the end of the world. It was the first time there had risen in his mind a definite thought of going to her — if she were alive. It startled him. It was like a shock. Go to her? Why? He drew forth the picture from his coat pocket and stared at the wonder-face of the Girl in the light of the blazing logs. *Why?* His heart trembled. He lifted his eyes to the grayish film of smoke rising between him and the balsam-covered tent, and slowly he saw another face take form, framed in that wraith-like mist of smoke — the face of a golden goddess, laughing at him, taunting him. *Laughing — laughing!* . . . He forced his gaze from it with a shudder. Again he looked at the picture of the Girl in his hand. "*She knows. She understands. She comforts me. "* He whispered the words. They were like a breath rising out of his soul. He replaced the picture in his pocket, and for a moment held it close against his breast.

The next day, as the swift-thickening gloom of northern night was descending about them again, the Missioner halted his team on the crest of a boulder-strewn ridge, and pointing down into the murky plain at their feet he said, with the satisfaction of one who has come to a journey's end:

"There is Tavish's."

CHAPTER XI

They went down into the plain. David strained his eyes, but he could see nothing where Father Roland had pointed except the purplish sea of forest growing black in the fading twilight. Ahead of the team Mukoki picked his way slowly and cautiously among the snow-hidden rocks, and with the Missioner David flung his weight backward on the sledge to keep it from running upon the dogs. It was a thick, wild place and it struck him that Tavish could not have chosen a spot of more sinister aspect in which to hide himself and his secret. A terribly lonely place it was, and still as death as they went down into it. They heard not even the howl of a dog, and surely Tavish had dogs. He was on the point of speaking, of asking the Missioner why Tavish, haunted by fear, should bury himself in a place like this, when the lead-dog suddenly stopped and a low, lingering whine drifted back to them. David had never heard anything like that whine. It swept through the line of dogs, from throat to throat, and the beasts stood stiff-legged and stark in their traces, staring with eight pairs of restlessly blazing eyes into the wall of darkness ahead. The Cree had turned, but the sharp command on his lips had frozen there. David saw him standing ahead of the team as silent and as motionless as rock. From him he looked into the Missioner's face. Father Roland was staring. There was a strange suspense in his breathing. And then, suddenly, the lead-dog sat back on his haunches and turning his gray muzzle up to the sky emitted a long and mournful howl. There was something about it that made David shiver. Mukoki came staggering back through the snow like a sick man.

"*Nipoo-win Ooyoo!*" he said, his eyes shining like points of flame. A shiver seemed to be running through him.

For a moment the Missioner did not seem to hear him. Then he cried:

"Give them the whip! Drive them on!"

The Cree turned, unwinding his long lash.

"*Nipoo-win Ooyoo!*" he muttered again.

The whip cracked over the backs of the huskies, the end of it stinging the rump of the lead-dog, who was master of them all. A snarl rose for an instant in his throat, then he straightened out, and the dogs lurched forward. Mukoki ran ahead, so that the lead-dog was close at his heels.

"What did he say?" asked David.

In the gloom the Missioner made a gesture of protest with his two hands. David could no longer see his face.

"He is superstitious," he growled. "He is absurd. He would make the very devil's flesh creep. He says that old Beaver has given the death howl. Bah!"

David could *feel* the other's shudder in the darkness. They went on for another hundred yards. With a low word Mukoki stopped the team. The dogs were whining softly, staring straight ahead, when David and the Missioner joined the Cree.

Father Roland pointed to a dark blot in the night, fifty paces beyond them. He spoke to David.

"There is Tavish's cabin. Come. We will see."

Mukoki remained with the team. They could hear the dogs whining as they advanced. The cabin took shape in their faces — grotesque, dark, lifeless. It was a foreboding thing, that cabin. He remembered in a flash all that the Missioner had told him about Tavish. His pulse was beating swiftly. A shiver ran up his back, and he was filled with a strange dread. Father Roland's voice startled him.

"Tavish! Tavish!" it called.

They stood close to the door, but heard no answer. Father Roland stamped with his foot, and scraped with his toe on the ground.

"See, the snow has been cleaned away recently," he said. "Mukoki is a fool. He is superstitious. He made me, for an instant — afraid."

There was a vast relief in his voice. The cabin door was unbolted and he flung it open confidently. It was pitch dark inside, but a flood of warm air struck their faces. The Missioner laughed.

"Tavish, are you asleep?" he called.

There was no answer. Father Roland entered.

"He has been here recently. There is a fire in the stove. We will make ourselves at home." He fumbled in his clothes and found a match. A moment later he struck it, and lighted a tin lamp that hung from the ceiling. In its glow his face was of a strange colour. He had been under strain. The hand that held the burning match was unsteady. "Strange, very strange," he was saying, as if to himself. And then: "Preposterous! I will go back and tell Mukoki. He is shivering. He is afraid. He believes that Tavish is in league with the devil. He says that the dogs know, and that they have warned him. Queer. Monstrously queer. And interesting. Eh?"

He went out. David stood where he was, looking about him in the blurred light of the lamp over his head. He almost expected Tavish to creep out from some dark corner; he half expected to see him move from under the dishevelled blankets in the bunk at the far end of the room. It was a big room, twenty feet from end to end, and almost as wide, and after a moment or two he knew that he was the only living thing in it, except a small, gray mouse that came fearlessly quite close to his feet. And then he saw a second mouse, and a third, and about him, and over him, he heard a creeping, scurrying noise, as of many tiny feet pattering. A paper on the table rustled, a series of squeaks came from the bunk, he felt something that was like a gentle touch on the toe of his moccasin, and looked down. The cabin was alive with mice! It was filled with the restless movement of them — little bright-eyed creatures who moved about him without fear, and, he thought, expectantly. He had not moved an inch when Father Roland came again into the cabin. He pointed to the floor.

"The place is alive with them!" he protested.

Father Roland appeared in great good humour as he slipped off his mittens and rubbed his hands over the stove.

"Tavish's pets," he chuckled. "He says they're company. I've seen a dozen of them on his shoulders at one time. Queer. Queer."

His hands made the rasping sound as he rubbed them. Suddenly he lifted a lid from the stove and peered into the fire-box.

"He put fuel in here less than an hour ago," he said. "Wonder where he can be mouching at this hour. The dogs are gone." He scanned the table. "No supper. Pans clean. Mice hungry. He'll be back soon. But we won't wait. I'm famished."

He spoke swiftly, and filled the stove with wood. Mukoki began bringing in the dunnage. The uneasy gleam was still in his eyes. His gaze was shifting and restless with expectation. He came and went noiselessly, treading as though he feared his footsteps would awaken some one, and David saw that he was afraid of the mice. One of them ran up his sleeve as they were eating supper, and he flung it from him with a strange, quick breath, his eyes blazing.

"*Muche Munito!*" he shuddered.

He swallowed the rest of his meat hurriedly, and after that took his blankets, and with a few words in Cree to the Missioner left the cabin.

"He says they are little devils — the mice," said Father Roland, looking after him reflectively. "He will sleep near the dogs. I wonder how far his intuition goes? He believes that Tavish harbours bad spirits in this cabin, and that they have taken the form of mice. Pooh! They're cunning little vermin. Tavish has taught them tricks. Watch this one feed out of my hand!"

Half a dozen times they had climbed to David's shoulders. One of them had nestled in a warm furry ball against his neck, as if waiting. They were certainly companionable — quite chummy, as the Missioner said. No wonder Tavish harboured them in his loneliness. David fed them and let them nibble from his fingers, and yet they gave him a distinctly unpleasant sensation. When the Missioner had finished his last cup of coffee he crumbled a thick chunk of bannock and placed it on the floor back of the stove. The mice gathered round it in a silent, hungry, nibbling horde. David tried to count them. There must have been twenty. He felt an impulse to scoop them up in something, Tavish's water pail for instance, and pitch them out into the night. The creatures became quieter after their gorge on bannock crumbs. Most of them disappeared.

For a long time David and the Missioner sat smoking their pipes, waiting for Tavish. Father Roland was puzzled and yet he was assured. He was puzzled because Tavish's snow shoes hung on their wooden peg in one of the cross logs and his rifle was in its rack over the bunk.

"I didn't know he had another pair of snow shoes," he said. "Still, it is quite a time since I have seen him — a number of weeks. I came down in the early November snow. He is not far away or he would have taken his rifle. Probably setting a few fresh poison-baits after the storm."

They heard the sweep of a low wind. It often came at night after a storm, usually from off the Barrens to the northwest. Something thumped gently against the outside of the cabin, a low, peculiarly heavy and soft sort of sound, like a padded object, with only the log wall separating it from the bunk. Their ears caught it quite distinctly.

"Tavish hangs his meat out there," the Missioner explained, observing the sudden direction of David's eyes. "A haunch of moose, or, if he has been lucky, of caribou. I had forgotten Tavish's cache or we might have saved our meat."

He ran a hand through his thick, grayish hair until it stood up about his head like a brush.

David tried not to reveal his restlessness as they waited. At each new sound he hoped that what he heard was Tavish's footsteps. He had quite decidedly planned his action. Tavish would enter, and of course there would be greetings, and possibly half an hour or more of smoking and talk before he brought up the Firepan Creek country, unless, as might fortuitously happen, Father Roland spoke of it ahead of him. After that he would show

Tavish the picture, and he would stand well in the light so that it would be impressed upon Tavish all at once. He noticed that the chimney of the lamp was sooty and discoloured, and somewhat to the Missioner's amusement he took it off and cleaned it. The light was much more satisfactory then. He wandered about the cabin, scrutinizing, as if out of curiosity, Tavish's belongings. There was not much to discover. Close to the bunk there was a small battered chest with riveted steel ribs. He wondered whether it was unlocked, and what it contained. As he stood over it he could hear plainly the *thud, thud, thud*, of the thing outside — the haunch of meat — as though some one were tapping fragments of the Morse code in a careless and broken sort of way. Then, without any particular motive, he stepped into the dark corner at the end of the bunk. An agonized squeak came from under his foot, and he felt something small and soft flatten out, like a wad of dough. He jumped back. An exclamation broke from his lips. It was unpleasant, though the soft thing was nothing more than a mouse.

"Confound it!" he said.

Father Roland was listening to the slow, pendulum-like *thud, thud, thud*, against the logs of the cabin. It seemed to come more distinctly as David crushed out the life of the mouse, as if pounding a protest upon the wall.

"Tavish has hung his meat low," he said concernedly. "Quite careless of him, unless it is a very large quarter."

He began slowly to undress.

"We might as well turn in," he suggested. "When Tavish shows up the dogs will raise bedlam and wake us. Throw out Tavish's blankets and put your own in his bunk. I prefer the floor. Always did. Nothing like a good, smooth floor. . . ."

He was interrupted by the opening of the cabin door. The Cree thrust in his head and shoulders. He came no farther. His eyes were afire with the smouldering gleam of garnets. He spoke rapidly in his native tongue to the Missioner, gesturing with one lean, brown hand as he talked. Father Roland's face became heavy, furrowed, perplexed. He broke in suddenly, in Cree, and when he ceased speaking Mukoki withdrew slowly. The last David saw of the Indian was his shifting, garnet-like eyes, disappearing like beads of blackish flame.

"*Pest!*" cried the Little Missioner, shrugging his shoulders in disgust. "The dogs are uneasy. Mukoki says they smell death. They sit on their haunches, he says, staring — staring at nothing, and whining like puppies. He is going back with them to the other side of the ridge. If it will ease his soul, let him go."

"I have heard of dogs doing that," said David.

"Of course they will do it," shot back Father Roland unhesitatingly. "Northern dogs always do it, and especially mine. They are accustomed to death. Twenty times in a winter, and sometimes more, I care for the dead. They always go with me, and they can smell death in the wind. But here — why, it is absurd! There is nothing dead here — unless it is that mouse, and Tavish's meat!" He shook himself, grumbling under his breath at Mukoki's folly. And then: "The dogs have always acted queerly when Tavish was near," he added in a lower voice. "I can't explain why; they simply do. Instinct, possibly. His presence makes them uneasy. An unusual man, this Tavish. I wish he would come. I am anxious for you to meet him."

That his mind was quite easy on the score of Tavish's physical well-being he emphasized by falling asleep very shortly after rolling himself up in his blankets on the floor. During their three nights in camp David had marvelled at and envied the ease with which Father Roland could drop off into profound and satisfactory slumber, this being, as his new friend had explained to him, the great and underlying virtue of a good stomach. Tonight, however, the Missioner's deep and regular breathing as he lay on the floor was a matter of vexation to him. He wanted him awake. He wanted him up and alive, thoroughly alive, when Tavish came. "Pounding his ear like a tenderfoot," he thought, "while I, a puppy in harness, couldn't sleep if I wanted to." He was nervously alert. He filled his pipe for the third or fourth time and sat down on the edge of the bunk, listening for Tavish. He was certain, from all that had been said, that Tavish would come. All he had to do was wait. There had been growing in him, a bit unconsciously at first, a feeling of animosity toward Tavish, an emotion that burned in him with a gathering fierceness as he sat alone in the dim light of the cabin, grinding out in his mental restlessness visions of what Tavish might have done. Conviction had never been stronger in him. Tavish, if he had guessed correctly, was a fiend. He would soon know. And if he was right, if Tavish had done that, if up in those mountains. . . .

His eyes blazed and his hands were clenched as he looked down at Father Roland. After a moment, without taking his eyes from the Missioner's recumbent form, he reached to the pocket of his coat which he had flung on the bunk and drew out the picture of the Girl. He looked at it a long time, his heart growing warm, and the tense lines softening in his face.

"It can't be," he whispered. "She is alive!"

As if the wind had heard him, and was answering, there came more distinctly the sound close behind him.

Thud! Thud! Thud!

There was a silence, in which David closed his fingers tightly about the picture. And then, more insistently:

Thud! Thud! Thud!

He put the picture back into his pocket, and rose to his feet. Mechanically he slipped on his coat. He went to the door, opened it softly, and passed out into the night. The moon was above him, like a great, white disc. The sky burned with stars. He could see now to the foot of the ridge over which Mukoki had gone, and the clearing about the cabin lay in a cold and luminous glory. Tavish, if he had been caught in the twilight darkness and had waited for the moon to rise, would be showing up soon.

He walked to the side of the cabin and looked back. Quite distinctly he could see Tavish's meat, suspended from a stout sapling that projected straight out from under the edge of the roof. It hung there darkly, a little in shadow, swinging gently in the wind that had risen, and tap-tap-tapping against the logs. David moved toward it, gazing at the edge of the forest in which he thought he had heard a sound that was like the creak of a sledge runner. He hoped it was Tavish returning. For several moments he listened with his back to the cabin. Then he turned. He was very close to the thing hanging from the sapling. It was swinging slightly. The moon shone on it, and then — Great God! A face — a human face! A face, bearded, with bulging, staring eyes, gaping mouth — a grin of agony frozen in it! And it was tapping, tapping, tapping!

He staggered back with a dreadful cry. He swayed to the door, groped blindly for the latch, stumbled in clumsily, like a drunken man. The horror of that lifeless, grinning face was in his voice. He had awakened the Missioner, who was sitting up, staring at him.

"Tavish . . ." cried David chokingly; "Tavish — is dead!" and he pointed to the end of the cabin where they could hear again that *tap-tap-tapping* against the log wall.

CHAPTER XII

Not until afterward did David realize how terribly his announcement of Tavish's death must have struck into the soul of Father Roland. For a few seconds the Missioner did not move. He was wide awake, he had heard, and yet he looked at David dumbly, his two hands gripping his blanket. When he did move, it was to turn his face slowly toward the end of the cabin where the thing was hanging, with only the wall between. Then, still slowly, he rose to his feet.

David thought he had only half understood.

"Tavish — is dead!" he repeated huskily, straining to swallow the thickening in his throat. "He is out there — hanging by his neck — dead!"

Dead! He emphasized that word — spoke it twice.

Father Roland still did not answer. He was getting into his clothes mechanically, his face curiously ashen, his eyes neither horrified nor startled, but with a stunned look in them. He did not speak when he went to the door and out into the night. David followed, and in a moment they stood close to the thing that was hanging where Tavish's meat should have been. The moon threw a vivid sort of spotlight on it. It was grotesque and horrible — very bad to look at, and unforgettable. Tavish had not died easily. He seemed to shriek that fact at them as he swung there dead; even now he seemed more terrified than cold. His teeth gleamed a little. That, perhaps, was the worst of it all. And his hands were clenched tight. David noticed that. Nothing seemed relaxed about him.

Not until he had looked at Tavish for perhaps sixty full seconds did Father Roland speak. He had recovered himself, judging from his voice. It was quiet and unexcited. But in his first words, unemotional as they were, there was a significance that was almost frightening.

"At last! She made him do that!"

He was speaking to himself, looking straight into Tavish's agonized face. A great shudder swept through David. *She!* He wanted to cry out. He wanted to know. But the Missioner now had his hands on the gruesome thing in the moonlight, and he was saying:

"There is still warmth in his body. He has not been long dead. He hanged himself, I should say, not more than half an hour before we reached the cabin. Give me a hand, David!"

With a mighty effort David pulled himself together. After all, it was nothing more than a dead man hanging there. But his hands were like ice as he seized hold of it. A knife gleamed in the moonlight over Tavish's head as the Missioner cut the rope. They lowered Tavish to the snow, and David went into the cabin for a blanket. Father Roland wrapped the blanket carefully about the body so that it would not freeze to the ground. Then they entered the cabin. The Missioner threw off his coat and built up the fire. When he turned he seemed to notice for the first time the deathly pallor in David's face.

"It shocked you — when you found it there," he said. "*Ugh!* I don't wonder. But I . . . David, I didn't tell you I was expecting something like this. I have feared for Tavish. And tonight when the dogs and Mukoki signalled death I was alarmed — until we found the fire in the stove. It didn't seem reasonable then. I thought Tavish would return. The dogs were gone, too. He must have freed them just before he went out there. Terrible! But justice — justice, I suppose. God sometimes works His ends in queer ways, doesn't He?"

"What do you mean?" cried David, again fighting that thickening in his throat. "Tell me, Father! I must know. Why did he kill himself?"

His hand was clutching at his breast, where the picture lay. He wanted to tear it out, in this moment, and demand of Father Roland whether this was the face — the girl's face — that had haunted Tavish.

"I mean that his fear drove him at last to kill himself," said Father Roland in a slow, sure voice, as if carefully weighing his words before speaking them. "I believe, now, that he terribly wronged some one, that his conscience was his fear, and that it haunted him by bringing up visions and voices until it drove him finally to pay his debt. And up here conscience is *mitoo aye chikoon* — the Little Brother of God. That is all I know. I wish Tavish had confided in me, I might have saved him."

"Or — punished," breathed David.

"My business is not to punish. If he had come to me, asking help for himself and mercy from his God, I could not have betrayed him."

He was putting on his coat again.

"I am going after Mukoki," he said. "There is work to be done, and we may as well get through with it by moonlight. I don't suppose you feel like sleep?"

David shook his head. He was calmer now, quite recovered from the first horror of his shock, when the door closed behind

Father Roland. In the thoughts that were swiftly readjusting themselves in his mind there was no very great sympathy for the man who had hanged himself. In place of that sympathy the oppression of a thing that was greater than disappointment settled upon him heavily, driving from him his own personal dread of this night's ghastly adventure, and adding to his suspense of the last forty-eight hours a hopelessness the poignancy of which was almost like that of a physical pain. Tavish was dead, and in dying he had taken with him the secret for which David would have paid with all he was worth in this hour. In his despair, as he stood there alone in the cabin, he muttered something to himself. The desire possessed him to cry out aloud that Tavish had cheated him. A strange kind of rage burned within him and he turned toward the door, with clenched hands, as if about to rush out and choke from the dead man's throat what he wanted to know, and force his glazed and staring eyes to look for just one instant on the face of the girl in the picture. In another moment his brain had cleared itself of that insane fire. After all, would Tavish kill himself without leaving something behind? Would there not be some kind of an explanation, written by Tavish before he took the final step? A confession? A letter to Father Roland? Tavish knew that the Missioner would stop at his cabin on his return into the North. Surely he would not kill himself without leaving some work for him — at least a brief accounting for his act!

He began looking about the cabin again, swiftly and eagerly at first, for if Tavish had written anything he would beyond all doubt have placed the paper in some conspicuous place: pinned it at the end of his bunk, or on the wall, or against the door. They might have overlooked it, or possibly it had fallen to the floor. To make his search surer David lowered the lamp from its bracket in the ceiling and carried it in his hand. He went into dark corners, scrutinized the floor as well as the walls, and moved garments from their wooden pegs. There was nothing. Tavish had cheated him again! His eyes rested finally on the chest. He placed the lamp on a stool, and tried the lid. It was unlocked. As he lifted it he heard voices indistinctly outside. Father Roland had returned with Mukoki. He could hear them as they went to where Tavish was lying with his face turned up to the moon.

On his knees he began pawing over the stuff in the chest. It was a third filled with odds and ends — little else but trash; tangled ends of *babiche*, a few rusted tools, nails and bolts, a pair of half worn shoe packs — a mere litter of disappointing rubbish. The door opened behind him as he was rising to his feet. He turned to face Mukoki and the Missioner.

"There is nothing," he said, with a gesture that took in the room. "He hasn't left any word that I can find."

Father Roland had not closed the door.

"Mukoki will help you search. Look in his clothing on the wall. Tavish must surely have left — something."

He went out, shutting the door behind him. For a moment he listened to make sure that David was not going to follow him. He hurried then to the body of Tavish, and stripped off the blanket. The dead man was terrible to look at, with his open glassy eyes and his distorted face, and the moonlight gleaming on his grinning teeth. The Missioner shuddered.

"I can't guess," he whispered, as if speaking to Tavish. "I can't guess — quite — what made you do it, Tavish. But you haven't died without telling me. I know it. It's there — in your pocket."

He listened again, and his lips moved. He bent over him, on one knee, and averted his eyes as he searched the pockets of Tavish's heavy coat. Against the dead man's breast he found it, neatly folded, about the size of foolscap paper — several pages of it, he judged, by the thickness of the packet. It was tied with fine threads of *babiche*, and in the moonlight he could make out quite distinctly the words, "For Father Roland, God's Lake — Personal." Tavish, after all, had not made himself the victim of sudden fright, of a momentary madness. He had planned the affair in a quite business-like way. Premeditated it with considerable precision, in fact, and yet in the end he had died with that stare of horror and madness in his face. Father Roland spread the blanket over him again after he had placed the packet in his own coat. He knew where Tavish's pick and shovel were hanging at the back of the cabin and he brought these tools and placed them beside the body. After that he rejoined David and the Cree.

They were still searching, and finding nothing.

"I have been looking through his clothes — out there," said the Missioner, with a shuddering gesture which intimated that his task had been as fruitless as their own. "We may as well bury him. A shallow grave, close to where his body lies. I have placed a pick and a shovel on the spot." He spoke to David: "Would you mind helping Mukoki to dig? I would like to be alone for a little while. You understand. There are things. . . ."

"I understand, Father."

For the first time David felt something of the awe of this thing that was death. He had forgotten, almost, that Father Roland was a servant of God, so vitally human had he found him, so unlike all other men of his calling he had ever known. But it was impressed upon him now, as he followed Mukoki. Father Roland wanted to be alone. Perhaps to pray. To ask mercy for Tavish's soul. To plead for its guidance into the Great Unknown. The thought quieted his own emotions, and as he began to dig in the hard snow and frozen earth he tried to think of Tavish as a man, and not as a monster.

In the cabin Father Roland waited until he heard the beat of the pick before he moved. Then he fastened the cabin door with a wooden bolt and sat himself down at the table, with the lamp close to his bent head and Tavish's confession in his hands. He cut the *babiche* threads with his knife, unfolded the sheets of paper and began to read, while Tavish's mice nosed slyly out of their murky corners wondering at the new and sudden stillness in the cabin and, it may be, stirred into restlessness by the absence of their master.

    *   *   *   *   *

The ground under the snow was discouragingly hard. To David the digging of the grave seemed like chipping out bits of flint from a solid block, and he soon turned over the pick to Mukoki. Alternately they worked for an hour, and each time that the Cree took his place David wondered what was keeping the Missioner so long in the cabin. At last Mukoki intimated with a sweep of his hands and a hunch of his shoulders that their work was done. The grave looked very shallow to David, and he was about to protest against his companion's judgment when it occurred to him that Mukoki had probably digged many holes such as this in the earth, and had helped to fill them again, so it was possible he knew his business. After all, why did people weigh down one's last slumber with six feet of soil overhead when three or four would leave one nearer to the sun, and make not quite so chill a bed? He was thinking of this as he took a last look at Tavish. Then he heard the Indian give a sudden grunt, as if some one had poked him unexpectedly in the pit of the stomach. He whirled about, and stared.

Father Roland stood within ten feet of them, and at sight of him an exclamation rose to David's lips and died there in an astonished gasp. He seemed to be swaying, like a sick man, in the moonlight, and impelled by the same thought Mukoki and David moved toward him. The Missioner extended an arm, as if to hold them back. His face was ghastly, and terrible — almost as terrible as Tavish's, and he seemed to be struggling with something in his throat before he could speak. Then he said, in a strange, forced voice that David had never heard come from his lips before:

"Bury him. There will be — no prayer."

He turned away, moving slowly in the direction of the forest. And as he went David noticed the heavy drag of his feet, and the unevenness of his trail in the snow.

CHAPTER XIII

For two or three minutes after Father Roland had disappeared in the forest David and Mukoki stood without moving. Amazed and a little stunned by the change they had seen in the Missioner's ghastly face, and perplexed by the strangeness of his voice and the unsteadiness of his walk as he had gone away from them, they looked expectantly for him to return out of the shadows of the timber. His last words had come to them with metallic hardness, and their effect, in a way, had been rather appalling: "There will be — no prayer." Why? The question was in Mukoki's gleaming, narrow eyes as he faced the dark spruce, and it was on David's lips as he turned at last to look at the Cree. There was to be no prayer for Tavish! David felt himself shuddering, when suddenly, breaking the silence like a sinister cackle, an exultant exclamation burst from the Indian, as though, all at once, understanding had dawned upon him. He pointed to the dead man, his eyes widening.

"Tavish — he great devil," he said. "*Mon Père* make no prayer. *Mey-oo!*" and he grinned in triumph, for had he not, during all these months, told his master that Tavish was a devil, and that his cabin was filled with little devils? "Mey-oo," he cried again, louder than before. "A devil!" and with a swift, vengeful movement he sprang to Tavish, caught him by his moccasined feet, and to David's horror flung him fiercely into the shallow grave. "A devil!" he croaked again, and like a madman began throwing in the frozen earth upon the body.

David turned away, sickened by the thud of the body and the fall of the clods on its upturned face — for he had caught a last unpleasant glimpse of the face, and it was staring and grinning up at the stars. A feeling of dread followed him into the cabin. He filled the stove, and sat down to wait for Father Roland. It was a long wait. He heard Mukoki go away. The mice rustled about him again. An hour had passed when he heard a sound at the door, a scraping sound, like the peculiar drag of claws over wood, and a moment later it was followed by a whine that came to him faintly. He opened the door slowly. Baree stood just outside the threshold. He had given him two fish at noon, so he knew that it was not hunger that had brought the dog to the cabin. Some mysterious instinct had told him that David was alone; he wanted to come in; his yearning gleamed in his eyes as he stood there stiff-legged in the moonlight. David held out a hand, on the point of enticing him through the door, when he heard the soft crunching of feet in the snow. A gray shadow, swift as the wind, Baree disappeared. David scarcely knew when he went. He was looking into the face of Father Roland. He backed into the cabin, without speaking, and the Missioner entered. He was smiling. He had, to an extent, recovered himself. He threw off his mittens and rasped his hands over the fire in an effort at cheerfulness. But there was something forced in his manner, something that he was making a terrific fight to keep under. He was like one who had been in great mental stress for many days instead of a single hour. His eyes burned with the smouldering glow of a fever; his shoulders hung loosely as though he had lost the strength to hold them erect; he shivered, David noticed, even as he rubbed his hands and smiled.

"Curious how this has affected me, David," he said apologetically. "It is incredible, this weakness of mine. I have seen death many scores of times, and yet I could not go and look on his face again. Incredible! Yet it is so. I am anxious to get away. Mukoki will soon be coming with the dogs. A devil, Mukoki says. Well, perhaps. A strange man at best. We must forget this night. It has been an unpleasant introduction for you into our North. We must forget it. We must forget Tavish." And then, as if he had omitted a fact of some importance, he added: "I will kneel at his graveside before we go."

"If he had only waited," said David, scarcely knowing what words he was speaking, "if he had waited until tomorrow, only, or the next day. . . ."

"Yes; if he had waited!"

The Missioner's eyes narrowed. David heard the click of his jaws as he dropped his head so that his face was hidden.

"If he had waited," he repeated, after David, "if he had only waited!" And his hands, spread out fan-like ever the stove, closed slowly and rigidly as if gripping at the throat of something.

"I have friends up in that country he came from," David forced himself to say, "and I had hoped he would be able to tell me something about them. He must have known them, or heard of them."

"Undoubtedly," said the Missioner, still looking at the top of the stove, and unclenching his fingers as slowly as he had drawn them together, "but he is dead."

There was a note of finality in his voice, a sudden forcefulness of meaning as he raised his head and looked at David.

"Dead," he repeated, "and buried. We are no longer privileged even to guess at what he might have said. As I told you once before, David, I am not a Catholic, nor a Church-of-England man, nor of any religion that wears a name, and yet I accepted a little of them all into my own creed. A wandering Missioner — and I am such a one — must obliterate to an extent his own deep-souled convictions and accept indulgently all articles of Christian faith; and there is one law, above all others, which he must hold inviolate. He must not pry into the past of the dead, nor speak aloud the secrets of the living. Let us forget Tavish."

His words sounded a knell in David's heart. If he had hoped that Father Roland would, at the very last, tell him something more about Tavish, that hope was now gone. The Missioner spoke in a voice that was almost gentle, and he came to David and put a hand on his shoulder as a father might have done with a son. He had placed himself, in this moment, beyond the reach of any questions that might have been in David's mind. With eyes and touch that spoke a deep affection he had raised a barrier between them as inviolable as that law of his creed which he had just mentioned. And with it had come a better understanding.

David was glad that Mukoki's voice and the commotion of the dogs came to interrupt them. They gathered up hurriedly the few things they had brought into the cabin and carried them to the sledge. David did not enter the cabin again but stood with the dogs in the edge of the timber, while Father Roland made his promised visit to the grave. Mukoki followed him, and as the Missioner stood over the dark mound in the snow, David saw the Cree slip like a shadow into the cabin, where a light was still burning. Then he noticed that Father Roland was kneeling, and a moment later the Indian came out of the cabin quietly, and without looking back joined him near the dogs. They waited.

Over Tavish's grave Father Roland's lips were moving, and out of his mouth strange words came in a low and unemotional voice that was not much above a whisper:

" . . . and I thank God that you did not tell me before you died, Tavish," he was saying. "I thank God for that. For if you had — I would have killed you!"

As he came back to them David noticed a flickering of light in the cabin, as though the lamp was sputtering and about to go out. They put on their snow shoes, and with Mukoki breaking the trail buried themselves in the moonlit forest.

Half an hour later they halted on the summit of a second ridge. The Cree looked back and pointed with an exultant cry. Where the cabin had been a red flare of flame was rising above the tree tops. David understood what the flickering light in the cabin had meant. Mukoki had spilled Tavish's kerosene and had touched a match to it so that the little devils might follow their master into the black abyss. He almost fancied he could hear the agonized squeaking of Tavish's pets.

* * * * *

Straight northward, through the white moonlight of that night, Mukoki broke their trail, travelling at times so swiftly that the Missioner commanded him to slacken his pace on David's account. Even David did not think of stopping. He had no desire to stop so long as their way was lighted ahead of them. It seemed to him that the world was becoming brighter and the forest gloom less cheerless as they dropped that evil valley of Tavish's farther and farther behind them. Then the moon began to fade, like a great lamp that had burned itself out of oil, and darkness swept over them like huge wings. It was two o'clock when they camped and built a fire.

So, day after day, they continued into the North. At the end of his tenth day — the sixth after leaving Tavish's — David felt that he was no longer a stranger in the country of the big snows. He did not say as much to Father Roland, for to express such a thought to one who had lived there all his life seemed to him to be little less than a bit of sheer imbecility. Ten days! That was all, and yet they might have been ten months, or as many years for that matter, so completely had they changed him. He was not thinking of himself physically — not a day passed that Father Roland did not point out some fresh triumph for him there. His limbs were nearly as tireless as the Missioner's; he knew that he was growing heavier; and he could at last chop through a tree without winding himself. These things his companions could see. His appetite was voracious. His eyes were keen and his hands steady, so that he was doing splendid practice shooting with both rifle and pistol, and each day when the Missioner insisted on their bout with the gloves he found it more and more difficult to hold himself in. "Not so hard, David," Father Roland frequently cautioned him, and in place of the first joyous grin there was always a look of settled anxiety in Mukoki's face as he watched them. The more David pummelled him, the greater was the Little Missioner's triumph. "I told you what this north country could do for you," was his exultant slogan; "I told you!"

Once David was on the point of telling him that he could see only the tenth part of what it had done for him, but the old shame held his tongue. He did not want to bring up the old story. The fact that it had existed, and had written itself out in human passion, remained with him still as a personal and humiliating degradation. It was like a scar on his own body, a repulsive sore which he wished to keep out of sight, even from the eyes of the man who had been his salvation. The growth of this revulsion within him had kept pace with his physical improvement, and if at the end of these ten days Father Roland had spoken of the woman who had betrayed him — the woman who had been his wife — he would have turned the key on that subject as decisively as the Missioner had banned further conversation or conjecture about Tavish. This was, perhaps, the best evidence that he had cut out the cancer in his breast. The Golden Goddess, whom he had thought an angel, he now saw stripped of her glory. If she had repented in that room, if she had betrayed fear even, a single emotion of mental agony, he would not have felt so sure of himself. But she had laughed. She was, like Tavish, a devil. He thought of her beauty now as that of a poisonous flower. He had unwittingly touched such a flower once, a flower of wonderful waxen loveliness, and it had produced a pustular eruption on his hand. She was like that. Poisonous. Treacherous. A creature with as little soul as that flower had perfume. It was this change in him, in his conception and his memory of her, that he would have given much to have Father Roland understand.

During this period of his own transformation he had observed a curious change in Father Roland. At times, after leaving Tavish's cabin, the Little Missioner seemed struggling under the weight of a deep and gloomy oppression. Once or twice, in the firelight, it had looked almost like sickness, and David had seen his face grow wan and old. Always after these fits of dejection there would follow a reaction, and for hours the Missioner would be like one upon whom had fallen a new and sudden happiness. As day added itself to day, and night to night, the periods of depression became shorter and less frequent, and at last Father Roland emerged from them altogether, as though he had been fighting a great fight, and had won. There was a new lustre in his eyes. David wondered whether it was a trick of his imagination that made him think the lines in the Missioner's face were not so deep, that he stood straighter, and that there was at times a deep and vibrant note in his voice which he had not heard before.

During these days David was trying hard to make himself believe that no reasonable combination of circumstances could have associated Tavish with the girl whose picture he kept in the breast pocket of his coat. He succeeded in a way. He tried also to dissociate the face in the picture from a living personality. In this he failed. More and more the picture became a living thing for him. He found a great comfort in his possession of it. He made up his mind that he would keep it, and that its sweet face, always on the point of speaking to him, should go with him wherever he went, guiding him in a way — a companion. He found that, in hours when the darkness and the emptiness of his life oppressed him, the face gave him new hope, and he saw new light. He ceased to think of it as a picture, and one night, speaking half aloud, he called her Little Sister. She seemed nearer to him after that. Unconsciously his hand learned the habit of going to his breast pocket when they were travelling, to make sure that she was there. He would have suffered physical torment before he would have confided all this to any living soul, but the secret thought that was growing more and more in his heart he told to Baree. The dog came into their camps now, but not until the Missioner and Mukoki had gone to bed. He would cringe down near David's feet, lying there motionless, oblivious of the other dogs and showing no inclination to disturb them. He was there on the tenth night, looking steadily at David with his two bloodshot eyes, wondering what it was that his master held in his hands. From the lips and eyes of the Girl, trembling and aglow in the firelight, David looked at Baree. In the bloodshot eyes he saw the immeasurable faith of an adoring slave. He knew that Baree would never leave him. And the Girl, looking at him as steadily as Baree, would never leave him. There was a tremendous thrill in the thought. He leaned over the dog, and with a tremulous stir in his voice, he whispered:

"Some day, boy, we may go to her."

Baree shivered with joy. David's voice, whispering to him in that way, was like a caress, and he whined softly as he crept an inch or two nearer to his master's feet.

That night Father Roland was restless. Hours later, when he was lying snug and warm in his own blankets, David heard him get up, and watched him as he scraped together the burned embers of the fire and added fresh fuel to them. The flap of the tent was back a little, so that he could see plainly. It could not have been later than midnight. The Missioner was fully dressed, and as the fire burned brighter David could see the ruddy glow of his face, and it struck him that it looked singularly boyish in the flame-glow. He did not guess what was keeping the Missioner awake until a little later he heard him among the dogs, and his voice came to him, low and exultingly, and as boyish as his face had seemed: "We'll be home tomorrow, boys — *home!*" That word — home — sounded oddly enough to David up here three hundred miles from civilization. He fancied that he heard the dogs shuffling in the snow, and the satisfied rasping of their master's hands.

Father Roland did not return into the tent again that night. David fell asleep, but was roused for breakfast at three o'clock, and they were away before it was yet light. Through the morning darkness Mukoki led the way as unerringly as a fox, for he was now on his own ground. As dawn came, with a promise of sun, David wondered in a whimsical sort of way whether his companions, both dogs and men, were going mad. He had not as yet experienced the joy and excitement of a northern homecoming, nor had he dreamed that it was possible for Mukoki's leathern face to break into wild jubilation. As the first rays of the sun shot over the forests, he began, all at once, to sing, in a low, chanting voice that grew steadily louder; and as he sang he kept time in a curious way with his hands. He did not slacken his pace, but kept steadily on, and suddenly the Little Missioner joined him in a voice that rang out like the blare of a bugle. To David's ears there was something familiar in that song as it rose wildly on the morning air.

> *"Pa sho ke non ze koon,*
> *Ta ba nin ga,*
> *Ah no go suh nuh guk,*
> *Na quash kuh mon;*
> *Na guh mo yah nin koo,*
> *Pa sho ke non ze koon,*
> *Pa sho ke non ze koon,*
> *Ta ba nin go."*

"What is it?" he asked, when Father Roland dropped back to his side, smiling and breathing deeply. "It sounds like a Chinese puzzle, and yet . . ."

The Missioner laughed. Mukoki had ended a second verse.

"Twenty years ago, when I first knew Mukoki, he would chant nothing but Indian legends to the beat of a tom-tom," he explained. "Since I've had him he has developed a passion for 'mission singing' — for hymns. That was 'Nearer, my God, to Thee.'"

Mukoki, gathering wind, had begun again.

"That's his favourite," explained Father Roland. "At times, when he is alone, he will chant it by the hour. He is delighted when I join in with him. It's 'From Greenland's Icy Mountains.'"

> *"Ke wa de noong a yah jig,*
> *Kuh ya 'gewh wah bun oong,*

E gewh an duh nuh ke jig,
E we de ke zhah tag,
Kuh ya puh duh ke woo waud
Palm e nuh sah wunzh eeg,
Ke nun doo me goo nah nig
Che shuh wa ne mung wah."

At first David had felt a slight desire to laugh at the Cree's odd chanting and the grotesque movement of his hands and arms, like two pump handles in slow and rhythmic action, as he kept time. This desire did not come to him again during the day. He remembered, long years ago, hearing his mother sing those old hymns in his boyhood home. He could see the ancient melodeon with its yellow keys, and the ragged hymn book his mother had prized next to her Bible; and he could hear again her sweet, quavering voice sing those gentle songs, like unforgettable benedictions — the same songs that Mukoki and the Missioner were chanting now, up here, a thousand miles away. That was a long time ago — a very, very long time ago. She had been dead many years. And he — he must be growing old. Thirty-eight! And he was nine then, with slender legs and tousled hair, and a worship for his mother that had mellowed and perhaps saddened his whole life. It was a long time ago. But the songs had lived. They must be known over the whole world — those songs his mother used to sing. He began to join in where he could catch the tunes, and his voice sounded strange and broken and unreal to him, for it was a long time since those boyhood days, and he had not lifted it in song since he had sung then — with his mother.

*   *   *   *   *

It was growing dusk when they came to the Missioner's home on God's Lake. It was almost a château, David thought when he first saw it, built of massive logs. Beyond it there was a smaller building, also built of logs, and toward this Mukoki hurried with the dogs and the sledge. He heard the welcoming cries of Mukoki's family and the excited barking of dogs as he followed Father Roland into the big cabin. It was lighted, and warm. Evidently some one had been keeping it in readiness for the Missioner's return. They entered into a big room, and in his first glance David saw three doors leading from this room: two of them were open, the third was closed. There was something very like a sobbing note in Father Roland's voice as he opened his arms wide, and said to David:

"Home, David — your home!"

He took off his things — his coat, his cap, his moccasins, and his thick German socks — and when he again spoke to David and looked at him, his eyes had in them a mysterious light and his words trembled with suppressed emotion.

"You will forgive me, David — you will forgive me a weakness, and make yourself at home — while I go alone for a few minutes into . . . that . . . room?"

He rose from the chair on which he had seated himself to strip off his moccasins and faced the closed door. He seemed to forget David after he had spoken. He went to it slowly, his breath coming quickly, and when he reached it he drew a heavy key from his pocket. He unlocked the door. It was dark inside, and David could see nothing as the Missioner entered. For many minutes he sat where Father Roland had left him, staring at the door.

"A strange man — a very strange man!" Thoreau had said. Yes, a strange man! What was in that room? Why its unaccountable silence? Once he thought he heard a low cry. For ten minutes he sat, waiting. And then — very faintly at first, almost like a wind soughing through distant tree tops and coming ever nearer, nearer, and more distinct — there came to him from beyond the closed door the gently subdued music of a violin.

CHAPTER XIV

In the days and weeks that followed, this room beyond the closed door, and what it contained, became to David more and more the great mystery in Father Roland's life. It impressed itself upon him slowly but resolutely as the key to some tremendous event in his life, some vast secret which he was keeping from all other human knowledge, unless, perhaps, Mukoki was a silent sharer. At times David believed this was so, and especially after that day when, carefully and slowly, and in good English, as though the Missioner had trained him in what he was to say, the Cree said to him:

"No one ever goes into that room, m'sieu. And no man has ever seen *mon Père's* violin."

The words were spoken in a low monotone without emphasis or emotion, and David was convinced they were a message from the Missioner, something Father Roland wanted him to know without speaking the words himself. Not again after that first night did he apologize for his visits to the room, nor did he ever explain why the door was always locked, or why he invariably locked it after him when he went in. Each night, when they were at home, he disappeared into the room, opening the door only enough to let his body pass through; sometimes he remained there for only a few minutes, and occasionally for a long time. At least once a day, usually in the evening, he played the violin. It was always the same piece that he played. There was never a variation, and David could not make up his mind that he had ever heard it before. At these times, if Mukoki happened to be in the Château, as Father Roland called his place, he would sit like one in a trance, scarcely breathing until the music had ceased. And when the Missioner came from the room his face was always lit up in a kind of halo. There was one exception to all this, David noticed. The door was never unlocked when there was a visitor. No other but himself and Mukoki heard the sound of the violin, and this fact, in time, impressed David with the deep faith and affection of the Little Missioner. One evening Father Roland came from the room with his face aglow with some strange happiness that had come to him in there, and placing his hands on David's shoulders he said, with a yearning and yet hopeless inflection in his voice:

"I wish you would stay with me always, David. It has made me younger, and happier, to have a son."

In David there was growing — but concealed from Father Roland's eyes for a long time — a strange insistent restlessness. It ran in his blood, like a thing alive, whenever he looked at the face of the Girl. He wanted to go on.

And yet life at the Château, after the first two weeks, was anything but dull and unexciting. They were in the heart of the great trapping country. Forty miles to the north was a Hudson's Bay post where an ordained minister of the Church of England had a mission. But Father Roland belonged to the forest people alone. They were his "children," scattered in their shacks and tepees over ten thousand square miles of country, with the Château as its centre. He was ceaselessly on the move after that first fortnight, and David was always with him. The Indians worshipped him, and the quarter-breeds and half-breeds and occasional French called him "*mon Père*" in very much the same tone of voice as they said "Our Father" in their prayers. These people of the trap-lines were a revelation to David. They were wild, living in a savage primitiveness, and yet they reverenced a divinity with a conviction that amazed him. And they died. That was the tragedy of it. They died — too easily. He understood, after a while, why a country ten times as large as the state of Ohio had altogether a population of less than twenty-five thousand, a fair-sized town. Their belts were drawn too tight — men, women, and little children — their belts too tight. That was it! Father Roland emphasized it. Too much hunger in the long, terrible months of winter, when to keep body and soul together they trapped the furred creatures for the hordes of luxurious barbarians in the great cities of the earth. Just a steady, gnawing hunger all through the winter — hunger for something besides meat, a hunger that got into the bones, into the eyes, into arms and legs — a hunger that brought sickness, and then death.

That winter he saw grown men and women die of measles as easily as flies that had devoured poison. They were over at Metoosin's, sixty miles to the west of the Château, when Metoosin returned to his shack with supplies from a Post. Metoosin had taken up lynx and marten and mink that would sell the next year in London and Paris for a thousand dollars, and he had brought back a few small cans of vegetables at fifty cents a can, a little flour at forty cents a pound, a bit of cheap cloth at the price of rare silk, some tobacco and a pittance of tea, and he was happy. A half season's work on the trap-line and his family could have eaten it all in a week — if they had dared to eat as much as they needed.

"And still they're always in the debt of the Posts," the Missioner said, the lines settling deeply on his face.

And yet David could not but feel more and more deeply the

thrill, the fascination, and, in spite of its hardships, the recompense of this life of which he had become a part. For the first time in his life he clearly perceived the primal measurements of riches, of contentment and of ambition, and these three things that he saw stripped naked for his eyes many other things which he had not understood, or in blindness had failed to see, in the life from which he had come. Metoosin, with that little treasure of food from the Post, did not know that he was poor, or that through many long years he had been slowly starving. He was rich! He was a great trapper! And his Cree wife I-owa, with her long, sleek braid and her great, dark eyes, was tremendously proud of her lord, that he should bring home for her and the children such a wealth of things — a little flour, a few cans of things, a few yards of cloth, and a little bright ribbon. David choked when he ate with them that night. But they were happy! That, after all, was the reward of things, even though people died slowly of something which they could not understand. And there were, in the domain of Father Roland, many Metoosins, and many I-owas, who prayed for nothing more than enough to eat, clothes to cover them, and the unbroken love of their firesides. And David thought of them, as the weeks passed, as the most terribly enslaved of all the slaves of Civilization — slaves of vain civilized women; for they had gone on like this for centuries, and would go on for other generations, giving into the hands of the great Company their life's blood which, in the end, could be accounted for by a yearly dole of food which, under stress, did not quite serve to keep body and soul together.

It was after a comprehension of these things that David understood Father Roland's great work. In this kingdom of his, running approximately fifty miles in each direction from the Château — except to the northward, where the Post lay — there were two hundred and forty-seven men, women, and children. In a great book the Little Missioner had their names, their ages, the blood that was in them, and where they lived; and by them he was worshipped as no man that ever lived in that vast country of cities and towns below the Height of Land. At every tepee and shack they visited there was some token of love awaiting Father Roland; a rare skin here, a pair of moccasins there, a pair of snow shoes that it had taken an Indian woman's hands weeks to make, choice cuts of meat, but mostly — as they travelled along — the thickly furred skins of animals; and never did they go to a place at which the Missioner did not leave something in return, usually some article of clothing so thick and warm that no Indian was rich enough to buy it for himself at the Post. Twice each winter Father Roland sent down to Thoreau a great sledge load of these contributions of his people, and Thoreau, selling them, sent back a still greater sledge load of supplies that found their way in this manner of exchange into the shacks and tepees of the forest people.

"If I were only rich!" said Father Roland one night at the Château, when it was storming dismally outside. "But I have nothing, David. I can do only a tenth of what I would like to do. There are only eighty families in this country of mine, and I have figured that a hundred dollars a family, spent down there and not at the Post, would keep them all in comfort through the longest and hardest winter. A hundred dollars, in Winnipeg, would buy as much as an Indian trapper could get at the Post for a thousand dollars' worth of fur, and five hundred dollars is a good catch. It is terrible, but what can I do? I dare not buy their furs and sell them for my people, because the Company would blacklist the whole lot and it would be a great calamity in the end. But if I had money — if I could do it with my own. . . ."

David had been thinking of that. In the late January snow two teams went down to Thoreau in place of one. Mukoki had charge of them, and with him went an even half of what David had brought with him — fifteen hundred dollars in gold certificates.

"If I live I'm going to make them a Christmas present of twice that amount each year," he said. "I can afford it. I fancy that I shall take a great pleasure in it, and that occasionally I shall return into this country to make a visit."

It was the first time that he had spoken as though he would not remain with the Missioner indefinitely. But the conviction that the time was not far away when he would be leaving him had been growing within him steadily. He kept it to himself. He fought against it even. But it grew. And, curiously enough, it was strongest when Father Roland was in the locked room playing softly on the violin. David never mentioned the room. He feigned an indifference to its very existence. And yet in spite of himself the mystery of it became an obsession with him. Something within it seemed to reach out insistently and invite him in, like a spirit chained there by the Missioner himself, crying for freedom. One night they returned to the Château through a blizzard from the cabin of a half-breed whose wife was sick, and after their supper the Missioner went into the mystery-room. He played the violin as usual. But after that there was a long silence. When Father Roland came out, and seated himself opposite David at the small table on which their books were scattered, David received a shock. Clinging to the Missioner's shoulder, shimmering like a polished silken thread in the lampglow, was a long, shining hair — a woman's hair. With an effort David choked back the word of amazement in his throat, and began turning over the pages of a book. And then suddenly, the Missioner saw that silken thread. David heard his quick breath. He saw, without raising his eyes, the slow, almost stealthy movement of his companion's fingers as he plucked the hair from his arm and shoulder, and when David looked up the hair was gone, and one of Father Roland's hands was closed tightly, so tightly that the veins stood out on it. He rose from the table, and again went into the room beyond the locked door. David's heart was beating like an unsteady hammer. He could not quite account for the strange effect this incident had upon him. He wanted more than ever to see that room beyond the locked door.

February — the Hunger Moon — of this year was a month of great storm in the Northland. This meant sickness, and a great deal of travel for Father Roland. He and David were almost ceaselessly on the move, and its hardships gave the finishing touches to David's education. The wilderness, vast and empty as it was, no longer held a dread for him. He had faced its bitterest storms; he had slept with the deep snow under his blankets; he had followed behind the Missioner through the blackest nights, when it had seemed as though no human soul could find its way; and he had looked on death. Once they ran swiftly to it through a night blizzard; again it came, three in a family, so far to the west that it was out of Father Roland's beaten trails; and again he saw it in the Madonna-like face of a young French girl, who had died clutching a cross to her breast. It was this girl's white face, sweet as a child's and strangely beautiful in death, that stirred David most deeply. She must have been about the age of the girl whose picture he carried next his heart.

Soon after this, early in March, he had definitely made up his mind. There was no reason now why he should not *go on*. He was physically fit. Three months had hardened him until he was like a rock. He believed that he had more than regained his weight. He could beat Father Roland with either rifle or pistol, and in one day he had travelled forty miles on snow shoes. That was when they had arrived just in time to save the life of Jean Croisset's little girl, who lived over on the Big Thunder. The crazed father had led them a mad race, but they had kept up with him. And just in time. There had not been an hour to lose. After that Croisset and his half-breed wife would have laid down their lives for Father

Roland — and for him. For the forest people had begun to accept him as a part of Father Roland; more and more he could see their growing love for him, their gladness when he came, their sorrow when he left, and it gave him what he thought of as a sort of *filling* satisfaction, something he had never quite fully experienced before in all his life. He knew that he would come back to them again some day — that, in the course of his life, he would spend a great deal of time among them. He assured Father Roland of this.

The Missioner did not question him deeply about his "friends" in the western mountains. But night after night he helped him to mark out a trail on the maps that he had at the Château, giving him a great deal of information which David wrote down in a book, and letters to certain good friends of his whom he would find along the way. As the slush snow came, and the time when David would be leaving drew nearer, Father Roland could not entirely conceal his depression, and he spent more time in the room beyond the locked door. Several times when about to enter the room he seemed to hesitate, as if there were something which he wanted to say to David. Twice David thought he was almost on the point of inviting him into the room, and at last he came to believe that the Missioner wanted him to know what was beyond that mysterious door, and yet was afraid to tell him, or ask him in. It was well along in March that the thing happened which he had been expecting. Only it came in a manner that amazed him deeply. Father Roland came from the room early in the evening, after playing his violin. He locked the door, and as he put on his cap he said:

"I shall be gone for an hour, David. I am going over to Mukoki's cabin."

He did not ask David to accompany him, and as he turned to go the key that he had held in his hand dropped to the floor. It fell with a quite audible sound. The Missioner must have heard it, and would have recovered it had it slipped from his fingers accidentally. But he paid no attention to it. He went out quickly, without glancing back.

For several minutes David stared at the key without moving from his chair near the table. It meant but one thing. He was invited to go into that room — *alone*. If he had had a doubt it was dispelled by the fact that Father Roland had left a light burning in there. It was not chance. There was a purpose to it all: the light, the audible dropping of the heavy key, the swift going of the Missioner. David made himself sure of this before he rose from his chair. He waited perhaps five minutes. Then he picked up the key.

At the door, as the key clicked in the lock, he hesitated. The thought came to him that if he was making a mistake it would be a terrible mistake. It held his hand for a moment. Then, slowly, he pushed the door inward and followed it until he stood inside. The first thing that he noticed was a big brass lamp, of the old style, brought over from England by the Company a hundred years ago, and he held his breath in anticipation of something tremendous impending. At first he saw nothing that impressed him forcibly. The room was a disappointment in that first glance. He could see nothing of its mystery, nothing of that strangeness, quite indefinable even to himself, which he had expected. And then, as he stood there staring about with wide-open eyes, the truth flashed upon him with a suddenness that drew a quick breath from his lips. He was standing in a *woman's room*! There was no doubt.

It looked very much as though a woman had left it only recently. There was a bed, fresh and clean, with a white counterpane. She had left on that bed a — nightgown; yes, and he noticed that it had a frill of lace at the neck. And on the wall were her garments, quite a number of them, and a long coat of a curious style, with a great fur collar. There was a small dresser, oddly antique, and on it were a brush and comb, a big red pin cushion, and odds and ends of a woman's toilet affairs. Close to the bed were a pair of shoes and a pair of slippers, with unusually high heels, and hanging over the edge of the counterpane was a pair of long stockings. The walls of the room were touched up, as if by a woman's hands, with pictures and a few ornaments. Where the garments were hanging David noticed a pair of woman's snow shoes, and a woman's moccasins under a picture of the Madonna. On the mantel there was a tall vase filled with the dried stems of flowers. And then came the most amazing discovery of all. There was a second table between the lamp and the bed, and it was set for two! Yes, for *two*! No, for *three*! For, a little in shadow, David saw a crudely made high-chair — a baby's chair — and on it were a little knife and fork, a baby spoon, and a little tin plate. It was astounding. Perfectly incredible. And David's eyes sought questingly for a door through which a woman might come and go mysteriously and unseen. There was none, and the one window of the room was so high up that a person standing on the ground outside could not look in.

And now it began to dawn upon David that all these things he was looking at were old — very old. In the Château the Missioner no longer ate on tin plates. The shoes and slippers must have been made a generation ago. The rag carpet under his feet had lost its vivid lines of colouring. Age impressed itself upon him. This was a woman's room, but the woman had not been here recently. And the child had not been here recently.

For the first time his eyes turned in a closer inspection of the table on which stood the big brass lamp. Father Roland's violin lay beside it. He made a step or two nearer, so that he could see beyond the lamp, and his heart gave a sudden jump. Shimmering on the faded red cloth of the table, glowing as brightly as though it had been clipped from a woman's head but yesterday, was a long, thick tress of hair! It was dark, richly dark, and his second impression was one of amazement at the length of it. The tress was as long as the table — fully a yard down the woman's back it must have hung. It was tied at the end with a bit of white ribbon.

David drew slowly back toward the door, stirred all at once by a great doubt. Had Father Roland meant him to look upon all this? A lump rose suddenly in his throat. He had made a mistake — a great mistake. He felt now like one who had broken into the sanctity of a sacred place. He had committed sacrilege. The Missioner had not dropped the key purposely. It must have been an accident. And he — David — was guilty of a great blunder. He withdrew from the room, and locked the door. He dropped the key where he had found it on the floor, and sat down again with his book. He did not read. He scarcely saw the lines of the printed page. He had not been in his chair more than ten minutes when he heard quick footsteps, followed by a hand at the door, and Father Roland came in. He was visibly excited, and his glance shot at once to the room which David had just left. Then his eyes scanned the floor. The key was gleaming where it had fallen, and with an exclamation of relief the Missioner snatched it up.

"I thought I had lost my key," he laughed, a bit nervously; then he added, with a deep breath: "It's snowing tonight. A heavy snow, and there will be good sledging for a few days. God knows I don't want you to leave me, but if it must be — we should take advantage of this snow. It will be the last. Mukoki and I will go with you as far as the Reindeer Lake country, two hundred miles northwest. David — *must* you go?"

It seemed to David that two tiny fists were pounding against his breast, where the picture lay.

"Yes, I must go," he said. "I have quite made up my mind to that. I must go."

CHAPTER XV

Ten days after that night when he had gone into the mystery-room at the Château, David and Father Roland clasped hands in a final farewell at White Porcupine House, on the Cochrane River, 270 miles from God's Lake. It was something more than a handshake. The Missioner made no effort to speak in these last moments. His team was ready for the return drive and he had drawn his travelling hood close about his face. In his own heart he believed that David would never return. He would go back to civilization, probably next autumn, and in time he would forget. As he said, on their last day before reaching the Cochrane, David's going was like taking a part of his heart away. He blinked now, as he dropped David's hand — blinked and turned his eyes. And David's voice had an odd break in it. He knew what the Missioner was thinking.

"I'll come back, *mon Père*," he called after him, as Father Roland broke away and went toward Mukoki and the dogs. "I'll come back next year!"

Father Roland did not look back until they were started. Then he turned and waved a mittened hand. Mukoki heard the sob in his throat. David tried to call a last word to him, but his voice choked. He, too, waved a hand. He had not known that there were friendships like this between men, and as the Missioner trailed steadily away from him, growing smaller and smaller against the dark rim of the distant forest, he felt a sudden fear and a great loneliness — a fear that, in spite of himself, they would not meet again, and the loneliness that comes to a man when he sees a world widening between himself and the one friend he has on earth. His one friend. The man who had saved him from himself, who had pointed out the way for him, who had made him fight. More than a friend; a father. He did not stop the broken sound that came to his lips. A low whine answered it, and he looked down at Baree, huddled in the snow within a yard of his feet. "My god and master," Baree's eyes said, as they looked up at him, "I am here." It was as if David had heard the words. He held out a hand and Baree came to him, his great wolfish body aquiver with joy. After all, he was not alone.

A short distance from him the Indian who was to take him over to Fond du Lac, on Lake Athabasca, was waiting with his dogs and sledge. He was a Sarcee, one of the last of an almost extinct tribe, so old that his hair was of a shaggy white, and he was so thin that he looked like a famine-stricken Hindu. "He has lived so long that no one knows his age," Father Roland had said, "and he is the best trailer between Hudson's Bay and the Peace." His name was Upso-Gee (the Snow Fox), and the Missioner had bargained with him for a hundred dollars to take David from White Porcupine House to Fond du Lac, three hundred miles farther northwest. He cracked his long caribou-gut whip to remind David that he was ready. David had said good-bye to the factor and the clerk at the Company store and there was no longer an excuse to detain him. They struck out across a small lake. Five minutes later he looked back. Father Roland, not much more than a speck on the white plain now, was about to disappear in the forest. It seemed to David that he had stopped, and again he waved his hand, though human eyes could not have seen the movement over that distance.

Not until that night, when David sat alone beside his campfire, did he begin to realize fully the vastness of this adventure into which he had plunged. The Snow Fox was dead asleep and it was horribly lonely. It was a dark night, too, with the shivering wailing of a restless wind in the tree tops; the sort of night that makes loneliness grow until it is like some kind of a monster inside, choking off one's breath. And on Upso-Gee's tepee, with the firelight dancing on it, there was painted in red a grotesque fiend with horns — a medicine man, or devil chaser; and this devil chaser grinned in a bloodthirsty manner at David as he sat near the fire, as if gloating over some dreadful fate that awaited him. It *was* lonely. Even Baree seemed to sense his master's oppression, for he had laid his head between David's feet, and was as still as if asleep. A long way off David could hear the howling of a wolf and it reminded him shiveringly of the lead-dog's howl that night before Tavish's cabin. It was like the death cry that comes from a dog's throat; and where the forest gloom mingled with the firelight he saw a phantom shadow — in the morning he found that it was a spruce bough, broken and hanging down — that made him think again of Tavish swinging in the moonlight. His thoughts bore upon him deeply and with foreboding. And he asked himself questions — questions which were not new, but which came to him tonight with a new and deeper significance. He believed that Father Roland would have gasped in amazement and that he would have held up his hands in incredulity had he known the truth of this astonishing adventure of his. An astonishing adventure — nothing less. To find a girl. A girl he had never seen, who might be in another part of the world, when he had got to the end of his journey — or married. And if he found her, what would he say? What would he do? Why did he want to find her? "God alone knows," he said aloud, borne down under his gloom, and went to bed.

Small things, as Father Roland had frequently said, decide great events. The next morning came with a glorious sun; the world again was white and wonderful, and David found swift answers to the questions he had asked himself a few hours before. Each day thereafter the sun was warmer, and with its increasing promise of the final "break-up" and slush snows, Upso-Gee's taciturnity and anxiety grew apace. He was little more talkative than the painted devil chaser on the blackened canvas of his tepee, but he gave David to understand that he would have a hard time getting back with his dogs and sledge from Fond du Lac if the thaw came earlier than he had anticipated. David marvelled at the old warrior's endurance, and especially when they crossed the forty miles of ice on Wollaston Lake between dawn and darkness. At high noon the snow was beginning to soften on the sunny slopes even then, and by the time they reached the Porcupine, Snow Fox was chanting his despairing prayer nightly before that grinning thing on his tepee. "Swas-tao (the thaw) she kam dam' queek," he said to David, grimacing his old face to express other things which he could not say in English. And it did. Four days later, when they reached Fond du Lac, there was water underfoot in places, and Upso-Gee turned back on the home trail within an hour.

This was in April, and the Post reminded David of a great hive to which the forest people were swarming like treasure-laden bees. On the last snow they were coming in with their furs from a hundred trap-lines. Luck was with David. On the first day Baree fought with a huge malemute and almost killed it, and David, in separating the dogs, was slightly bitten by the malemute. A friendship sprang up instantly between the two masters. Bouvais was a Frenchman from Horseshoe Bay, fifty miles from Fort Chippewyan, and a hundred and fifty straight west of Fond du Lac. He was a fox hunter. "I bring my furs over here, m'sieu," he explained, "because I had a fight with the factor at Fort Chippewyan and broke out two of his teeth," which was sufficient explanation. He was delighted when he learned that David wanted to go west. They started two days later with a sledge heavily laden with supplies. The runners sank deep in the growing slush, but under them was always the thick ice of Lake Athabasca, and going was not bad, except that David's feet were always wet. He was surprised that he did not take a "cold." "A cold — what is that?" asked Bouvais, who had lived along the Barrens all his life.

David described a typical case of sniffles, with running at eyes and nose, and Bouvais laughed. "The only cold we have up here is when the lungs get touched by frost," he said, "and then you die — the following spring. Always then. The lungs slough away." And then he asked: "Why are you going west?"

David found himself face to face with the question, and had to answer. "Just to toughen up a bit," he replied. "Wandering. Nothing else to do." And after all, he thought later, wasn't that pretty near the truth? He tried to convince himself that it was. But his hand touched the picture of the Girl, in his breast pocket. He seemed to feel her throbbing against it. A preposterous imagination! But it was pleasing. It warmed his blood.

For a week David and Baree remained at Horseshoe Bay with the Frenchman. Then they went on around the end of the lake toward Fort Chippewyan. Bouvais accompanied them, out of friendship purely, and they travelled afoot with fifty-pound packs on their shoulders, for in the big, sunlit reaches the ground was already growing bare of snow. Bouvais turned back when they were ten miles from Fort Chippewyan, explaining that it was a nasty matter to have knocked two teeth down a factor's throat, and particularly down the throat of the head factor of the Chippewyan and Athabasca district. "And they went down," assured Bouvais. "He tried to spit them out, but couldn't." A few hours later David met the factor and observed that Bouvais had spoken the truth; at least there were two teeth missing, quite conspicuously. Hatchett was his name. He looked it; tall, thin, sinewy, with bird-like eyes that were shifting this way and that at all times, as though he were constantly on the alert for an ambush, or feared thieves. He was suspicious of David, coming in alone in this No Man's Land with a pack on his back; a white man, too, which made him all the more suspicious. Perhaps a possible free trader looking for a location. Or, worse still, a spy of the Company's hated competitors, the Revilon Brothers. It took some time for Father Roland's letter to convince him that David was harmless. And then, all at once, he warmed up like a birch-bark taking fire, and shook David's hand three times within five minutes, so hungry was he for a white man's companionship — an *honest* white man's, mind you, and not a scoundrelly competitor's! He opened four cans of lobsters, left over from Christmas, for their first meal, and that night beat David at seven games of cribbage in a row. He wasn't married, he said; didn't even have an Indian woman. Hated women. If it wasn't for breeding a future generation of trappers he would not care if they all died. No good. Positively no good. Always making trouble, more or less. That's why, a long time ago, there was a fort at Chippewyan — sort of blockhouse that still stood there. Two men, of two different tribes, wanted same woman; quarrelled; fought; one got his blamed head busted; tribes took it up; raised hell for a time — all over that rag of a woman! Terrible creatures, women were. He emphasized his belief in short, biting snatches of words, as though afraid of wearing out his breath or his vocabulary or both. Maybe his teeth had something to do with it. Where the two were missing he carried the stem of his pipe, and when he talked the stem clicked, like a Castanet.

David had come at a propitious moment — a "most propichus moment," Hatchett told him. He had done splendidly that winter. His bargains with the Indians had been sharp and exceedingly profitable for the Company and as soon as he got his furs off to Fort McMurray on their way to Edmonton he was going on a long journey of inspection, which was his reward for duty well performed. His fur barges were ready. All they were waiting for was the breaking up of the ice, when the barges would start up the Athabasca, which meant *south*; while he, in his big war canoe, would head up the Peace, which meant *west*. He was going as far as Hudson's Hope, and this was within two hundred and fifty miles of where David wanted to go. He proved that fact by digging up an old Company map. David's heart beat an excited tattoo. This was more than he had expected. Almost too good to be true. "You can *work* your way up there with me," declared Hatchett, clicking his pipe stem. "Won't cost you a cent. Not a dam' cent. Work. Eat. Smoke. Fine trip. Just for company. A man needs company once in a while — decent company. Ice will go by middle of May. Two weeks. Meanwhile, have a devil of a time playing cribbage."

They did. Cribbage was Hatchett's one passion, unless another was — beating the Indians. "Rascally devils," he would say, driving his cribbage pegs home. "Always trying to put off poor fur on me for good. Deserve to be beat. And I beat 'em. Dam-if-I-don't."

"How did you lose your teeth?" David asked him at last. They were playing late one night.

Hatchett sat up in his chair as if stung. His eyes bulged as he looked at David, and his pipe stem clicked fiercely.

"Frenchman," he said. "Dirty pig of a Frenchman. No use for 'em. None. Told him women were no good — all women were bad. Said he had a woman. Said I didn't care — all bad just the same. Said the woman he referred to was his wife. Told him he was a fool to have a wife. No warning — the pig! He biffed me. Knocked those two teeth out — *down*! I'll get him some day. Flay him. Make dog whips of his dirty hide. All Frenchmen ought to die. Hope to God they will. Starve. Freeze."

In spite of himself David laughed. Hatchett took no offense, but the grimness of his long, sombre countenance remained unbroken. A day or two later he discovered Hatchett in the act of giving an old, white-haired, half-breed cripple a bag of supplies. Hatchett shook himself, as if caught in an act of crime.

"I'm going to kill that old Dog Rib soon as the ground's soft enough to dig a grave," he declared, shaking a fist fiercely after the old Indian. "Beggar. A sneak. No good. Ought to die. Giving him just enough to keep him alive until the ground is soft."

After all, Hatchett's face belied his heart. His tongue was like a cleaver. It ripped things generally — was terrible in its threatening, but harmless, and tremendously amusing to David. He liked Hatchett. His cadaverous countenance, never breaking into a smile, was the oddest mask he had ever seen a human being wear. He believed that if it once broke into a laugh it would not straighten back again without leaving a permanent crack. And yet he liked the man, and the days passed swiftly.

It was the middle of May before they started up the Peace, three days after the fur barges had gone down the Athabasca. David had never seen anything like Hatchett's big war canoe, roomy as a small ship, and light as a feather on the water. Four powerful Dog Ribs went with them, making six paddles in all. When it came to a question of Baree, Hatchett put down his foot with emphasis. "What! Make a dam' passenger of a dog? Never. Let him follow ashore — or die."

This would undoubtedly have been Baree's choice if he had had a voice in the matter. Day after day he followed the canoe, swimming streams and working his way through swamp and forest. It was no easy matter. In the deep, slow waters of the Lower Peace the canoe made thirty-five miles a day; twice it made forty. But Hatchett kept Baree well fed, and each night the dog slept at David's feet in camp. On the sixth day they reached Fort Vermilion, and Hatchett announced himself like a king. For he was on inspection. Company inspection, mind you. Important! A week later they arrived at Peace River landing, two hundred miles farther west, and on the twentieth day came to Fort St. John, fifty miles from Hudson's Hope. From here David saw his first of the mountains. He made out their snowy peaks clearly, seventy miles away, and with his finger on a certain spot on Hatchett's map his heart thrilled. He was almost there! Each day the mountains grew nearer. From Hudson's Hope he fancied that he could almost see the dark blankets of timber on their sides. Hatchett grunted. They were still forty miles away. And Mac Veigh, the factor at Hudson's Hope, looked at David in a curious sort of way when David told him where he was going.

"You're the first white man to do it," he said — an inflection of doubt in his voice. "It's not bad going up the Finly as far as the Kwadocha. But from there. . . ."

He shook his head. He was short and thick, and his jaw hung heavy with disapproval.

"You're still seventy miles from the Stikine when you end up at the Kwadocha," he went on, thumbing the map. "Who the devil will you get to take you on from there? Straight over the backbone of the Rockies. No trails. Not even a Post there. Too rough a country. Even the Indians won't live in it." He was silent for a moment, as if reflecting deeply. "Old Towaskook and his tribe are on the Kwadocha," he added, as if seeing a glimmer of hope. "*He might.* But I doubt it. They're a lazy lot of mongrels, Towaskook's people, who carve things out of wood, to worship. Still, he *might.* I'll send up a good man with you to influence him, and you'd better take along a couple hundred dollars in supplies as a further inducement."

The man was a half-breed. Three days later they left Hudson's Hope, with Baree riding amidships. The mountains loomed up swiftly after this, and the second day they were among them. After that it was slow work fighting their way up against the current of the Finly. It was tremendous work. It seemed to David that half their time was spent amid the roar of rapids. Twenty-seven times within five days they made portages. Later on it took them two days to carry their canoe and supplies around a mountain. Fifteen days were spent in making eighty miles. Easier travel followed then. It was the twentieth of June when they made their last camp before reaching the Kwadocha. The sun was still up; but they were tired, utterly exhausted. David looked at his map and at the figures in the notebook he carried. He had come close to fifteen hundred miles since that day when he and Father Roland and Mukoki had set out for the Cochrane. Fifteen hundred miles! And he had less than a hundred more to go! Just over those mountains — somewhere beyond them. It looked easy. He would not be afraid to go alone, if old Towaskook refused to help him. Yes, alone. He would find his way, somehow, he and Baree. He had unbounded confi-

dence in Baree. Together they could fight it out. Within a week or
two they would find the Girl.

And then . . .?

He looked at the picture a long time in the glow of the setting
sun.

CHAPTER XVI

It was the week of the Big Festival when David and his half-breed arrived at Towaskook's village. Towaskook was the "farthest east" of the totem-worshippers, and each of his forty or fifty people reminded David of the devil chaser on the canvas of the Snow Fox's tepee. They were dressed up, as he remarked to the half-breed, "like fiends." On the day of David's arrival Towaskook himself was disguised in a huge bear head from which protruded a pair of buffalo horns that had somehow drifted up there from the western prairies, and it was his special business to perform various antics about his totem pole for at least six hours between sunrise and sunset, chanting all the time most dolorous supplications to the squat monster who sat, grinning, at the top. It was "the day of good hunting," and Towaskook and his people worked themselves into exhaustion by the ardour of their prayers that the game of the mountains might walk right up to their tepee doors to be killed, thus necessitating the smallest possible physical exertion in its capture. That night Towaskook visited David at his camp, a little up the river, to see what he could get out of the white man. He was monstrously fat — fat from laziness; and David wondered how he had managed to put in his hours of labour under the totem pole. David sat in silence, trying to make out something from their gestures, as his half-breed, Jacques, and the old chief talked.

Jacques repeated it all to him after Towaskook, sighing deeply, had risen from his squatting posture, and left them. It was a terrible journey over those mountains, Towaskook had said. He had been on the Stikine once. He had split with his tribe, and had started eastward with many followers, but half of them had died — died because they would not leave their precious totems behind — and so had been caught in a deep snow that came early. It was a ten-day journey over the mountains. You went up above the clouds — many times you had to go above the clouds. He would never make the journey again. There was one chance — just one. He had a young bear hunter, Kio, his face was still smooth. He had not won his spurs, so to speak, and he was anxious to perform a great feat, especially as he was in love with his medicine man's daughter Kwak-wa-pisew (the Butterfly). Kio might go, to prove his valour to the Butterfly. Towaskook had gone for him. Of course, on a mission of this kind, Kio would accept no pay. That would go to Towaskook. The two hundred dollars' worth of supplies satisfied him.

A little later Towaskook returned with Kio. He was exceedingly youthful, slim-built as a weazel, but with a deep-set and treacherous eye. He listened. He would go. He would go as far as the confluence of the Pitman and the Stikine, if Towaskook would assure him the Butterfly. Towaskook, eyeing greedily the supplies which Jacques had laid out alluringly, nodded an agreement to that. "The next day," Kio said, then, eager now for the adventure. "The next day they would start."

That night Jacques carefully made up the two shoulder packs which David and Kio were to carry, for thereafter their travel would be entirely afoot. David's burden, with his rifle, was fifty pounds. Jacques saw them off, shouting a last warning for David to "keep a watch on that devil-eyed Kio."

Kio was not like his eyes. He turned out, very shortly, to be a communicative and rather likable young fellow. He was ignorant of the white man's talk. But he was a master of gesticulation; and when, in climbing their first mountain, David discovered muscles in his legs and back that he had never known of before, Kio laughingly sympathized with him and assured him in vivid pantomime that he would soon get used to it. Their first night they camped almost at the summit of the mountain. Kio wanted to make the warmth of the valley beyond, but those new muscles in David's legs and back declared otherwise. Strawberries were ripening in the deeper valleys, but up where they were it was cold. A bitter wind came off the snow on the peaks, and David could smell the pungent fog of the clouds. They were so high that the scrub twigs of their fire smouldered with scarcely sufficient heat to fry their bacon. David was oblivious of the discomfort. His blood ran warm in hope and anticipation. He was almost at the end of his journey. It had been a great fight, and he had won. There was no doubt in his mind now. After this he could face the world again.

Day after day they made their way westward. It was tremendous, this journey over the backbone of the mountains. It gave one a different conception of men. They like ants on these mountains, David thought — insignificant, crawling ants. Here was where one might find a soul and a religion if he had never had one before. One's littleness, at times, was almost frightening. It made one think, impressed upon one that life was not much more than an accident in this vast scale of creation, and that there was great necessity for a God. In Kio's eyes, as he sometimes looked down into the valleys, there was this thing; the thought which perhaps he couldn't analyze, the great truth which he couldn't understand, but felt. It made a worshipper of him — a devout worshipper of the totem. And it occurred to David that perhaps the spirit of God was in that totem even as much as in finger-worn rosaries and the ivory crosses on women's breasts.

Early on the eleventh day they came to the confluence of the Pitman and the Stikine rivers, and a little later Kio turned back on his homeward journey, and David and Baree were alone. This aloneness fell upon them like a thing that had a pulse and was alive. They crossed the Divide and were in a great sunlit country of amazing beauty and grandeur, with wide valleys between the mountains. It was July. From up and down the valley, from the breaks between the peaks and from the little gullies cleft in shale and rock that crept up to the snow lines, came a soft and droning murmur. It was the music of running water. That music was always in the air, for the rivers, the creeks, and the tiny streams, gushing down from the snow that lay eternally up near the clouds, were never still. There were sweet perfumes as well as music in the air. The earth was bursting with green; the early flowers were turning the sunny slopes into coloured splashes of red and white and purple — splashes of violets and forget-me-nots, of wild asters and hyacinths. David looked upon it all, and his soul drank in its wonders. He made his camp, and he remained in it all that day, and the next. He was eager to go on, and yet in his eagerness he hesitated, and waited. It seemed to him that he must become acquainted with this empty world before venturing farther into it — alone; that it was necessary for him to understand it a little, and get his bearings. He could not lose himself. Jacques had assured him of that, and Kio had pantomimed it, pointing many times at the broad, shallow stream that ran ahead of him. All he had to do was to follow the river. In time, many weeks, of course, it would bring him to the white settlement on the ocean. Long before that he would strike Firepan Creek. Kio had never been so far; he had never been farther than this junction of the two streams, Towaskook had informed Jacques. So it was not fear that held David. It was the *aloneness*. He was taking a long mental breath. And, meanwhile, he was repairing his boots, and doctoring Baree's feet, bruised and sore by their travel over the shale of the mountain tops.

He thought that he had experienced the depths of loneliness after leaving the Missioner. But here it was a much larger thing. This night, as he sat under the stars and a great white moon, with Baree at his feet, it engulfed him; not in a depressing way, but awesomely. It was not an unpleasant loneliness, and yet he felt that it had no limit, that it was immeasurable. It was as vast as the mountains that shut him in. Somewhere, miles to the east of him now, was Kio. That was all. He knew that he would never be able to describe it, this loneliness — or aloneness; one man, and a dog, with a world to themselves. After a time, as he looked up at the stars and listened to the droning sound of the waters in the valley, it began to thrill him with a new kind of intelligence. Here was peace as vast as space itself. It was not troubled by the struggling existence of men, and women, and it seemed to him that he must remain very still under the watchfulness of those billions of sentinels in the sky, with the white moon floating under them. The second night he made himself and Baree a small fire. The third morning he shouldered his pack and went on.

Baree kept close at his master's side, and the eyes of the two were constantly on the alert. They were in a splendid game country, and David watched for the first opportunity that would give Baree and himself fresh meat. The white sand bars and gravelly shores of the stream were covered with the tracks of the wild dwellers of the valley and the adjoining ranges, and Baree sniffed hungrily whenever he came to the warm scent of the last night's spoor. He was hungry. He had been hungry all the way over the mountains. Three times that day David saw a caribou at a distance. In the afternoon he saw a grizzly on a green slope. Toward evening he ran into luck. A band of sheep had come down from a mountain to drink, and he came upon them suddenly, the wind in his favour. He killed a young ram. For a full minute after firing the shot he stood in his tracks, scarcely breathing. The report of his rifle was like an explosion. It leaped from mountain to mountain, echoing, deepening, coming back to him in murmuring intonations, and dying out at last in a sighing gasp. It was a weird and disturbing sound. He fancied that it could be heard many miles away. That night the two feasted on fresh meat.

It was their fifth day in the valley when they came to a break in the western wall of the range, and through this break flowed a stream that was very much like the Stikine, broad and shallow and ribboned with shifting bars of sand. David made up his mind that it must be the Firepan, and he could feel his pulse quicken as he started up it with Baree. He must be quite near to Tavish's cabin, if it had not been destroyed. Even if it had been burned on account of the plague that had infested it, he would surely discover the charred ruins of it. It was three o'clock when he started up the creek, and he was — inwardly — much agitated. He grew more and more positive that he was close to the end of his adventure. He would soon come upon life — human life. And then? He tried to dispel the unsteadiness of his emotions, the swiftly growing discomfort of a great anxiety. The first, of course, would be Tavish's cabin, or the ruins of it. He had taken it for granted that Tavish's location would be here, near the confluence of the two streams. A hunter or prospector would naturally choose such a position.

He travelled slowly, questing both sides of the stream, and listening. He expected at any moment to hear a sound, a new kind of sound. And he also scrutinized closely the clean, white bars of sand. There were footprints in them, of the wild things. Once his heart gave a sudden jump when he saw a bear track that looked very much like a moccasin track. It was a wonderful bear country. Their signs were everywhere along the stream, and their number and freshness made Baree restless. David travelled until dark. He had the desire to go on even then. He built a small fire instead, and cooked his supper. For a long time after that he sat in the moonlight smoking his pipe, and still listening. He tried not to think. The next day would settle his doubts. The Girl? What would he find? He went to sleep late and awoke with the summer dawn.

The stream grew narrower and the country wilder as he progressed. It was noon when Baree stopped dead in his tracks, stiff-legged, the bristles of his spine erect, a low and ominous growl in his throat. He was standing over a patch of white sand no larger than a blanket.

"What is it, boy?" asked David.

He went to him casually, and stood for a moment at the edge of the sand without looking down, lighting his pipe.

"What is it?"

The next moment his heart seemed rising up into his throat. He had been expecting what his eyes looked upon now, and he had been watching for it, but he had not anticipated such a tremendous shock. The imprint of a moccasined foot in the sand! There was no doubt of it this time. A human foot had made it — one, two, three, four, five times — in crossing that patch of sand! He stood with the pipe in his mouth, staring down, apparently without power to move or breathe. It was a small footprint. Like a boy's. He noticed, then, with slowly shifting eyes, that Baree was bristling and growling over another track. A bear track, huge, deeply impressed in the sand. The beast's great spoor crossed the outer edge of the sand, following the direction of the moccasin tracks. It was thrillingly fresh, if Baree's bristling spine and rumbling voice meant anything.

David's eyes followed the direction of the two trails. A hundred yards upstream he could see where gravel and rock were replaced entirely by sand, quite a wide, unbroken sweep of it,

across which those clawed and moccasined feet must have travelled if they had followed the creek. He was not interested in the
bear, and Baree was not interested in the Indian boy; so when they
came to the sand one followed the moccasin tracks and the other
the claw tracks. They were not at any time more than ten feet
apart. And then, all at once, they came together, and David saw
that the bear had crossed the sand last and that his huge paws had
obliterated a part of the moccasin trail. This did not strike him as
unusually significant until he came to a point where the moccasins turned sharply and circled to the right. The bear followed. A
little farther — and David's heart gave a sudden thump! At first it
might have been coincidence, a bit of chance. It was chance no
longer. It was deliberate. The claws were on the trail of the moccasins. David halted and pocketed his pipe, on which he had not
drawn a breath in several minutes. He looked at his rifle, making
sure that it was ready for action. Baree was growling. His white
fangs gleamed and lurid lights were in his eyes as he gazed ahead
and sniffed. David shuddered. Without doubt the claws had overtaken the moccasins by this time.

It was a grizzly. He guessed so much by the size of the spoor.
He followed it across a bar of gravel. Then they turned a twist in
the creek and came to other sand. A cry of amazement burst from
David's lips when he looked closely at the two trails again.

The moccasins were now following the grizzly!

He stared, for a few moments disbelieving his eyes. Here, too,
there was no room for doubt. The feet of the Indian boy had
trodden in the tracks of the bear. The evidence was conclusive; the
fact astonishing. Of course, it was barely possible. . . .

Whatever the thought might have been in David's mind, it
never reached a conclusion. He did not cry out at what he saw
after that. He made no sound. Perhaps he did not even breathe.
But it was there — under his eyes; inexplicable, amazing, not to be
easily believed. A third time the order of the mysterious footprints
in the sand was changed — and the grizzly was now following the
boy, obliterating almost entirely the indentures in the sand of his
small, moccasined feet. He wondered whether it was possible that
his eyes had gone bad on him, or that his mind had slipped out of
its normal groove and was tricking him with weirdly absurd hallu-
cinations. So what happened in almost that same breath did not
startle him as it might otherwise have done. It was for a brief
moment simply another assurance of his insanity; and if the
mountains had suddenly turned over and balanced themselves on
their peaks their gymnastics would not have frozen him into a

more speechless stupidity than did the Girl who rose before him just then, not twenty paces away. She had emerged like an apparition from behind a great boulder — a little older, a little taller, a bit wilder than she had seemed to him in the picture, but with that same glorious hair sweeping about her, and that same questioning look in her eyes as she stared at him. Her hands were in that same way at her side, too, as if she were on the point of running away from him. He tried to speak. He believed, afterward, that he even made an effort to hold out his arms. But he was powerless. And so they stood there, twenty paces apart, staring as if they had met from the ends of the earth.

Something happened then to whip David's reason back into its place. He heard a crunching — heavy, slow. From around the other end of the boulder came a huge bear. A monster. Ten feet from the girl. The first cry rushed out of his throat. It was a warning, and in the same instant he raised his rifle to his shoulder. The girl was quicker than he — like an arrow, a flash, a whirlwind of burnished tresses, as she flew to the side of the great beast. She stood with her back against it, her two hands clutching its tawny hair, her slim body quivering, her eyes flashing at David. He felt weak. He lowered his rifle and advanced a few steps.

"Who . . . what . . ." he managed to say; and stopped. He was powerless to go on. But she seemed to understand. Her body stiffened.

"I am Marge O'Doone," she said defiantly, "and this is my bear!"

CHAPTER XVII

She was splendid as she stood there, an exquisite human touch in the savageness of the world about her — and yet strangely wild as she faced David, protecting with her own quivering body the great beast behind her. To David, in the first immensity of his astonishment, she had seemed to be a woman; but now she looked to him like a child, a very young girl. Perhaps it was the way her hair fell in a tangled riot of curling tresses over her shoulders and breast; the slimness of her; the shortness of her skirt; the unfaltering clearness of the great, blue eyes that were staring at him; and, above all else, the manner in which she had spoken her name. The bear might have been nothing more than a rock to him now, against which she was leaning. He did not hear Baree's low growling. He had travelled a long way to find her, and now that she stood there before him in flesh and blood he was not interested in much else. It was a rather difficult situation. He had known her so long, she had been with him so constantly, filling even his dreams, that it was difficult for him to find words in which to begin speech. When they did come they were most commonplace; his voice was quiet, with an assured and protecting note in it.

"My name is David Raine," he said. "I have come a great distance to find you."

It was a simple and unemotional statement of fact, with nothing that was alarming in it, and yet the girl shrank closer against her bear. The huge brute was standing without the movement of a muscle, his small reddish eyes fixed on David.

"I won't go back!" she said. "I'll — fight!"

Her voice was clear, direct, defiant. Her hands appeared from behind her, and her little fists were clenched. With a swift movement she tossed her hair back from about her face. Her eyes were blue, but dark as thunder clouds in their gathering fierceness. She was like a child, and yet a woman. A ferocious little person. Ready to fight. Ready to spring at him if he approached. Her eyes never left his face.

"I won't go back!" she repeated. "I won't!"

He was noticing other things about her. Her moccasins were in tatters. Her short skirt was torn. Her shining hair was in tangles. As she swept it back from her face he saw under her eyes the darkness of exhaustion; in her cheeks a wanness, which he did not know just then was caused by hunger, and by her struggle to get away from something. On the back of one of her clenched hands was a deep, red scratch. The look in his face must have given the girl some inkling of the truth. She leaned a little forward, quickly and eagerly, and demanded:

"Didn't you come from the Nest? Didn't they send you — after me?"

She pointed down the narrow valley, her lips parted as she waited for his answer, her hair rioting over her breast again as she bent toward him.

"I've come fifteen hundred miles — from that direction," said David, swinging an arm toward the backward mountains. "I've never been in this country before. I don't know where the Nest is, or what it is. And I'm not going to take you back to it unless you want to go. If some one is coming after you, and you're bound to fight. I'll help you. Will that bear bite?"

He swung off his pack and put down his gun. For a moment the girl stared at him with widening eyes. The fear went out of them slowly. Her hand unclenched, and suddenly she turned to the big grizzly and clasped her bared arms about the shaggy monster's neck.

"Tara, Tara, it isn't one of them!" she cried. "It isn't one of them — and we thought it was!"

She whirled on David with a suddenness that took his breath away. It was like the swift turning of a bird. He had never seen a movement so quick.

"Who are you?" she flung at him, as if she had not already heard his name. "Why are you here? What business have you going up there — to the Nest?"

"I don't like that bear," said David dubiously, as the grizzly made a slow movement toward him.

"Tara won't hurt you," she said. "Not unless you put your hands on me, and I scream. I've had him ever since he was a baby and he has never hurt any one yet. But — he will!" Her eyes glowed darkly again, and her voice had a strange, hard little note in it. "I've been . . . training him," she added. "Tell me — why are you going to the Nest?"

It was a point-blank, determined question, with still a hint of suspicion in it; and her eyes, as she asked it, were the clearest, steadiest, bluest eyes he had ever looked into.

He was finding it hard to live up to what he had expected of himself. Many times he had thought of what he would say when he found this girl, if he ever did find her; but he had anticipated something a little more conventional, and had believed that it would be quite the easiest matter in the world to tell who he was, and why he had come, and to tell it all convincingly and understandably. He had not, in short, expected the sort of little person who stood there against her bear — a very difficult little person to approach easily and with assurance — half woman and half child, and beautifully wild. She was not disappointing. She was greatly appealing. When he surveyed her in a particularizing way, as he did swiftly, there was an exquisiteness about her that gave him pleasureable thrills. But it was all wild. Even her hair, an amazing glory of tangled curls, was wild in its disorder; she seemed palpitating with that wildness, like a fawn that had been run into a corner — no, not a fawn, but some beautiful creature that could and would fight desperately if need be. That was his impression. He was undergoing a smashing of his conceptions of this girl as he had visioned her from the picture, and a readjustment of her as she existed for him now. And he was not disappointed. He had never seen anything quite like this Marge O'Doone and her bear. *O'Doone!* His mind had harked back quickly, at her mention of that name, to the woman in the coach of the Transcontinental, the woman who was seeking a man by the name of Michael O'Doone. Of course the woman was her mother. Her name, too, must have been O'Doone.

Very slowly the girl detached herself from her bear, and came until she stood within three steps of David.

"Tara won't hurt you," she assured him again, "unless I scream. He would tear you to pieces, then."

If she had betrayed a sudden fear at his first appearance, it was gone now. Her eyes were like dark rock-violets and again he thought them the bluest and most fearless eyes he had ever seen. She was less a child now, standing so close to him; her slimness made her appear taller than she was. David knew that she was going to question him, and before she could speak he asked:

"Why are you afraid of some one coming after you from the Nest, as you call it?"

"Because," she replied with quiet fearlessness, "I am running away from it."

"Running away!" he gasped. "How long. . . ."

"Two days."

He understood now — her ragged moccasins, her frayed skirt, her tangled hair, the look of exhaustion about her. It came upon him all at once that she was standing unsteadily, swaying slightly like the slender stem of a flower stirred by a breath of air, and that he had not noticed these things because of the steadiness and clearness of her wonderful eyes. He was at her side in an instant.

He forgot the bear. His hand seized hers — the one with the deep, red scratch on it — and drew her to a flat rock a few steps away. She followed him, keeping her eyes on him in a wondering sort of way. The grizzly's reddish eyes were on David. A few yards away Baree was lying flat on his belly between two stones, his eyes on the bear. It was a strange scene and rather weirdly incongruous. David no longer sensed it. He still held the girl's hand as he seated her on the rock, and he looked into her eyes, smiling confidently. She was, after all, his little chum — the Girl who had been with him ever since that first night's vision in Thoreau's cabin, and who had helped him to win that great fight he had made; the girl who had cheered and inspired him during many months, and whom he had come fifteen hundred miles to see. He told her this. At first she possibly thought him a little mad. Her eyes betrayed that suspicion, for she uttered not a word to break in on his story; but after a little her lips parted, her breath came a little more quickly, a flush grew in her cheeks. It was a wonderful thing in her life, this story, no matter if the man was a bit mad, or even an impostor. He at least was very real in this moment, and he had told the story without excitement, and with an immeasurable degree of confidence and quiet tenderness — as though he had been simplifying the strange tale for the ears of a child, which in fact he had been endeavouring to do; for with the flush in her cheeks, her parted lips, and her softening eyes, she looked to him more like a child now than ever. His manner gave her great faith. But of course she was, deep in her trembling soul, quite incredulous that he should have done all these things for *her* — incredulous until he ended his story with that day's travel up the valley, and then, for the first time, showed to her — as a proof of all he had said — the picture.

She gave a little cry then. It was the first sound that had broken past her lips, and she clutched the picture in her hands and stared at it; and David, looking down, could see nothing but that shining disarray of curls, a rich and wonderful brown, in the sunlight, clustering about her shoulders and falling thickly to her waist. He thought it indescribably beautiful, in spite of the manner in which the curls and tresses had tangled themselves. They hid her face as she bent over the picture. He did not speak. He waited, knowing that in a moment or two all that he had guessed at would be clear, and that when the girl looked up she would tell him about the picture, and why she happened to be here, and not with the woman of the coach, who must have been her mother.

When at last she did look up from the picture her eyes were big and staring and filled with a mysterious questioning.

David, feeling quite sure of himself, said:

"How did it happen that you were away up here, and not with your mother that night when I met her on the train?"

"She wasn't my mother," replied the girl, looking at him still in that strange way. "My mother is dead."

CHAPTER XVIII

After that quietly spoken fact that her mother was dead, David waited for Marge O'Doone to make some further explanation. He had so firmly convinced himself that the picture he had carried was the key to all that he wanted to know — first from Tavish, if he had lived, and now from the girl — that it took him a moment or two to understand what he saw in his companion's face. He realized then that his possession of the picture and the manner in which it had come into his keeping were matters of great perplexity to her, and that the woman whom he had met in the Transcontinental held no significance for her at all, although he had told her with rather marked emphasis that this woman — whom he had thought was her mother — had been searching for a man who bore her own name, O'Doone. The girl was plainly expecting him to say something, and he reiterated this fact — that the woman in the coach was very anxious to find a man whose name was O'Doone, and that it was quite reasonable to suppose that *her* name was O'Doone, especially as she had with her this picture of a girl bearing that name. It seemed to him a powerful and utterly convincing argument. It was a combination of facts difficult to get away from without certain conclusions, but this girl who was so near to him that he could almost feel her breath did not appear fully to comprehend their significance. She was looking at him with wide-open, wondering eyes, and when he had finished she said again:

"My mother is dead. And my father is dead, too. And my aunt is dead — up at the Nest. There isn't any one left but my uncle Hauck, and he is a brute. And Brokaw. He is a bigger brute. It was he who made me let him take this picture — two years ago. I have been training Tara to kill — to kill any one that touches me, when I scream."

It was wonderful to watch her eyes darken, to see her pupils grow big and luminous. She did not look at the picture clutched in her hands, but straight at him.

"He caught me there, near the creek. He *frightened* me. He *made* me let him take it. He wanted me to take off my. . . ."

A flood of wild blood rushed into her face. In her heart was a fury.

"I wouldn't be afraid now — not of him alone," she cried. "I would scream — and fight, and Tara would tear him into pieces. Oh, Tara knows how to do it — *now*! I have trained him."

"He compelled you to let him take the picture," urged David

gently. "And then. . . ."

"I saw one of the pictures afterward. My aunt had it. I wanted to destroy it, because I hated it, and I hated him. But she said it was necessary for her to keep it. She was sick then. I loved her. She would put her arms around me every day. She used to kiss me, nights, when I went to bed. But we were afraid of Hauck — I don't call him 'uncle.' *She* was afraid of him. Once I jumped at him and scratched his face when he swore at her, and he pulled my hair. *Ugh*, I can feel it now! After that she used to cry, and she always put her arms around me closer than ever. She died that way, holding my head down to her, and trying to say something. But I couldn't understand. I was crying. That was six months ago. Since then I've been training Tara — to kill."

"And why have you trained Tara, little girl?"

David took her hand. It lay warm and unresisting in his, a firm, very little hand. He could feel a slight shudder pass through her.

"I heard — something," she said. "The Nest is a terrible place. Hauck is terrible. Brokaw is terrible. And Hauck sent away somewhere up there" — she pointed northward — "for Brokaw. He said — I belonged to Brokaw. What did he mean?"

She turned so that she could look straight into David's eyes. She was hard to answer. If she had been a woman. . . .

She saw the slow, gathering tenseness in David's face as he looked for a moment away from her bewildering eyes — the hardening muscles of his jaws; and her own hand tightened as it lay in his.

"What did Hauck mean?" she persisted. "Why do I belong to Brokaw — that great, red brute?"

The hand he had been holding he took between both his palms in a gentle, comforting way. His voice was gentle, too, but the hard lines did not leave his face.

"How old are you, Marge?" he asked.

"Seventeen," she said.

"And I am — thirty-eight." He turned to smile at her. "See. . . ." He raised a hand and took off his hat. "My hair is getting gray!"

She looked up swiftly, and then, so suddenly that it took his breath away, her fingers were running back through his thick blond hair.

"A little," she said. "But you are not old."

She dropped her hand. Her whole movement had been innocent as a child's.

"And yet I am *quite* old," he assured her. "Is this man Brokaw at the Nest, Marge?"

She nodded.

"He has been there a month. He came after Hauck sent for him, and went away again. Then he came back."

"And you are now running away from him?"

"From all of them," she said. "If it were just Brokaw I wouldn't be afraid. I would let him catch me, and scream. Tara would kill him for me. But it's Hauck, too. And the others. They are worse since Nisikoos died. That is what I called her — Nisikoos — my aunt. They are all terrible, and they all frighten me, especially since they began to build a great cage for Tara. Why should they build a cage for Tara, out of small trees? Why do they want to shut him up? None of them will tell me. Hauck says it is for another bear that Brokaw is bringing down from the Yukon. But I know they are lying. It is for Tara." Suddenly her fingers clutched tightly at his hand, and for the first time he saw under her long, shimmering lashes the darkening fire of a real terror. "Why do I belong to Brokaw?" she asked again, a little tremble in her voice. "Why did Hauck say that? Can — can a man — buy a girl?"

The nails of her slender fingers were pricking his flesh. David did not feel their hurt.

"What do you mean?" he asked, trying to keep his voice steady. "Did that man — Hauck — sell you?"

He looked away from her as he asked the question. He was afraid, just then, that something was in his face which he did not want her to see. He began to understand; at least he was beginning to picture a very horrible possibility.

"I — don't — know," he heard her say, close to his shoulder. "It was night before last I heard them quarrelling, and I crept close to a door that was a little open, and looked in. Brokaw had given my uncle a bag of gold, a little sack, like the miners use, and I heard him swear at my uncle, and say: 'That's more than she is worth but I'll give in. *Now* she's mine!' I don't know why it frightened me so. It wasn't Brokaw. I guess it was the terrible look in that man's face — my uncle's. Tara and I ran away that night. Why do you suppose they want to put Tara in a cage? Do you think Brokaw was buying *Tara* to put into that cage? He said 'she,' not 'he'."

He looked at her again. Her eyes were not so fearless now.

"Was he buying Tara, or me?" she insisted.

"Why do you have that thought — that he was buying *you*?" David asked. "Has anything — happened?"

A second time a fury of blood leapt into her face and her lashes shadowed a pair of blazing stars.

"He — that red brute — caught me in the dark two weeks ago, and held me there — and kissed me!" She fairly panted at him, springing to her feet and standing before him. "I would have screamed, but it was in the house, and Tara couldn't have come to me. I scratched him, and fought, but he bent my head back until it hurt. He tried it again the day he gave my uncle the gold, but I struck him with a stick, and got away. Oh, I *hate* him! And he knows it. And my uncle cursed me for striking him! And that's why . . . I'm running away."

"I understand," said David, rising and smiling at her confidently, while in his veins his blood was running like little streams of fire. "Don't you believe, now, all that I've told you about the picture? How it tried so hard to talk to me, and tell me to hurry? It got me here just about in time, didn't it? It'll be a great joke on Brokaw, little girl. And your uncle Hauck. A great joke, eh?" He laughed. He felt like laughing, even as his blood pounded through him at fever heat. "You're a little brick, Marge — you and your bear!"

It was the first time he had thought of the bear since Marge had detached herself from the big beast to come to him, and as he looked in its direction he gave a startled exclamation.

Baree and the grizzly had been measuring each other for some time. To Baree this was the most amazing experience in all his life, and flattened out between the two rocks he was at a loss to comprehend why his master did not either run or shoot. He wanted to jump out, if his master showed fight, and leap straight at that ugly monster, or he wanted to run away as fast as his legs would carry him. He was shivering in indecision, waiting a signal from David to do either one or the other. And Tara was now moving slowly toward the dog! His huge head was hung low, swinging slightly from side to side in a most terrifying way; his great jaws were agape, and the nearer he came to Baree the smaller the dog seemed to grow between the rocks. At David's sudden cry the girl had turned, and he was amazed to hear her laughter, clear and sweet as a bell. It was funny, that picture of the dog and the bear, if one was in the mood to see the humour of it!

"Tara won't hurt him," she hurried to say, seeing David's uneasiness. "He loves dogs. He wants to play with . . . what is his name?"

"Baree. And mine is David."

"Baree — David. See!"

Like a bird she had left his side and in an instant, it seemed, was astride the big grizzly, digging her fingers into Tara's thick coat — smiling back at him, her radiant hair about her like a cloud, filled with marvellous red-and-gold fires in the sun.

"Come," she said, holding out a hand to David. "I want Tara to know you are our friend. Because" — the darkness came into her eyes again — "I have been *training him*, and I want him to know he must not hurt *you*."

David went to them, little fancying the acquaintance he was about to make, until Marge slipped off her bear and put her two arms unhesitatingly about his shoulders, and drew him down with her close in front of Tara's big head and round, emotionless eyes. For a thrilling moment or two she pressed her face close to his, looking all the time straight at Tara, and talking to him steadily. David did not sense what she was saying, except that in a general way she was telling Tara that he must never hurt this man, no matter what happened. He felt the warm crush of her hair on his neck and face. It billowed on his breast for a moment. The girl's hand touched his cheek, warm and caressing. He made no movement of his own, except to rise rigidly when she unclasped her arms from about his shoulders.

"There; he won't hurt you now!" she exclaimed in triumph.

Her cheeks were flaming, but not with embarrassment. Her eyes were as clear as the violets he had crushed under his feet in the mountain valleys. He looked at her as she stood before him, so much like a child, and yet enough of a woman to make his own cheeks burn. And then he saw a sudden changing expression come into her face. There was something pathetic about it, something that made him see again what he had forgotten — her exhaustion, the evidences of her struggle. She was looking at his pack.

"We haven't had anything to eat since we ran away," she said simply. "I'm hungry."

He had heard children say "I'm hungry" in that same voice, with the same hopeful and entreating insistence in it; he had spoken those words himself a thousand times, to his mother, in just that same way, it seemed to him; and as she stood there, looking at his pack, he was filled with a very strong desire to crumple her close in his arms — not as a woman, but as a child. And this desire held him so still for a moment that she thought he was waiting for her to explain.

"I fastened our bundle on Tara's back and we lost it in the night coming up over the mountain," she said. "It was so steep that in places I had to catch hold of Tara and let him drag me up."

In another moment he was at his pack, opening it, and tossing things to right and left on the white sand, and the girl watched him, her eyes very bright with anticipation.

"Coffee, bacon, bannock, and potatoes," he said, making a quick inventory of his small stock of provisions.

"Potatoes!" cried the girl.

"Yes — dehydrated. See? It looks like rice. One pound of this equals fourteen pounds of potatoes. And you can't tell the difference when it's cooked right. Now for a fire!"

She was darting this way and that, collecting small dry sticks in the sand before he was on his feet. He could not resist standing for a moment and watching her. Her movements, even in her quick and eager quest of fuel, were the most graceful he had ever seen in a human being. And yet she was tired! She was hungry! And he believed that her feet, concealed in those rock-torn moccasins, were bruised and sore. He went down to the stream for water, and in the few moments that he was gone his mind worked swiftly. He believed that he understood, perhaps even more than the girl herself. There was something about her that was so sweetly childish — in spite of her age and her height and her amazing prettiness that was not all a child's prettiness — that he could not feel that she had realized fully the peril from which she was fleeing when he found her. He had guessed that her dread was only partly for herself and that the other part was for Tara, her bear. She had asked him in a sort of plaintive anxiety and with rather more of wonderment and perplexity in her eyes than fear, whether she belonged to Brokaw, and what it all meant, and whether a man could buy a girl. It was not a mystery to him that the "red brute" she had told him about should want her. His puzzlement was that such a thing could happen, if he had guessed right, among men. Buy her? Of course down there in the big cities such a thing had happened hundreds and thousands of times — were happening every day — but he could not easily picture it happening up here, where men lived because of their strength. There must surely be other men at the Nest than the two hated and feared by the girl — Hauck, her uncle, and Brokaw, the "red brute."

She had built a little pile of sticks and dry moss ready for the touch of a match when he returned. Tara had stretched himself out lazily in the sun and Baree was still between the two rocks, eyeing him watchfully. Before David lighted the fire he spread his one blanket out on the sand and made the Girl sit down. She was close to him, and her eyes did not leave his face for an instant. Whenever he looked up she was gazing straight at him, and when he went down to the creek for another pail of water he felt that her eyes were still on him. When he turned to come back, with fifty paces between them, she smiled at him and he waved his hand at her. He asked her a great many questions while he prepared their dinner. The Nest, he learned, was a free-trading place, and Hauck was its proprietor. He was surprised when he learned that he was not on Firepan Creek after all. The Firepan was over the range, and there were a good many Indians to the north and west of it. Miners came down frequently from the Taku River country and the edge of the Yukon, she said. At least she thought they were miners, for that is what Hauck used to tell Nisikoos, her aunt. They came after whisky. Always whisky. And the Indians came for liquor, too. It was the chief article that Hauck, her uncle, traded in. He brought it from the coast, in the winter time — many sledge loads of it; and some of those "miners" who came down from the north carried away much of it. If it was summer they would take it away on pack horses. What would they do with so much liquor, she wondered? A little of it made such a beast of Hauck, and a beast of Brokaw, and it drove the Indians wild. Hauck would no longer allow the Indians to drink it at the Nest. They had to take it away with them — into the mountains. Just now there was quite a number of the "miners" down from the north, ten or twelve of them. She had not been afraid when Nisikoos, her aunt, was alive. But now there was no other woman at the Nest, except an old Indian woman who did Hauck's cooking. Hauck wanted no one there. And she was afraid of those men. They all feared Hauck, and she knew that Hauck was afraid of Brokaw. She didn't know why, but he was. And she was afraid of them all, and hated them all. She had been quite happy when Nisikoos was alive. Nisikoos had taught her to read out of books, had taught her things ever since she could remember. She could write almost as well as Nisikoos. She said this a bit proudly. But since her aunt had gone, things were terribly changed. Especially the men. They had made her more afraid, every day.

"None of them is like you," she said with startling frankness, her eyes shining at him. "I would love to be with you!"

He turned, then, to look at Tara dozing in the sun.

CHAPTER XIX

They ate, facing each other, on a clean, flat stone that was like a table. There was no hesitation on the girl's part, no false pride in the concealment of her hunger. To David it was a joy to watch her eat, and to catch the changing expressions in her eyes, and the little half smiles that took the place of words as he helped her diligently to bacon and bannock and potatoes and coffee. The bright glow went only once out of her eyes, and that was when she looked at Tara and Baree.

"Tara has been eating roots all day," she said, "But what will he eat?" and she nodded at the dog.

"He had a whistler for breakfast," David assured her. "Fat as butter. He wouldn't eat now anyway. He is too much interested in the bear." She had finished, with a little sigh of content, when he asked: "What do you mean when you say that you have trained Tara to kill? Why have you trained him?"

"I began the day after Brokaw did that — held me there in his arms, with my head bent back. *Ugh!* he was terrible, with his face so close to mine!" She shuddered. "Afterward I washed my face, and scrubbed it hard, but I could still *feel* it. I can feel it now!" Her eyes were darkening again, as the sun darkens when a thunder cloud passes under it. "I wanted to make Tara understand what he must do after that, so I stole some of Brokaw's clothes and carried them up to a little plain on the side of the mountain. I stuffed them with grass, and made a . . . what do you call it? In Indian it is *issena-koosewin.* . . ."

"A dummy," he said.

She nodded.

"Yes, that is it. Then I would go with it a little distance from Tara, and would begin to struggle with it, and scream. The third time, when Tara saw me lying under it, kicking and screaming, he gave it a blow with his paw that ripped it clean in two! And after that. . . ."

Her eyes were glorious in their wild triumph.

"He would tear it into bits," she cried breathlessly. "It would take me a whole day to mend it again, and at last I had to steal more clothes. I took Hauck's this time. And soon they were gone, too. That is just what Tara will do to a man — when I fight and scream!"

"And a little while ago you were ready to jump at me, and fight and scream!" he reminded her, smiling across their rock table.

"Not after you spoke to me," she said, so quickly that the

words seemed to spring straight from her heart. "I wasn't afraid then. I was — glad. No, I wouldn't scream — not even if you held me like Brokaw did!"

He felt the warm blood rising under his skin again. It was impossible to keep it down. And he was ashamed of it — ashamed of the thought that for an instant was in his mind. The soul of the wild, little mountain creature was in her eyes. Her lips made no concealment of its thoughts or its emotions, pure as the blue skies above them and as ungoverned by conventionality as the winds that shifted up and down the valleys. She was a new sort of being to him, a child-woman, a little wonder-nymph that had grown up with the flowers. And yet not so little after all. He had noticed that the top of her shining head came considerably above his chin.

"Then you will not be afraid to go back to the Nest — with me?" he asked.

"No," she said with a direct and amazing confidence. "But I'd rather run away with you." Then she added quickly, before he could speak: "Didn't you say you came all that way — hundreds of miles — to find *me*? Then why must we go back?"

He explained to her as clearly as he could, and as reason seemed to point out to him. It was impossible, he assured her, that Brokaw or Hauck or any other man could harm her now that he was here to take care of her and straighten matters out. He was as frank with her as she had been with him. Her eyes widened when he told her that he did not believe Hauck was her uncle, and that he was certain the woman whom he had met that night on the Transcontinental, and who was searching for an O'Doone, had some deep interest in her. He must discover, if possible, how the picture had got to her, and who she was, and he could do this only by going to the Nest and learning the truth straight from Hauck. Then they would go on to the coast, which would be an easy journey. He told her that Hauck and Brokaw would not dare to cause them trouble, as they were carrying on a business of which the provincial police would make short work, if they knew of it. They held the whip hand, he and Marge. Her eyes shone with increasing faith as he talked.

She had leaned a little over the narrow rock between them so that her thick curls fell in shining clusters under his eyes, and suddenly she reached out her arms through them and her two hands touched his face.

"And you will take me away? You promise?"

"My dear child, that is just what I came for," he said, feigning to be surprised at her questions. "Fifteen hundred miles for just that. *Now* don't you believe all that I've told you about the picture?"

"Yes," she nodded.

She had drawn back, and was looking at him so steadily and with such wondering depths in her eyes that he found himself compelled for an instant to turn his own gaze carelessly away.

"And you used to talk to it," she said, "and it seemed *alive*?"

"Very much alive, Marge."

"And you *dreamed* about me?"

He *had* said that, and he felt again that warm rise of blood. He felt himself in a difficult place. If she had been older, or even younger. . . .

"Yes," he said truthfully.

He feared one other question was quite uncomfortably near. But it didn't come. The girl rose suddenly to her feet, flung back her hair, and ran to Tara, dozing in the sun. What she was saying to the beast, with her arms about his shaggy neck, David could only guess. He found himself laughing again, quietly of course, with his back to her, as he picked up their dinner things. He had not anticipated such an experience as this. It rather unsettled him. It was amusing — and had a decided thrill to it. Undoubtedly Hauck and Brokaw were rough men; from what she had told him he was convinced they were lawless men, engaged in a very wide "underground" trade in whisky. But he believed that he would not find them as bad as he had pictured them at first, even though the Nest was a horrible place for the girl. Her running away was the most natural thing in the world — for her. She was an amazingly spontaneous little creature, full of courage and a fierce determination to fight some one, but probably today or tomorrow she would have been forced to turn homeward, quite exhausted with her adventure, and nibbling roots along with Tara to keep herself alive. The thought of her hunger and of the dire necessity in which he had found her, drove the smile from his lips. He was finishing his pack when she left the bear and came to him.

"If we are to get over the mountain before dark we must hurry," she said. "See — it is a big mountain!"

She pointed to a barren break in the northward range, close up to the snow-covered peaks.

"And it's cold up there when night comes," she added.

"Can you make it?" David asked. "Aren't you tired? Your feet sore? We can wait here until morning. . . ."

"I can climb it," she cried, with an excitement which he had not seen in her before. "I can climb it — and travel all night — to tell Brokaw and Hauck I don't belong to them any more, and that we're going away! Brokaw will be like a mad beast, and before we go I'll scratch his eyes out!"

"Good Lord!" gasped David under his breath.

"And if Hauck swears at me I'll scratch *his* out!" she declared, trembling in the glorious anticipation of her vengeance. "I'll . . . I'll scratch *his* out, anyway, for what he did to Nisikoos!"

David stared at her. She was looking away from him, her eyes on the break between the mountains, and he noticed how tense her slender body had become and how tightly her hands were clenched.

"They won't dare to touch me or swear at me when you are there," she added, with sublime faith.

She turned in time to catch the look in his face. Swiftly the excitement faded out of her own. She touched his arm, hesitatingly.

"Wouldn't . . . you want me . . . to scratch out their eyes?" she asked.

He shook his head.

"It wouldn't do," he said. "We must be very careful. We mustn't let them know you ran away. We must tell them you climbed up the mountain, and got lost."

"I never get lost," she protested.

"But we must tell them that just the same," he insisted. "Will you?"

She nodded emphatically.

"And now, before we start, tell me why they haven't followed you?"

"Because I came over the mountain," she replied, pointing again toward the break. "It's all rock, and Tara left no marks. They wouldn't think we'd climb over the range. They've been looking for us in the other valley if they have hunted for us at all. We were going to climb over *that* range, too." She turned so that she was pointing to the south.

"And then?"

"There are people over there. I've heard Hauck talk about them."

"Did you ever hear him speak of a man by the name of Tavish?" he asked, watching her closely.

"Tavish?" She pursed her lips into a red "O," and little lines gathered thoughtfully between her eyes. "Tavish? No-o-o, I never have."

"He lived at one time on Firepan Creek. Had small-pox," said

David.

"That is terrible," the girl shuddered. "The Indians die of it up here. Hauck says that my father and mother died of small-pox, before I could remember. It is all like a dream. I can see a woman's face sometimes, and I can remember a cabin, and snow, and lots of dogs. Are you ready to go?"

He shouldered his pack, and as he arranged the straps Marge ran to Tara. At her command the big beast rose slowly and stood before her, swinging his head from side to side, his jaws agape. David called to Baree and the dog came to him like a streak and stood against his leg, snarling fiercely.

"Tut, tut," admonished David, softly, laying a hand on Baree's head. "We're all friends, boy. Look here!"

He walked straight over to the grizzly and tried to induce Baree to follow him. Baree came half way and then sat himself on his haunches and refused to budge another inch, an expression so doleful in his face that it drew from the girl's lips a peal of laughter in which David found it impossible not to join. It was delightfully infectious; he was laughing more with her than at Baree. In the same breath his merriment was cut short by an unexpected and most amazing discovery. Tara, after all, had his usefulness. His mistress had vaulted astride of him, and was nudging him with her heels, leaning forward so that with one hand she was pulling at his left ear. The bear turned slowly, his finger-long claws clicking on the stones, and when his head was in the right direction Marge released his ear and spoke sharply, beating a tattoo with her heels at the same time.

"*Neah*, Tara, *Neah*!" she cried.

After a moment's hesitation, in which the grizzly seemed to be getting his bearings, Tara struck out straight for the break between the mountains, with his burden. The girl turned and waved a beckoning hand at David.

"*Pao*! you must hurry!" she called to him, laughing at the astonishment in his face.

He had started to fill his pipe, but for the next few minutes he forgot that the pipe was in his hand. His eyes did not leave the huge beast, ambling along a dozen paces ahead of him, or the slip of a girl who rode him. He had caught a glimpse of Baree, and the dog's eyes seemed to be bulging. He half believed that his own mouth was open when the girl called to him. What had happened was most startlingly unexpected, and what he stared at now was a wondrous sight! Tara travelled with the rolling, slouching gait typical of the wide-quartered grizzly, and the girl was a sinuous part of him — by all odds the most wonderful thing in the world to David at this moment. Her hair streamed down her back in a cascade of sunlit glory. She flung back her head, and he thought of a wonderful golden-bronze flower. He heard her laugh, and cry out to Tara, and when the grizzly climbed up a bit of steep slide she leaned forward and became a part of the bear's back, her curls shimmering in the thick ruff of Tara's neck. As he toiled upward in their wake, he caught a glimpse of her looking back at him from the top of the slide, her eyes shining and her lips smiling at him. She reminded him of something he had read about Leucosia, his favorite of the "Three Sirens," only in this instance it was a siren of the mountains and not of the sea that was leading him on to an early doom — if he had to keep up with that bear! His breath came more quickly. In ten minutes he was gasping for wind, and in despair he slackened his pace as the bear and his rider disappeared over the crest of the first slope. She was waving at him then, fully two hundred yards up that infernal hill, and he was sure that she was laughing. He had almost reached the top when he saw her sitting in the shade of a rock, watching him as he toiled upward. There was a mischievous seriousness in the blue of her eyes when he reached her side.

"I'm sorry, *Sakewawin*," she said, lowering her eyes until they were hidden under the silken sheen of her long lashes, "I couldn't make Tara go slowly. He is hungry, and he knows that he is going home."

"And I thought you had sore feet," he managed to say.

"I don't ride him going *down* a mountain," she explained, thrusting out her ragged little feet. "I can't hang on, and I slip over his head. You must walk ahead of Tara. That will hold him back."

He tried this experiment when they continued their ascent, and Tara followed so uncomfortably close that at times David could feel his warm breath against his hand. When they reached the second slope the girl walked beside him. For a half mile it was not a bad climb and there was soft grass underfoot. After that came the rock and shale, and the air grew steadily colder. They had started at one o'clock and it was five when they reached the first snow. It was six when they stood at the summit. Under them lay the valley of the Firepan, a broad, sun-filled sweep of scattered timber and green plain, and the girl pointed into it, north and west.

"Off there is the Nest," she said. "We could almost see it if it weren't for that big, red mountain."

She was very tired, though she had ridden Tara at least two

thirds of the distance up the mountains. In her eyes was the mistiness of exhaustion, and as a chill wind swept about them she leaned against David, and he could feel that her endurance was nearly gone. As they had come up to the snow line he had made her put on the light woollen shirt he carried in his pack; and the big handkerchief, in which he had so long wrapped the picture, he had fastened scarf-like about her head, so she was not cold. But she looked pathetically childlike and out of place, standing here beside him at the very top of the world, with the valley so far down that the clumps of timber in it were like painted splashes. It was a half mile down to the first bit of timber — a small round patch of it in a narrow dip — and he pointed to it encouragingly.

"We'll camp there and have supper. I believe it is far enough down for a fire. And if it is impossible for you to ride Tara — I'm going to carry you!"

"You can't, *Sakewawin*" she sighed, letting her head touch his arm for a moment. "It is more difficult to carry a load down a mountain than up. I can walk."

Before he could stop her she had begun to descend. They went down quickly — three times as quickly as they had climbed the other side — and when, half an hour later, they reached the timber in the dip, he felt as if his back were broken. The girl had persistently kept ahead of him, and with a little cry of triumph she dropped down at the foot of the first balsam they came to. The pupils of her eyes were big and dark as she looked up at him, quivering with the strain of the last great effort, and yet she tried to smile at him.

"You may carry me — some time — but not down a mountain," she said, and laid her head wearily on the pillow of her arm, so that her face was concealed from him. "And now — please get supper, *Sakewawin*."

He spread his blanket over her before he began searching for a camp site. He noticed that Tara was already hunting for roots. Baree followed close at his master's heels. Quite near, David found a streamlet that trickled down from the snow line, and to a grassy plot on the edge of this he dragged a quantity of dry wood and built a fire. Then he made a thick couch of balsam boughs and went to his little companion. In the half hour he had been at work she had fallen asleep. Utter exhaustion was in the limpness of her slender body as he raised her gently in his arms. The handkerchief had slipped back over her shoulder and she was wonderfully sweet, and helpless, as she lay with her head on his breast. She was still asleep when he placed her on the balsams, and it was dark when he awakened her for supper. The fire was burning brightly. Tara had stretched himself out in a huge, dark bulk in the outer glow of it. Baree was close to the fire. The girl sat up, rubbed her eyes, and stared at David.

"*Sakewawin*," she whispered then, looking about her in a moment's bewilderment.

"Supper," he said, smiling. "I did it all while you were napping, little lady. Are you hungry?"

He had spread their meal so that she did not have to move from her balsams, and he had brought a short piece of timber to place as a rest at her back, cushioned by his shoulder pack and the blanket. After all his trouble she did not eat much. The mistiness was still in her eyes, so after he had finished he took away the timber and made of the balsams a deep pillow for her, that she might lie restfully, with her head well up, while he smoked. He did not want her to go to sleep. He wanted to talk. And he began by asking how she had so carelessly run away with only a pair of moccasins on her feet and no clothes but the thin garments she was wearing.

"They were in Tara's pack, *Sakewawin*," she explained, her eyes glowing like sleepy pools in the fireglow. "They were lost."

He began then to tell her about Father Roland. She listened, growing sleepier, her lashes drooping slowly until they formed dark curves on her cheeks. He was close enough to marvel at their length, and as he watched them, quivering in her efforts to keep awake and listen to him, they seemed to him like the dark petals of two beautiful flowers closing slumbrously for the night. It was a wonderful thing to see them open suddenly and find the full glory of the sleep-filled eyes on him for an instant, and then to watch them slowly close again as she fought valiantly to conquer her irresistible drowsiness, the merest dimpling of a smile on her lips. The last time she opened them he had her picture in his hands, and was looking at it, quite close to her, with the fire lighting it up. For a moment he thought the sight if it had awakened her completely.

"Throw it into the fire," she said. "Brokaw made me let him take it, and I hate it. I hate Brokaw. I hate the picture. Burn it."

"But I must keep it," he protested. "Burn it! Why it's. . . ."

"You won't want it — after tonight."

Her eyes were closing again, heavily, for the last time.

"Why?" he asked, bending over her.

"Because, *Sakewawin* . . . you have me . . . now," came her voice, in drowsy softness; and then the long lashes lay quietly against her cheeks.

CHAPTER XX

He thought of her words a long time after she had fallen asleep. Even in that last moment of her consciousness he had found her voice filled with a strange faith and a wonderful assurance as it had drifted away in a whisper. He would not want the picture any more — because he had *her*! That was what she had said, and he knew it was her soul that had spoken to him as she had hovered that instant between consciousness and slumber. He looked at her, sleeping under his eyes, and he felt upon him for the first time the weight of a sudden trouble, a gloomy foreboding — and yet, under it all, like a fire banked beneath dead ash, was the warm thrill of his possession. He had spread his blanket over her, and now he leaned over and drew back her thick curls. They were warm and soft in his fingers, strangely sweet to touch, and for a moment or two he fondled them while he gazed steadily into the childish loveliness of her face, dimpled still by that shadow of a smile with which she had fallen asleep. He was beginning to feel that he had accepted for himself a tremendous task, and that she, not much more than a child, had of course scarcely foreseen its possibilities. Her faith in him was a pleasurable thing. It was absolute. He realized it more as the hours dragged on and he sat alone by the fire. So great was it that she was going back fearlessly to those whom she hated and feared. She was returning not only fearlessly but with a certain defiant satisfaction. He could fancy her saying to Hauck, and the Red Brute: "I've come back. Now touch me if you dare!" What would he have to do to live up to that surety of her confidence in him? A great deal, undoubtedly. And if he won for her, as she fully expected him to win, what would he do with her? Take her to the coast — put her into a school somewhere down south? That was his first notion. For to him she looked more than ever like a child as she lay asleep on her bed of balsams.

He tried to picture Brokaw. He tried to see Hauck in his mental vision, and he thought over again all that the girl had told him about herself and these men. As he looked at her now — a little, softly breathing thing under his gray blanket — it was hard for him to believe anything so horrible as she had suggested. Perhaps her fears had been grossly exaggerated. The exchange of gold between Hauck and the Red Brute had probably been for something else. Even men engulfed in the brutality of the trade they were in would not think of such an appalling crime. And then — with a fierceness that made his blood boil — came the thought of that time when Brokaw had caught her in his arms, and had held her head back until it *hurt* — and had kissed her! Baree had crept between his knees, and David's fingers closed so tightly in the loose skin of his neck that the dog whined. He rose to his feet and stood gazing down at the girl. He stood there for a long time without moving or making a sound.

"A little woman," he whispered to himself at last. "Not a child."

From that moment his blood was hot with a desire to reach the Nest. He had never thought seriously of physical struggle with men except in the way of sport. His disposition had always been to regard such a thing as barbarous, and he had never taken advantage of his skill with the gloves as the average man might very probably have done. To fight was to lower one's self-respect enormously, he thought. It was not a matter of timidity, but of very strong conviction — an entrenchment that had saved him from wreaking vengeance — in the hour when another man would have killed. But there, in that room in his home, he had stood face to face with a black, revolting sin. There had been nothing left to shield, nothing to protect. Here it was different. A soul had given itself into his protection, a soul as pure as the stars shining over the mountain tops, and its little keeper lay there under his eyes sleeping in the sweet faith that it was safe with him. A little later his fingers tingled with an odd thrill as he took his automatic out of his pack, loaded it carefully, and placed it in his pocket where it could be easily reached. The act was a declaration of something ultimately definite. He stretched himself out near the fire and went to sleep with the force of this declaration brewing strangely within him.

He was awake with the summer dawn and the sun was beginning to tint up the big red mountain when they began the descent into the valley. Before they started he loaned the girl his comb and single military brush, and for fifteen minutes sat watching her while she brushed the tangles out of her hair until it fell about her in a thick, waving splendour. At the nape of her neck she tied it with a bit of string which he found for her, and after that, as they travelled downward, he observed how the rebellious tresses, shimmering and dancing about her, persisted in forming themselves into curls again. In an hour they reached the valley, and for a few moments they sat down to rest, while Tara foraged among the rocks for marmots. It was a wonderful valley into which they had come. From where they sat, it was like an immense park. Green slopes reached almost to the summits of the mountains, and to a point half way up these slopes — the last timber line —

clumps of spruce and balsam trees were scattered over the green as if set there by hands of men. Some of these timber patches were no larger than the decorative clumps in a city park, and others covered acres and tens of acres; and at the foot of the slopes on either side, like decorative fringes, were thin and unbroken lines of forest. Between these two lines of forest lay the open valley of soft and undulating meadow, dotted with its purplish bosks of buffalo-, willow-, and mountain-sage, its green coppices of wild rose and thorn, and its clumps of trees. In the hollow of the valley ran a stream.

And this was her home! She was telling him about it as they sat there, and he listened to her, and watched her bird-like movements, without breaking in to ask questions which the night had shaped in his mind. She pointed out gray summits on which she had stood. Off there, just visible in the gray mist of early sunshine, was the mountain where she had found Tara five years ago — a tiny cub who must have lost his mother. Perhaps the Indians had killed her. And that long, rock-strewn slide, so steep in places that he shuddered when he thought of what she had done, was where she and Tara had climbed over the range in their flight. She chose the rocks so that Tara would leave no trail. He regarded that slide as conclusive evidence of the very definite resolution that must have inspired her. A fit of girlish temper would not have taken her up that rock slide, and in the night. He thought it time to speak of what was weighing upon his mind.

"Listen to me, Marge," he said, pointing toward the red mountain ahead of them. "Off there, you say, is the Nest. What are we going to do when we arrive there?"

The little lines gathered between her eyes again as she looked at him.

"Why — tell them," she said.

"Tell them what?"

"That you've come for me, and that we're going away, *Sakewawin*."

"And if they object? If Brokaw and Hauck say you cannot go?"

"We'll go anyway, *Sakewawin*."

"That's a pretty name you've given me," he mused, thinking of something else. "I like it."

For the first time she blushed — blushed until her face was like one of the wild roses in those prickly copses of the valley.

And then he added:

"You must not tell them too much — at first, Marge. Remember that you were lost, and I found you. You must give me time to get acquainted with Hauck and Brokaw."

She nodded, but there was a moment's anxiety in her eyes, and he saw for an instant the slightest quiver in her throat.

"You won't — let them — keep me? No matter what they say — you won't let them keep me?"

He jumped up with a laugh and tilted her chin so that he looted straight into her eyes; and her faith filled them again in a flood.

"No — you're going with me," he promised. "Come. I'm quite anxious to meet Hauck and the Red Brute!"

It seemed singular to David that they met no one in the valley that day, and the girl's explanation that practically all travel came from the north and west, and stopped at the Nest, did not fully satisfy him. He still wondered why they did not encounter one of the searching parties that must have been sent out for her — until she told him that, since Nisikoos died, she and Tara had gone quite frequently into the mountains and remained all night, so that perhaps no search had been made for her after all. Hauck had not seemed to care. More frequently than otherwise he had not missed her. Twice she had been away for two nights and two days. It was only because Brokaw had given that gold to Hauck that she had feared pursuit. If Hauck had bought her. . . .

She spoke of that possible sale as if she might have been the merest sort of chattel. And then she startled him by saying:

"I have known of those white men from the north buying Indian girls. I have seen them sold for whisky. *Ugh!*" She shuddered. "Nisikoos and I overheard them one night. Hauck was selling a girl for a little sack of gold — like *that*. Nisikoos held me more tightly than ever, that night. I don't know why. She was terribly afraid of that man — Hauck. Why did she live with him if she was afraid of him? Do you know? *I* wouldn't. I'd run away."

He shook his head.

"I'm afraid I can't tell you, my child."

Her eyes turned on him suddenly.

"Why do you call me that — a child?"

"Because you're not a woman; because you're so very, very young, and I'm so very old," he laughed.

For a long time after that she was silent as they travelled steadily toward the red mountain.

They ate their dinner in the sombre shadow of it. Most of the afternoon Marge rode her bear. It was sundown when they stopped for their last meal. The Nest was still three miles farther on, and the stars were shining brilliantly before they came to the little, wooded plain in the edge of which Hauck had hidden away his place of trade. When they were some hundred yards away they came over a knoll and David saw the glow of fires. The girl stopped suddenly and her hand caught his arm. He counted four of those fires in the open. A fifth glowed faintly, as if back in timber. Sounds came to them — the slow, hollow booming of a tom-tom, and voices. They could see shadows moving. The girl's fingers were pinching David's arm.

"The Indians have come in," she whispered.

There was a thrill of uneasiness in her words. It was not fear. He could see that she was puzzled, and that she had not expected to find fires or those moving shadows. Her eyes were steady and shining as she looked at him. It seemed to him that she had grown taller, and more like a woman, as they stood there. Something in her face made him ask:

"Why have they come?"

"I don't know," she said.

She started down the knoll straight for the fires. Tara and Baree filed behind them. Beyond the glow of the camp a dark bulk took shape against the blackness of the forest. David guessed that it was the Nest. He made out a deep, low building, unlighted so far as he could see. Then they entered into the fireglow. Their appearance produced a strange and instant quiet. The beating of the tom-tom ceased. Voices died. Dark faces stared — and that was all. There were about fifty of them about the fires, David figured. And not a white man's face among them. They were all Indians. A lean, night-eyed, sinister-looking lot. He was conscious that they were scrutinizing him more than they were the girl. He could almost feel the prick of their eyes. With her head up, his companion walked between the fires and beyond them, looking neither to one side nor the other. They turned the end of the huge log building and on this side it was glowing dimly with light, and David faintly heard voices. The girl passed swiftly into a hollow of gloom, calling softly to Tara. The bear followed her, a grotesque, slowly moving hulk, and David waited. He heard the clink of a chain. A moment later she returned to him.

"There is a light in Hauck's room," she said. "His council room, he calls it — where he makes bargains. I hope they are both there, *Sakewawin* — both Hauck and Brokaw." She seized his hand, and held it tightly as she led him deeper into darkness. "I wonder why so many of the Indians are in? I did not know they were coming. It is the wrong time of year for — a crowd like that!"

He felt the quiver in her voice. She was quite excited, he knew.

And yet not about the Indians, nor the strangeness of their presence. It was her *triumph* that made her tremble in the darkness, a wonderful anticipation of the greatest event that had ever happened in her life. She hoped that Hauck and Brokaw were in that room! She would confront them there, with *him*. That was it. She felt her bondage — her prisonment — in this savage place was ended; and she was eager to find them, and let them know that she was no longer afraid, or alone — no longer need obey or fear them. He felt the thrill of it in the hot, fierce little clasp of her hand. He saw it glowing in her eyes when they passed through the light of a window. Then they turned again, at the back of the building. They paused at a door. Not a ray of light broke the gloom here. The stars seemed to make the blackness deeper. Her fingers tightened.

"You must be careful," he said. "And — remember."

"I will," she whispered.

It was his last warning. The door opened slowly, with a creaking sound, and they entered into a long, gloomy hall, illumined by a single oil lamp that sputtered and smoked in its bracket on one of the walls. The hall gave him an idea of the immensity of the building. From the far end of it, through a partly open door, came a reek of tobacco smoke, and loud voices — a burst of coarse laughter, a sudden volley of curses that died away in a still louder roar of merriment. Some one closed the door from within. The girl was staring toward the end of the hall, and shuddering.

"That is the way it has been — growing worse and worse since Nisikoos died," she said. "In there the white men who come down from the north, drink, and gamble, and quarrel. They are always quarrelling. This room is ours — Nisikoos' and mine." She touched with her hand a door near which they were standing. Then she pointed to another. There were half a dozen doors up and down the hall. "And that is Hauck's."

He threw off his pack, placed it on the floor, with his rifle across it. When he straightened, the girl was listening at the door of Hauck's room. Beckoning to him she knocked on it lightly, and then opened it. David entered close behind her. It was a rather large room — his one impression as he crossed the threshold. In the centre of it was a table, and over the table hung an oil lamp with a tin reflector. In the light of this lamp sat two men. In his first glance he made up his mind which was Hauck and which was Brokaw. It was Brokaw, he thought, who was facing them as they entered — a man he could hate even if he had never heard of him before. Big. Loose-shouldered. A carnivorous-looking giant with a mottled, reddish face and bleary eyes that had an amazed and watery stare in them. Apparently the girl's knock had not been heard, for it was a moment before the other man swung slowly about in his chair so that he could see them. That was Hauck. David knew it. He was almost a half smaller than the other, with round, bullish shoulders, a thick neck, and eyes wherein might lurk an incredible cruelty. He popped half out of his seat when he saw the girl, and a stranger. His jaws seemed to tighten with a snap. A snap that could almost be heard. But it was Brokaw's face that held David's eyes. He was two thirds drunk. There was no doubt about it, if he was any sort of judge of that kind of imbecility. One of his thick, huge hands was gripping a bottle. Hauck had evidently been reading him something out of a ledger, a Post ledger, which he held now in one hand. David was surprised at the quiet and unemotional way in which the girl began speaking. She said that she had wandered over into the other valley and was lost when this stranger found her. He had been good to her, and was on his way to the settlement on the coast. His name was. . . .

She got no further than that. Brokaw had taken his devouring gaze from her and was staring at David. He lurched suddenly to his feet and leaned over the table, a new sort of surprise in his heavy countenance. He stretched out a hand. His voice was a bellow.

"McKenna!"

He was speaking directly at David — calling him by name. There was as little doubt of that as of his drunkenness. There was also an unmistakable note of fellowship in his voice. McKenna! David opened his mouth to correct him when a second thought occurred to him in a mildly inspirational way. Why not McKenna? The girl was looking at him, a bit surprised, questioning him in the directness of her gaze. He nodded, and smiled at Brokaw. The giant came around the table, still holding out his big, red hand.

"Mac! God! You don't mean to say you've forgotten. . . ."

David took the hand.

"Brokaw!" he chanced.

The other's hand was as cold as a piece of beef. But it possessed a crushing strength. Hauck was staring from one to the other, and suddenly Brokaw turned to him, still pumping David's hand.

"McKenna — that young devil of Kicking Horse, Hauck! You've heard me speak of him. McKenna. . . ."

The girl had backed to the door. She was pale. Her eyes were shining, and she was looking straight at David when Brokaw released his hand.

"Good-night, *Sakewawin!*" she said.

It was very distinct, that word — *Sakewawin!* David had never heard it come quite so clearly from her lips. There was something of defiance and pride in her utterance of it — and intentional and decisive emphasis to it. She smiled at him as she went through the door, and in that same breath Hauck had followed her. They disappeared. When David turned he found Brokaw backed against the table, his hands gripping the edge of it, his face distorted by passion. It was a terrible face to look into — to stand before, alone in that room — a face filled with menace and murder. So sudden had been the change in it that David was stunned for a moment. In that space of perhaps a quarter of a minute neither uttered a sound. Then Brokaw leaned slowly forward, his great hands clenched, and demanded in a hissing voice:

"What did she mean when she called you that — *Sakewawin?* What did she mean?"

It was not now the voice of a drunken man, but the voice of a man ready to kill.

CHAPTER XXI

"*Sakewawin!* What did she mean when she called you that?"

It was Brokaw's voice again, turning the words round but repeating them. He made a step toward David, his hands clenched more tightly and his whole hulk growing tense. His eyes, blazing as if through a very thin film of water — water that seemed to cling there by some strange magic — were horrible, David thought. *Sakewawin!* A pretty name for himself, he had told the girl — and here it was raising the very devil with this drink-bloated colossus. He guessed quickly. It was decidedly a matter of guessing quickly and of making prompt and satisfactory explanation — or, a throttling where he stood. His mind worked like a race-horse. "Sakewawin" meant something that had enraged Brokaw. A jealous rage. A rage that had filled his aqueous eyes with a lurid glare. So David said, looking into them calmly, and with a little feigned surprise:

"Wasn't she speaking to you, Brokaw?"

It was a splendid shot. David scarcely knew why he made it, except that he was moved by a powerful impulse which just now he had not time to analyze. It was this same impulse that had kept him from revealing himself when Brokaw had mistaken him for someone else. Chance had thrown a course of action into his way and he had accepted it almost involuntarily. It had suddenly occurred to him that he would give much to be alone with this half drunken man for a few hours — as McKenna. He might last long enough in that disguise to discover things. But not with Hauck watching him, for Hauck was four fifths sober, and there was a depth to his cruel eyes which he did not like. He watched the effect of his words on Brokaw. The tenseness left his body, his hands unclenched slowly, his heavy jaw relaxed — and David laughed softly. He felt that he was out of deep water now. This fellow, half filled with drink, was wonderfully credulous. And he was sure that his watery eyes could not see very well, though his ears had heard distinctly.

"She was looking at you, Brokaw — straight at you — when she said good-night," he added.

"You sure — sure she said it to me, Mac?"

David nodded, even as his blood ran a little cold.

A leering grin of joy spread over Brokaw's face.

"The — the little devil!" he said, gloatingly.

"What does it mean?" David asked. "*Sakewawin* — I had never heard it." He lied calmly, turning his head a bit out of the light.

Brokaw stared at him a moment before answering.

"When a girl says that — it means — *she* belongs to you," he said. "In Indian it means — *possession*! Dam' . . . of course you're right! She said it to me. She's mine. She belongs to me. I own her. And I thought. . . ."

He caught up the bottle and turned out half a glass of liquor, swaying unsteadily:

"Drink, Mac?"

David shook his head.

"Not now. Let's go to your shack if you've got one. Lots to talk about — old times — Kicking Horse, you know. And this girl? I can't believe it! If it's true, you're a lucky dog."

He was not thinking of consequences — of tomorrow. Tonight was all he asked for — alone with Brokaw. That mountain of flesh, stupefied with liquor, was no match for him now. Tomorrow he might hold the whip hand, if Hauck did not return too soon.

"Lucky dog! Lucky dog!" He kept repeating that. It was like music in Brokaw's ears. And such a girl! An angel! He couldn't believe it! Brokaw's face was like a red fire in his exultation, his lustful joy, his great triumph. He drank the liquor he had proffered David, and drank a second time, rumbling in his thick chest like some kind of animal. Of course she was an angel! Hadn't he, and Hauck, and that woman who had died, made her grow into an angel — just for him? She belonged to him. Always had belonged to him, and he had waited a long time. If she had ever called any other man that name — Sakewawin — he would have killed him. Certain. Killed him dead. This was the first time she had ever called him that. Lucky dog? You bet he was. They'd go to his shack — and talk. He drank a third time. He rolled heavily as they entered the hall, David praying that they would not meet Hauck. He had his victim. He was sure of him. And the hall was empty. He picked up his gun and pack, and held to Brokaw's arm as they went out into the night. Brokaw staggered guidingly into a wall of darkness, talking thickly about lucky dogs. They had gone perhaps a hundred paces when he stopped suddenly, very close to something that looked to David like a section of tall fence built of small trees. It was the cage. He jumped at that conclusion before he could see it clearly in the clouded starlight. From it there came a growling rumble, a deep breath that was like air escaping from a pair of bellows, and he saw faintly a huge, motionless shape beyond the stripped and upright sapling trunks.

"Grizzly," said Brokaw, trying to keep himself on an even balance. "Big bear-fight tomorrow, Mac. My bear — her bear — a great fight! Everybody in to see it. Nothing like a bear-fight, eh? S'prise her, won't it — pretty little wench! When she sees her bear fighting mine? Betchu hundred dollars my bear kills Tara!"

"Tomorrow," said David. "I'll bet tomorrow. Where's the shack?"

He was anxious to reach that, and he hoped it was a good distance away. He feared every moment that he would hear Hauck's voice or his footsteps behind them, and he knew that Hauck's presence would spoil everything. Brokaw, in his cups, was talkative — almost garrulous. Already he had explained the mystery of the cage, and the Indians. The big fight was to take place in the cage, and the Indians had come in to see it. He found himself wondering, as they went through the darkness, how it had all been kept from the girl, and why Brokaw should deliberately lower himself still more in her esteem by allowing the combat to occur. He asked him about it when they entered the shack to which Brokaw guided him, and after they had lighted a lamp. It was a small, gloomy, whisky-smelling place. Brokaw went directly to a box nailed against the wall and returned with a quart flask that resembled an army canteen, and two tin cups. He sat down at a small table, his bloated, red face in the light of the lamp, that queer animal-like rumbling in his throat, as he turned out the liquor. David had heard porcupines make something like the same sound. He pulled his hat lower over his eyes to hide the gleam of them as Brokaw told him what he and Hauck had planned. The bear in the cage belonged to him — Brokaw. A big brute. Fierce. A fighter. Hauck and he were going to bet on his bear because it would surely kill Tara. Make a big clean-up, they would. Tara was soft. Too easy living. And they needed money because those scoundrels over on the coast had failed to get in enough whisky for their trade. The girl had almost spoiled their plans by going away with Tara. And he — Mac — was a devil of a good fellow for bringing her back! They'd pull off the fight tomorrow. If the girl — that little bird-devil that belonged to him — didn't like it. . . .

He brought the canteen down with a bang, and shoved one of the cups across to David.

"Of course, she belongs to you," said David, encouragingly, "but — confound you — I can't believe it, you old dog! I can't believe it!" He leaned over and gave Brokaw a jocular slap, forcing a laugh out of himself. "She's too pretty for you. Prettiest kid I ever saw! How did it happen? Eh? You — *lucky* — dog!"

He was fairly trembling as he saw the red fire of satisfaction, of gloating pleasure, deepen in Brokaw's face.

"She hasn't belonged to you very long, eh?"

"Long time, long time," replied Brokaw, pausing with his cup half way to his mouth. "Years ago."

Suddenly he lowered the cup so forcefully that half the liquor in it was spilled over the table. He thrust his huge shoulders and red face toward David, and in an instant there was a snarl on his thick lips.

"Hauck said she didn't," he growled. "What do you think of that, Mac? — said she didn't belong to me any more, an' I'd have to pay for her keep! Gawd, I did. I gave him a lot of gold!"

"You were a fool," said David, trying to choke back his eagerness. "A fool!"

"I should have killed him, shouldn't I, Mac — killed him an' *took* her?" cried Brokaw huskily, his passion rising as he knotted his huge fists on the table. "Killed him like you killed the Breed for that long-haired she-devil over at Copper Cliff!"

"I — don't — know," said David, slowly, praying that he might not say the wrong thing now. "I don't know what claim you had on her, Brokaw. If I knew. . . ."

He waited. Brokaw did not seem altogether like a drunken man now, and for a moment he feared that discovery had come. He leaned over the table. The watery film seemed to drop from his eyes for an instant and his teeth gleamed wolfishly. David was glad the lamp chimney was black with soot, and that the rim of his hat shadowed his face, for it seemed to him that Brokaw's vision had grown suddenly better.

"I should have killed him, an' took her," repeated Brokaw, his voice heavy with passion. "I should have had her long ago, but Hauck's woman kept her from me. She's been mine all along, ever since. . . ." His mind seemed to lag. He drew his hulking shoulders back slowly. "But I'll have her tomorrow," he mumbled, as if he had suddenly forgotten David and was talking to himself. "Tomorrow. Next day we'll start north. Hauck can't say anything now. I've paid him. She's mine — mine now — tonight! By. . . ."

David shuddered at what he saw in the brute's revolting face. It was the dawning of a sudden, terrible idea. Tonight! It blazed there in his eyes, grown watery again. Quickly David turned out more liquor, and thrust one of the cups into Brokaw's hand. The giant drank. His body sank into piggish laxness. For a moment the danger was past. David knew that time was precious. He must force his hand.

"And if Hauck troubles you," he cried, striking the table a blow with his fist, "I'll help you settle for him, Brokaw! I'll do it for old time's sake. I'll do to him what I did to the Breed. The girl's yours. She's belonged to you for a long time, eh? Tell me about it, Brokaw — tell me before Hauck comes!"

Could he never make that bloated fiend tell him what he wanted to know? Brokaw stared at him stupidly, and then all at once he started, as if some one had pricked him into consciousness, and a slow grin began to spread over his face. It was a reminiscent, horrible sort of leer, not a smile — the expression of a man who gloats over a revolting and unspeakable thing.

"She's mine — been mine ever since she was a baby," he confided, leaning again over the table. "Good friend, give her to me, Mac — good friend but a dam' fool," he chuckled. He rubbed his huge hands together and turned out more liquor. "Dam' fool!" he repeated. "Any man's a dam' fool to turn down a pretty woman, eh, Mac? An' she was pretty, he says. *My* girl's mother, you know. She must have been pretty. It was off there — in the bush country — years ago. The kid you brought in today was a baby then — alone with her mother. Ho, ho! deuced easy — deuced easy! But he was a darn' fool!"

He drank with incredible slowness, it seemed to David. It was torture to watch him, with the fear, every instant, that Hauck would come.

"What happened?" he urged.

"Bucky — my friend — in love with that woman, O'Doone's wife," resumed Brokaw. "Dead crazy, Mac. Crazier'n you were over the Breed's woman, only he didn't have the nerve. Just moped around — waiting — keeping out of O'Doone's way. Trapper, O'Doone was — or a Company runner. Forgot which. Anyway he went on a long trip, in winter, and got laid up with a broken leg long way from home. Wife and baby alone, an' Bucky sneaked up one day and found the woman sick with fever. Out of her head! Dead out, Bucky says — an' my Gawd! If she didn't think he was her husband come back! That easy, Mac — an' he lacked the nerve! Crazy in love with her, he was, an' didn't dare play the part. Told me it was conscience. Bah! it wasn't. He was afraid. Scared. A fool. Then he said the fever must have touched him. Ho, ho! it was funny. He was a scared fool. Wish *I'd* been there, Mac; wish *I* had!"

His eyes half closed, gleaming in narrow, shining slits. His chin dropped on his chest. David prodded him on.

"Bucky got her to run away with him," continued Brokaw.

"Her and the kid, while she was still out of her head. Bucky even got her to write a note, he said, telling O'Doone she was sick of him an' was running away with another man. Bucky didn't give his own name, of course. An' the woman didn't know what she was doing. They started west with the kid, and all the time Bucky was *afraid*! He dragged the woman on a sledge, and snow covered their trail. He hid in a cabin a hundred miles from O'Doone's, an' it was there the woman come to her senses. Gawd! it must have been exciting! Bucky says she was like a mad woman, and that she ran screeching out into the night, leaving the kid with him. He followed but he couldn't find her. He waited, but she never came back. A snow storm covered her trail. Then Bucky says *he* went mad — the fool! He waited till spring, keeping that kid, and then he made up his mind to get it back to Papa O'Doone in some way. He sneaked back where the cabin had been, and found nothing but char there. It had been burned. Oh, the devil, but it was funny! And after all this trouble he hadn't dared to take O'Doone's place with the woman. Conscience? Bah! He was a fool. You don't get a pretty woman like that very often, eh, Mac?" Unsteadily he tilted the flask to turn himself out another drink. His voice was thickening. David rejoiced when he saw that the flask was empty.

"Dam'!" said Brokaw, shaking it.

"Go on," insisted David. "You haven't told me how you came by the girl, Brokaw?"

The watery film was growing thicker over Brokaw's eyes. He brought himself back to his story with an apparent effort.

"Came west, Bucky did — with the kid," he went on. "Struck my cabin, on the Mackenzie, a year later. Told me all about it. Then one day he sneaked away and left her with me, begging me to put her where she'd be safe. I did. Gave her to Hauck's woman, and told her Bucky's story. Later, Hauck came over here and built this place. Three years ago I come down from the Yukon, and saw the kid. Pretty? Gawd, she was! Almost a woman. And she was *mine*. I told 'em so. Mebby the woman would have cheated me, but I had Hauck on the hip because I saw him kill a man when he was drunk — a white man from Fort MacPherson. Helped him hide the body. And then — oh, it was funny! — I ran across Bucky! He was living in a shack a dozen miles from here, an' he didn't know Marge was the O'Doone baby. I told him a big lie — told him the kid died, an' that I'd heard the woman had killed herself, and that O'Doone was in a lunatic asylum. Mebby he did have a conscience, the fool! Guess he was a little crazy himself. Went away soon after that. Never heard of him since. An' I've been hanging round until the girl was old enough to live with a man. Ain't I done right, Mac? Don't she belong to me? An' tomorrow. . . ."

His head rolled. He recovered himself with an effort, and leaned heavily against the table. His face was almost barren of human expression. It was the face of a monster, unlighted by reason, stripped of mind and soul. And David, glaring into it across the table, questioned him once more, even as he heard the crunch of footsteps outside, and knew that Hauck was coming — coming in all probability to unmask him in the part he had played. But Hauck was too late. He was ready to fight now, and as he held himself prepared for the struggle he asked that question.

"And this man — Bucky; what was his other name, Brokaw?"

Brokaw's thick lips moved, and then came his voice, in a husky whisper:

"Tavish!"

CHAPTER XXII

The next instant Hauck was at the open door. He did not cross the threshold at once, but stood there for perhaps twenty seconds — his gray, hard face looking in on them with eyes in which there was a cold and sinister glitter. Brokaw, with the fumes of liquor thick in his brain, tried to nod an invitation for him to enter; his head rolled grotesquely and his voice was a croak. David rose slowly to his feet, thrusting back his chair. From contemplating Brokaw's sagging body, Hauck's eyes were levelled at him. And then his lips parted. One would not have called it a smile. It revealed to David a deadly animosity which the man was trying to hide under the disguise of that grin, and he knew that Hauck had discovered that he was not McKenna. Swiftly David shot a glance at Brokaw. The giant's head and shoulders lay on the table, and he made a sudden daring effort to save a little more time for himself.

"I'm sorry," he said. "He's terribly drunk."

Hauck nodded his head — he kept nodding it, that cold glitter in his eyes, the steady, insinuating grin still there.

"Yes, he's drunk," he said, his voice as hard as a rock. "Better come to the house. I've got a room for you. There's only one bunk in here — McKenna."

He dragged out the name slowly, a bit tauntingly it seemed to David. And David laughed. Might as well play his last card well, he thought.

"My name isn't McKenna," he said. "It's David Raine. He made a mistake, and he's so drunk I haven't been able to explain."

Without answering, Hauck backed out of the door. It was an invitation for David to follow. Again he carried his pack and gun with him through the darkness, and Hauck uttered not a word as they returned to the Nest. The night was brighter now, and David could see Baree close at his heels, following him as silently as a shadow. The dog slunk out of sight when they came to the building. They did not enter from the rear this time. Hauck led the way to a door that opened into the big room from which had come the sound of cursing and laughter a little before. There were ten or a dozen men in that room, all white men, and, upon entering, David was moved by a sudden suspicion that they were expecting him — that Hauck had prepared them for his appearance. There was no liquor in sight. If there had been bottles and glasses on the tables, they had been cleared away — but no one had thought to wipe away certain liquid stains that David saw shimmering wetly in the glow of the three big lamps hanging from the ceiling. He looked the men over quickly as he followed the free trader. Never, he thought, had he seen a rougher or more unpleasant-looking lot. He caught more than one eye filled with the glittering menace he had seen in Hauck's. Not a man nodded at him, or spoke to him. He passed close to one raw-boned individual, so close that he brushed against him, and there was an unconcealed and threatening animosity in this man's face as he glared up at him. By the time he had passed through the room his suspicion had become a conviction. Hauck had purposely put him on parade, and there was a deep and sinister significance in the attitude of these men.

They passed through the hall into which he and Marge had entered from the opposite side of the Nest, and Hauck paused at the door of a room almost opposite to the one which the girl had said belonged to her.

"This will be your room while you are our guest," he said. The glitter in his eyes softened as he nodded at David. He tried to speak a bit affably, but David felt that his effort was rather unsuccessful. It failed to cover the hard note in his voice and the curious twitch of his upper lip — a snarl almost — as he forced a smile. "Make yourself at home," he added. "We'll have breakfast in the morning with my niece." He paused for a moment and then said, looking keenly at David: "I suppose you tried hard to make Brokaw understand he had made a mistake, and that you wasn't McKenna? Brokaw is a good fellow when he isn't drunk."

David was glad that he turned away without waiting for an answer. He did not want to talk with Hauck tonight. He wanted to turn over in his mind what he had learned from Brokaw, and tomorrow act with the cool judgment which was more or less characteristic of him. He did not believe even now that there would be anything melodramatic in the outcome of the affair. There would be an unpleasantness, of course; but when both Hauck and Brokaw were confronted with a certain situation, and with the peculiarly significant facts which he now held in his possession, he could not see how they would be able to place any very great obstacle in the way of his determination to take Marge from the Nest. He did not think of personal harm to himself, and as he entered his room, where a lamp had been lighted for him, his mind had already begun to work on a plan of action. He would compromise with them. In return for the loss of the girl they should have his promise — his oath, if necessary — not to reveal the secret of the traffic in which they were engaged, or of that still more important affair between Hauck and the white man from

Fort MacPherson. He was certain that, in his drunkenness, Brokaw had spoken the truth, no matter what he might deny tomorrow. They would not hazard an investigation, though to lose the girl now, at the very threshold of his exultant realization, would be like taking the earth from under Brokaw's feet. In spite of the tenseness of the situation David found himself chuckling with satisfaction. It would be unpleasant — very — he repeated that assurance to himself; but that self-preservation would be the first law of these rascals he was equally positive, and he began thinking of other things that just now were of more thrilling import to him.

It was Tavish, then — that half mad hermit in his mice-infested cabin — who had been at the bottom of it all! Tavish! The discovery did not amaze him profoundly. He had never been able to dissociate Tavish from the picture, unreasoning though he confessed himself to be, and now that his mildly impossible conjectures had suddenly developed into facts, he was not excited. It was another thought — or other thoughts — that stirred him more deeply, and brought a heat into his blood. His mind leaped back to that scene of years ago, when Marge O'Doone's mother had run shrieking out in the storm of night to escape Tavish. *But she had not died!* That was the thought that burned in David's brain now. She had lived. She had searched for her husband — Michael O'Doone; a half mad wanderer of the forests at first, she may have been. She had searched for years. And she was still searching for him when he had met her that night on the Transcontinental! For it was she — Marge O'Doone, the mother, the wife, into whose dark, haunting eyes he had gazed from out the sunless depths of his own despair! *Her* mother. Alive. Seeking a Michael O'Doone — seeking — seeking. . . .

He was filled with a great desire to go at once to the Girl and tell her this wonderful new fact that had come into her life, and he found himself suddenly at the door of his room, with his fingers on the latch. Standing there, he shrugged his shoulders, laughing softly at himself as he realized how absurdly sensational he was becoming all at once. Tomorrow would be time. He filled and lighted his pipe, and in the whitish fumes of his tobacco he could picture quite easily the gray, dead face of Tavish, hanging at the end of his meat rack. Pacing restlessly back and forth across his room, he recalled the scenes of that night, and of days and nights that had followed. Brokaw had given him the key that was unlocking door after door. "Guess he was a little crazy," Brokaw had said, speaking of Tavish as he had last known him on the

Firepan. Crazy! Going mad! And at last he had killed himself. Was it possible that a man of Tavish's sort could be haunted for so long by spectres of the past? It seemed unreasonable. He thought of Father Roland and of the mysterious room in the Château, where he worshipped at the shrine of a woman and a child who were gone.

He clenched his hands, and stopped himself. What had leapt into his mind was as startling to his inner consciousness as the unexpected flash of magnesium in a dark room. It was unthinkable — impossible; and yet, following it, he found himself face to face with question after question which he made no effort to answer. He was dazed for a moment as if by the terrific impact of a thing which had neither weight nor form. Tavish, the woman, the girl — Father Roland! Absurd. He shook himself, literally shook himself, to get rid of that wildly impossible idea. He drove his mind back to the photograph of the girl — and the woman. How had she come into possession of the picture which Brokaw had taken? What had Nisikoos tried to say to Marge O'Doone in those last moments when she was dying — whispered words which the girl had not heard because she was crying, and her heart was breaking? Did Nisikoos know that the mother was alive? Had she sent the picture to her when she realized that the end of her own time was drawing near? There was something unreasonable in this too, but it was the only solution that came to him.

He was still pacing his room when the creaking of the door stopped him. It was opening slowly and steadily and apparently with extreme caution. In another moment Marge O'Doone stood inside. He had not seen her face so white before. Her eyes were big and glowing darkly — pools of quivering fear, of wild and imploring supplication. She ran to him, and clung to him with her hands at his shoulders, her face close to his.

"*Sakewawin* — dear *Sakewawin* — we must go; we must hurry — tonight!"

She was trembling, fairly shivering against him, with one hand touching his face now, and he put his arms about her gently.

"What is it, child?" he whispered, his heart choking suddenly. "What has happened?"

"We must run away! We must hurry!"

At the touch of his arms she had relaxed against his breast. The last of her courage seemed gone. She was limp, and terrified, and was looking up at him in such a strange way that he was filled with alarm.

"I didn't tell him anything," she whispered, as if afraid he

would not believe her. "I didn't tell him you weren't that man —
Mac — McKenna. He heard you and Brokaw go when you passed
my room. Then he went to the men. I followed — and listened. I
heard him telling them about you — that you were a spy — that
you belonged to the provincial police. . . ."

A sound in the hall interrupted her. She grew suddenly tense
in his arms, then slipped from them and ran noiselessly to the
door. There were shuffling steps outside, a thick voice growling
unintelligibly. The sounds passed. Marge O'Doone was whiter
still when she faced David.

"Hauck — and Brokaw!" She stood there, with her back to the
door. "We must hurry, *Sakewawin*. We must go — tonight!"

David looked at her. A spy? Police? Quite the first thing for
Hauck to suspect, of course. That law of self-preservation again —
the same law that would compel them to give up the girl to him
tomorrow. He found himself smiling at his frightened little companion, backed there against the door, white as death. His calm-
ness did not reassure her.

"He said — you were a spy," she repeated, as if he must understand what that meant. "They wanted to follow you to Brokaw's
cabin — and — and kill you!"

This was coming to the bottom of her fear with a vengeance. It
sent a mild sort of a shiver through him, and corroborated with
rather disturbing emphasis what he had seen in the men's faces as
he passed among them.

"And Hauck wouldn't let them? Was that it?" he asked.

She nodded, clutching a hand at her throat.

"He told them to do nothing until he saw Brokaw. He wanted
to be certain. And then. . . ."

His amazing and smiling composure seemed to choke back
the words on her lips.

"You must return to your room, Marge," he said quickly.
"Hauck has now seen Brokaw and there will be no trouble such as
you fear. I can promise you that. Tomorrow we will leave the Nest
openly — and with Hauck's and Brokaw's permission. But should
they find you here now — in my room — I am quite sure we
should have immediate trouble on our hands. I've a great deal to
tell you — much that will make you glad, but I half expect another
visit from Hauck, and you must hurry to your room."

He opened the door slightly, and listened.

"Good-night," he whispered, putting a hand for an instant to
her hair.

"Good night, *Sakewawin*."

She hesitated for just a moment at the doors and then, with the faintest sobbing breath, was gone. What wonderful eyes she had! How they had looked at him in that last moment! David's fingers were trembling a little as he locked his door. There was a small mirror on the table and he held it up to look at himself. He regarded his reflection with grim amusement. He was not beautiful. The scrub of blond beard on his face gave him rather an outlawish appearance. And the gray hair over his temples had grown quite conspicuous of late, quite conspicuous indeed. Heredity? Perhaps — but it was confoundedly remindful of the fact that he was thirty-eight!

He went to bed, after placing the table against the door, and his automatic under his pillow — absurd and unnecessary details of caution, he assured himself. And while Marge O'Doone sat awake close to the door of her room all night, with a little rifle that had belonged to Nisikoos across her lap, David slept soundly in the amazing confidence and philosophy of that perilous age — thirty-eight!

CHAPTER XXIII

A series of sounds that came to him at first like the booming of distant cannon roused David from his slumber. He awoke to find broad day in his room and a knocking at his door. He began to dress, calling out that he would open it in a moment, and was careful to place the automatic in his pocket before he lifted the table without a sound to its former position in the room. When he flung open the door he was surprised to find Brokaw standing there instead of Hauck. It was not the Brokaw of last night. A few hours had produced a remarkable change in the man. One would not have thought that he had been recently drunk. He was grinning and holding out one of his huge hands as he looked into David's face.

"Morning, Raine," he greeted affably. "Hauck sent me to wake you up for the fun. You've got just time to swallow your breakfast before we put on the big scrap — the scrap I told you about last night, when I was drunk. Head-over-heels drunk, wasn't I? Took you for a friend I knew. Funny. You don't look a dam' bit like him!"

David shook hands with him. In his first astonishment Brokaw's manner appeared to him to be quite sincere, and his voice to be filled with apology. This impression was gone before he had dropped his hand, and he knew why Hauck's partner had come. It was to get a good look at him — to make sure that he was not McKenna; and it was also with the strategic purpose of removing whatever suspicions David might have by an outward show of friendship. For this last bit of work Brokaw was crudely out of place. His eyes, like a bad dog's, could not conceal what lay behind them — hatred, a deep and intense desire to grip the throat of this man who had tricked him; and his grin was forced, with a subdued sort of malevolence about it. David smiled back.

"You *were* drunk," he said. "I had a deuce of a time trying to make you understand that I wasn't McKenna."

That amazing lie seemed for a moment to daze Brokaw. David realized the audacity of it, and knew that Brokaw would remember too well what had happened to believe him. Its effect was what he was after, and if he had had a doubt as to the motive of the other's visit that doubt disappeared almost as quickly as he had spoken. The grin went out of Brokaw's face, his jaws tightened, the red came nearer to the surface in the bloodshot eyes. As plainly as if he were giving voice to his thought he was saying: "You lie!" But he kept back the words, and as David noted carelessly the slow clenching and unclenching of his hands, he believed that Hauck was not very far away, and that it was his warning and the fact that he was possibly listening to them, that restrained Brokaw from betraying himself completely. As it was, the grin returned slowly into his face.

"Hauck says he's sorry he couldn't have breakfast with you," he said. "Couldn't wait any longer. The Indian's going to bring your breakfast here. You'd better hurry if you want to see the fun."

With this he turned and walked heavily toward the end of the hall. David glanced across at the door of Marge's room. It was closed. Then he looked at his watch. It was almost nine o'clock! He felt like swearing as he thought of what he had missed — that breakfast with Hauck and the Girl. He would undoubtedly have had an opportunity of seeing Hauck alone for a little while — a quarter of an hour would have been enough; or he could have settled the whole matter in Marge's presence. He wondered where she was now. In her room?

Approaching footsteps caused him to draw back deeper into his own and a moment later his promised breakfast appeared, carried on a big Company *keyakun*, by an old Indian woman — undoubtedly the woman that Marge had told him about. She placed the huge plate on his table and withdrew without either looking at him or uttering a sound. He ate hurriedly, and finished dressing himself after that. It was a quarter after nine when he went into the hall. In passing Marge's door he knocked. There came no response from within. He turned and passed through the big room in which he had seen so many unfriendly faces the night before. It was empty now. The stillness of the place began to fill him with uneasiness, and he hurried out into the day. A low tumult of sound was in the air, unintelligible and yet thrilling. A dozen steps brought him to the end of the building and he looked toward the cage. For a space after that he stood without moving, filled with a sudden, sickening horror as he realized his helplessness in this moment. If he had not overslept, if he had talked with Hauck, he might have prevented this monstrous thing that was happening — he might have demanded that Tara be a part of their bargain. It was too late now. An excited and yet strangely quiet crowd was gathered about the cage — a crowd so tense and motionless that he knew the battle was on. A low, growling roar came to him, and again he heard that tumult of human voices, like a great gasp rising spontaneously out of half a hundred throats, and in response to the sound he gave a sudden cry of rage. Tara was already battling for his life — Tara, that great, big-souled brute who had learned to follow his little mistress like a protecting dog, and who had accepted *him* as a friend — Tara, grown soft and lazy and unwarlike because of his voluntary slavery, had been offered to the sacrifice which Brokaw had told him was inevitable!

And the Girl! Where was she? He was unconscious of the fact that his hand was gripping hard at the automatic in his pocket. For a space his brain burned red, seething with a physical passion, a consuming anger which, in all his life, had never been roused so terrifically within him. He rushed forward and took his place in the thin circle of watching men. He did not look at their faces. He did not know whether he stood next to white men or Indians. He did not see the blaze in their eyes, the joyous trembling of their bodies, their silent, savage exultation in the spectacle.

He was looking at the cage.

It was 20 feet square — built of small trees almost a foot in diameter, with 18-inch spaces between — and out of it came a sickening, grinding smash of jaws. The two beasts were down, a ton of flesh and bone, in what seemed to him to be a death embrace. For a moment he could not tell which was Tara and which was Brokaw's grizzly. They separated in that same breath, gained their feet, and stood facing each other. They must have been fighting for some minutes. Tara's jaws were foaming with blood and out of the throat of Brokaw's bear there rolled a rumbling, snarling roar that was like the deep-chested bellow of an angry bull. With that roar they came together again, Tara waiting stolidly and with panting sides for the rush of his enemy. It was hard for David to see what was happening in that twisting contortion of huge bodies, but as they rolled heavily to one side he saw a great red splash of blood where they had lain. It looked as if some one had poured it there out of a pail.

Suddenly a hand fell on his shoulder. He looked round. Brokaw was leering at him.

"Great scrap, eh?"

There was a look in his red face that revealed the pitiless savagery of a cat. David's clenched hand was as hard as iron and his brain was filled with a wild desire to strike. He fought to hold himself in.

"Where is — the Girl?" he demanded.

Brokaw's face revealed his hatred now, the taunting triumph of his power over this man who was a spy. He bared his yellow teeth in an exultant grin.

"Tricked her," he snarled. "Tricked her — like you tricked me! Got the Indian woman to steal her clothes, an' she's up there in her room — alone — *an' naked*! An' she won't have any clothes until I say so, for she's mine — body and soul. . . ."

David's clenched hand shot out, and in his blow was not alone the cumulated force of all his years of training but also of the one great impulse he had ever had to kill. In that instant he wanted to strike a man dead — a red-visaged monster, a fiend; and his blow sent Brokaw's huge body reeling backward, his head twisted as if his neck had been broken. He had not time to see what happened after that blow. He did not see Brokaw fall. A piercing interruption — a scream that startled every drop of blood in his body — turned him toward the cage. Ten paces from him, standing at the inner edge of that circle of astounded and petrified men, was the Girl! At first he thought she was standing naked there — naked under the staring eyes of the fiends about him. Her white arms gleamed bare, her shoulders and breast were bare, her slim, satiny body was naked to the waist, about which she had drawn tightly — as if in a wild panic of haste — an old and ragged skirt! It was the Indian woman's skirt. He caught the glitter of beads on it, and for a moment he stared with the others, unable to move or cry out her name. And then a breath of wind flung back her hair and he saw her face the colour of marble. She was like a piece of glistening statuary, without a quiver of life that his eyes could see, without a movement, without a breath. Only her hair moved, stirred by the air, flooded by the sun, floating about her shoulders and down her bare back in a lucent cloud of red and gold fires — and out of this she was staring at the cage, stunned into that lifeless and unbreathing posture of horror by what she saw. David did not follow her eyes. He heard the growl and roar and clashing jaws of the fighting beasts; they were down again; one of the 6-inch trees that formed the bars of the cage snapped like a walking stick as their great bodies lurched against it; the earth shook, the very air seemed to tremble with the terrific force of the struggle — and only the Girl was looking at that struggle. Every eye was on her now, and David sprang suddenly forth from the circle of men, calling her name.

Ten paces separated them; half that distance lay between the Girl and the cage. With the swiftness of an arrow sprung from the bow she had leaped into life and crossed that space. In a tenth part of a second David would have been at her side. He was that tenth of a second too late. A gleaming shaft, she had passed between the bars and a tumult of horrified voices rose above the roar of battle as the girl sprang at the beasts with her naked hands.

Her voice came to David in a scream.

"Tara — Tara — Tara — — "

His brain reeled when he saw her down — down! — with her little fists pummelling at a great, shaggy head; and in him there was the sickening weakness of a drunken man as he squeezed through that 18-inch aperture and almost fell at her side. He did not know that he had drawn his automatic; he scarcely realized that as fast as his fingers could press the trigger he was firing shot after shot, with the muzzle of his pistol so close to the head of Tara's enemy that the reports of the weapon were deadened as if muffled under a thick blanket. It was a heavy weapon. A stream of lead burned its way into the grizzly's brain. There were eleven shots and he fired them all in that wild, blood-red frenzy; and when he stood up he had the girl close in his arms, her naked breast throbbing pantingly against him. The clasp of his hands against her warm flesh cleared his head, and while Tara was rending at the throat of his dying foe, David drew her swiftly out of the cage and flung about her the light jacket he had worn.

"Go to your room," he said. "Tara is safe. I will see that no harm comes to him now."

The cordon of men separated for them as he led her through. The crowd was so silent that they could hear Tara's low throat-growling. And then, breaking that silence in a savage cry, came Brokaw's voice.

"Stop!"

He faced them, huge, terrible, quivering with rage. A step behind him was Hauck, and there was no longer in his face an effort to conceal his murderous intentions. Close behind Hauck there gathered quickly his white-faced whisky-mongers like a pack of wolves waiting for a lead-cry. David expected that cry to come from Brokaw. The Girl expected it, and she clung to David's shoulders, her bloodless face turned to the danger.

It was Brokaw who gave the signal to the men.

"Clear out the cage!" he bellowed. "This damned spy has killed my bear and he's got to fight me! Do you understand? Clear out the cage!"

He thrust his head and bull shoulders forward until his foul, hot breath touched their faces, and his red neck was swollen like the neck of a cobra with the passion of his jealousy and hatred.

"And in that fight — I'm going to kill you!" he hissed.

It was Hauck who put his hands on the Girl.

"Go with him," whispered David, as her arms tightened about his shoulders. "You must go with him, Marge — if I am to have a chance!"

Her face was against him. She was talking, low, swiftly, for his ears alone — with Hauck already beginning to pull her away.

"I will go to the house. When you see me at that window, fall on your face. I have a rifle — I will shoot him dead — from the window. . . ."

Perhaps Hauck heard. David wondered as he caught the glitter in his eyes when he drew the Girl away. He heard the crash of the big gate to the cage, and Tara, ambled out and took his way slowly and limpingly toward the edge of the forest. When he saw the Girl again, he was standing in the centre of the cage, his feet in a pool of blood that smeared the ground. She was struggling with Hauck, struggling to break from him and get to the house. And now he knew that Hauck had heard, and that he would hold her there, and that her eyes would be on him while Brokaw was killing him. For he knew that Brokaw would fight to kill. It would not be a square fight. It would be murder — if the chance came Brokaw's way. The thought did not frighten him. He was growing strangely calm in these moments. He realized the advantage of being unencumbered, and he stripped off his shirt, and tightened his belt. And then Brokaw entered. The giant had stripped himself to the waist, and he stood for a moment looking at David, a monster with the lust of murder in his eyes. It was frightfully unequal — this combat. David felt it, he was blind if he did not see it, and yet he was still unafraid. A great silence fell. Cutting it like a knife came the Girl's voice:

"*Sakewawin — Sakewawin. . . .*"

A brutish growl rose out of Brokaw's chest. He had heard that cry, and it stung him like an asp.

"Tonight, she will be with me," he taunted David and lowered his head for battle.

CHAPTER XXIV

David no longer saw the horde of faces beyond the thick bars of the cage. His last glance, shot past the lowered head and hulking shoulders of his giant adversary, went to the Girl. He noticed that she had ceased her struggling and was looking toward him. After that his eyes never left Brokaw's face. Until now it had not seemed that Brokaw was so big and so powerful, and, sizing up his enemy in that moment before the first rush, he realized that his one hope was to keep him from using his enormous strength at close quarters. A clinch would be fatal. In Brokaw's arms he would be helpless; he was conscious of an unpleasant thrill as he thought how easy it would be for the other to break his back, or snap his neck, if he gave him the opportunity. Science! What would it avail him here, pitted against this mountain of flesh and bone that looked as though it might stand the beating of clubs without being conquered! His first blow returned his confidence, even if it had wavered slightly. Brokaw rushed. It was an easy attack to evade, and David's arm shot out and his fist landed against Brokaw's head with a sound that was like the crack of a whip. Hauck would have gone down under that blow like a log. Brokaw staggered. Even he realized that this was science — the skill of the game — and he was grinning as he advanced again. He could stand a hundred blows like that — a grim and ferocious Achilles with but one vulnerable point, the end of his jaw. David waited and watched for his opportunity as he gave ground slowly. Twice they circled about the blood-spattered arena, Brokaw following him with leisurely sureness, and yet delaying his attack as if in that steady retreat of his victim he saw torture too satisfying to put an end to at once. David measured his carelessness, the slow almost unguarded movement of his great body, his unpreparedness for a *coup de main* — and like a flash he launched himself forward with all the weight of his body behind his effort.

It missed the other's jaw by two inches, that catapeltic blow — striking him full in the mouth, breaking his yellow teeth and smashing his thick lips so that the blood sprang out in a spray over his hairy chest, and as his head rocked backward David followed with a swift left-hander, and a second time missed the jaw with his right — but drenched his clenched fist in blood. Out of Brokaw there came a cry that was like the low roar of a beast; a cry that was the most inhuman sound David had ever heard from a human throat, and in an instant he found himself battling not for victory, not for that opportunity he twice had missed, but for his life.

Against that rushing bulk, enraged almost to madness, the ingenuity of his training alone saved him from immediate extinction. How many times he struck in the 120 seconds following his blow to Brokaw's mouth he could never have told. He was red with Brokaw's blood. His face was warm with it. His hands were as if painted, so often did they reach with right and left to Brokaw's gory visage. It was like striking at a monstrous thing without the sense of hurt, a fiend that had no brain that blows could sicken, a body that was not a body but an enormity that had strangely taken human form. Brokaw had struck him once — only once — in those two minutes, but blows were not what he feared now. He was beating himself to pieces, literally beating himself to pieces as a ship might have hammered itself against a reef, and fighting with every breath to keep himself out of the fatal clinch. His efforts were costing him more than they were costing his antagonist. Twice he had reached his jaw, twice Brokaw's head had rocked back on his shoulders — and then he was there again, closing in on him, grinning, dripping red to the soles of his feet, unconquerable. Was there no fairness out there beyond the bars of the cage? Were they all like the man he was fighting — devils? An intermission — only half a minute. Enough to give him a chance. The slow, invincible beast he was hammering almost had him as his thoughts wandered. He only half fended the sledge-like blow that came straight for his face. He ducked, swung up his guard like lightning, and was saved from death by a miracle. That blow would have crushed in his face — killed him. He knew it. Brokaw's huge fist landed against the side of his head and grazed off like a bullet that had struck the slanting surface of a rock. Yet the force of it was sufficient to send him crashing against the bars — and *down*.

In that moment he thanked God for Brokaw's slowness. He had a clear recollection afterward of almost having spoken the words as he lay dazed and helpless for an infinitesimal space of time. He expected Brokaw to end it there. But Brokaw stood mopping the blood from his face, as if partly blinded by it, while from beyond the cage there came a swiftly growing rumble of voices. He heard a scream. It was the scream — the agonized cry — of the Girl, that brought him to his feet while Brokaw was still wiping the hot flow from his dripping jaw. It was that cry that cleared his brain, that called out to him in its despair that he *must* win, that all was lost for her as well as for himself if he was vanquished — for more positively than at any other time during the fight he felt now that defeat would mean death. It had come to him definitely in the savage outcry of joy when he was down. There was to be no mercy. He had read the ominous decree. And Brokaw. . . .

He was like a madman as he came toward him again. There was no longer the leer on his face. There was in his battered and swollen countenance but one emotion. Blood and hurt could not hide it. It blazed like fires in his half closed eyes. It was the desire to kill. The passion which quenches itself in the taking of life, and every fibre in David's brain rose to meet it. He knew that it was no longer a matter of blows on his part — it was like the David of old facing Goliath with his bare hands. Curiously the thought of Goliath came to him in these flashing moments. Here, too, there must be trickery, something unexpected, a deadly stratagem, and his brain must work out his salvation quickly. Another two or three minutes and it would be over one way or the other. He made his decision. The tricks of his own art were inadequate, but there was still one hope — one last chance. It was the so-called "knee-break" of the bush country, a horrible thing, he had thought, when Father Roland had taught it to him. "Break your opponent's knees," the Missioner had said, "and you've got him." He had never practised it. But he knew the method, and he remembered the Little Missioner's words — "when he's straight facing you, with all your weight, like a cannon ball!" And suddenly he shot himself out like that, as Brokaw was about to rush upon him — a hundred and sixty pounds of solid flesh and bone against the joints of Brokaw's knees!

The shock dazed him. There was a sharp pain in his left shoulder, and with that shock and pain he was conscious of a terrible cry as Brokaw crashed over him. He was on his feet when Brokaw was on his knees. Whether or not they were really broken he could not tell. With all the strength in his body he sent his right again and again to the bleeding jaw of his enemy. Brokaw reached up and caught him in his huge arms, but that jaw was there, unprotected, and David battered it as he might have battered a rock with a hammer. A gasping cry rose out of the giant's throat, his head sank backward — and through a red fury, through blood that spattered up into his face, David continued to strike until the arms relaxed about him, and with a choking gurgle of blood in his throat, Brokaw dropped back limply, as if dead.

And then David looked again beyond the bars. The staring faces had drawn nearer to the cage, bewildered, stupefied, disbelieving, like the faces of stone images. For a space it was so quiet that it seemed to him they must hear his panting breath and the choking gurgle that was still in Brokaw's throat. The victor! He flung back his shoulders and held up his head, though he had great desire to stagger against one of the bars and rest. He could see the Girl and Hauck — and now the girl was standing alone, looking at him. She had seen him! She had seen him beat that giant beast, and a great pride rose in his breast and spread in a joyous light over his bloody face. Suddenly he lifted his hand and waved it at her. In a flash she was coming to him. She would have broken her way through the cordon of men, but Hauck stopped her. He had seen Hauck talking swiftly to two of the white men. And now Hauck caught the girl and held her back. David knew that he was dripping red and he was glad that she came no nearer. Hauck was telling her to go to the house, and David nodded, and with a movement of his hand made her understand that she must obey. Not until he saw her going did he pick up his shirt and step out among the men. Three or four of the whites went to Brokaw. The rest stared at him still in that amazed silence as he passed among them. He nodded and smiled at them, as though beating Brokaw had not been such a terrible task after all. He noticed there was scarcely an expression in the faces of the Indians. And then he found himself face to face with Hauck, and a step or two behind Hauck were the two white men he had talked to so hurriedly. One of them was the man David had brushed against in passing through the big room. There was a grin in his face now. There was a grin in Hauck's face, and a grin in the face of the third man, and to David's astonishment Hauck thrust out his hand.

"Shake, Raine! I'd have bet a thousand to fifty you were loser, but there wasn't a dollar going your way. A great fight!"

He turned to the other two.

"Take Raine to his room, boys. Help 'im wash up. I've got to see to Brokaw — an' this crowd."

David protested. He was all right. He needed only water and soap, both of which were in his room, but Hauck insisted that it wasn't square, and wouldn't look right, if he didn't have friends as well as Brokaw. Brokaw had forced the affair so suddenly that none of them had had time or thought to speak an encouraging or friendly word before the fight. Langdon and Henry would go with him now. He walked between the two to the Nest, and entered his room with them. Langdon, the tall man who had looked hatred at him last night, poured water into a tin basin while Henry, the smaller man, closed his door. They appeared quite companionable, especially Langdon.

"Didn't like you last night," he confessed frankly. "Thought you was one of them damned police, running your nose into our business mebby."

He stood beside David, with the pail of water in his hand, and as David bent over the basin Henry was behind him. He had drawn something from his pocket, and was edging up close. As David dipped his hands in the water he looked up into Langdon's face, and he saw there a strange and unexpected change — that deadly malignity of last night. In that moment the object in Henry's hand fell with terrific force on his head and he crumpled down over the basin. He was conscious of a single agonizing pain, like a hot iron thrust suddenly through him, and then a great and engulfing pit of darkness closed about him.

CHAPTER XXV

In that chaotic night in which he was drifting, David experienced neither pain nor very much of the sense of life. And yet, without seeing or feeling, he seemed to be living. All was dead within him but that last consciousness, which is almost the spirit; he might have been dreaming, and minutes, hours, or even years might have passed in that dream. For a long time he seemed to be sinking through the blackness; and then something stopped him, without jar or shock, and he was rising. He could hear nothing at first. There was a vast silence about him, a silence as deep and unbroken as the abysmal pit in which he seemed to be floating. After that he felt himself swaying and rocking, as though tossed gently on the billows of a sea. This was the first thought that took shape in his struggling brain — he was at sea; he was on a ship in the heart of a black night, and he was alone. He tried to call out, but his tongue seemed gone. It seemed a long time before day broke, and then it was strange day. Little needles of light pricked his eyes; silver strings shot like flashes of wave-like lightning through the darkness, and he began to feel, and to hear. A dozen hands seemed holding him down until he could move neither arms nor feet. He heard voices. There appeared to be many of them at first, an unintelligible rumble of voices, and then very swiftly they became two.

He opened his eyes. The first thing that he observed was a bar of sunlight against the eastern wall of his room. That bit of sunlight was like a magnet thrown there to reassemble the faculties that had drifted away from him in the dark night of his unconsciousness. It tried to tell him, first of all, that it was afternoon — quite late in the afternoon. He would have sensed that fact in another moment or two, but something came between him and the radiance flung by the westward slant of the sun. It was a face, two faces — first Hauck's and then Brokaw's! Yes, Brokaw was there! Staring down at him. A fiend still. And almost unrecognizable. He was no longer stripped, and he was no longer bloody. His countenance was swollen; his lips were raw, one eye was closed — but the other gleamed like a devil's. David tried to sit up. He managed with an effort, and balanced himself on the edge of his cot. His head was dizzy, and he felt clumsy and helpless as a stuffed bag. His hands were tied behind him, and his feet were bound. He thought Hauck looked like an exultant gargoyle as he stood there with a horrible grin on his face, and Brokaw. . . .

It was Brokaw who bent over him, his thick fingers knotting, his open eyes fairly livid.

"I'm glad you ain't dead, Raine."

His voice was husky, muffled by the swollen thickness of his battered lips.

"Thanks," said David. The dizziness was leaving him, but there was a steady pain in his head. He tried to smile. "Thanks!" It was rather idiotic of him to say that. Brokaw's hands were moving slowly toward his throat when Hauck drew him back.

"I won't touch him — not now," he growled. "But tonight — oh, God!"

His knuckles snapped.

"You — liar! You — spy! You — sneak!" he cursed through his broken teeth. David saw where they *had* been — a cavity in that cruel, battered mouth. "And you think, after that. . . ."

Again Hauck tried to draw him away. Brokaw flung off his hands angrily.

"I won't touch him — but I'll *tell* him, Hauck! The devil take me body and soul if I don't! I want him to know. . . ."

"You're a fool!" cried Hauck. "Stop, or by Heaven! . . ."

Brokaw opened his mouth and laughed, and David saw the havoc of his blows.

"You'll do *what*, Hauck? Nothing — that's what you'll do! Ain't I told him you killed that *napo* from MacPherson? Ain't I told him enough to set us both swinging?" He bent over David until his breath struck his face. "I'm glad you didn't die, Raine," he repeated, "because I want to see you when you shuffle off. We're only waiting for the Indians to go. Old Wapi starts with his tribe at sunset. I'm sorry, but we can't get the heathen away any earlier because he says it's good luck to start a journey at sunset in the moulting moon. You'll start yours a little later — as soon as they're out of sound of a rifle shot. You can't trust Indians, eh? You made a hit with old Wapi, and it wouldn't do to let him know we're going to send you where you sent my bear. Eh — would it?"

"You mean — you're going to murder me?" said David

"If standing you up against a tree and putting a bullet through your heart is murder — yes," gloated Brokaw.

"Murder — " repeated David.

He seemed powerless to say more than that. An overwhelming dizziness was creeping over him, the pain was splitting his head, and he swayed backward. He fought to recover himself, to hold himself up, but that returning sickness reached from his brain to the pit of his stomach, and with a groan he sank face downward on the cot. Brokaw was still talking, but he could no longer understand his words. He heard Hauck's sharp voice, their retreating footsteps, the opening and closing of the door — fighting all the time to keep himself from falling off into that black and bottomless pit again. It was many minutes before he drew himself to a sitting posture on the edge of his cot, this time slowly and guardedly, so that he would not rouse the pain in his head. It was there. He could feel it burning steadily and deeply, like one of his old-time headaches.

The bar of sunlight was gone from the wall, and through the one small window in the west end of his room he saw the fading light of day outside. It was morning when he had fought Brokaw; it was now almost night. The wash-basin was where it had fallen when Henry struck him. He saw a red stain on the floor where he must have dropped. Then again he looked at the window. It was rather oddly out of place, so high up that one could not look in from the outside — a rectangular slit to let in light, and so narrow that a man could not have wormed his way through it. He had seen nothing particularly significant in its location last night, or this morning, but now its meaning struck him as forcibly as that of the pieces of *babiche* thong that bound his wrists and ankles. A guest might be housed in this room without suspicion and at the turn of a key be made a prisoner. There was no way of escape unless one broke down the heavy door or cut through the log walls.

Gradually he was overcoming his sensation of sickness. His head was clearing, and he began to breathe more deeply. He tried to move his cramped arms. They were without feeling, lifeless weights hung to his shoulders. With an effort he thrust out his feet. And then — through the window — there came to him a low, thrilling sound.

It was the muffled *boom, boom, boom* of a tom-tom.

Wapi and his Indians were going, and he heard now a weird and growing chant, a savage paean to the wild gods of the Moulting Moon. A gasp rose in his throat. It was almost a cry. His last hope was going — with Wapi and his tribe! Would they help him if they knew? If he shouted? If he shrieked for them through that open window? It was a mad thought, an impossible thought, but it set his heart throbbing for a moment. And then — suddenly — it seemed to stand still. A key rattled, turned; the door opened — and Marge O'Doone stood before him!

She was panting — sobbing, as if she had been running a long distance. She made no effort to speak, but dropped at his feet and began sawing at the caribou *babiche* with a knife. She had come prepared with that knife! He felt the bonds snap, and before either had spoken she was at his back, and his hands were free. They were like lead. She dropped the knife then, and her hands were at his face — dark with dry stain of blood, and over and over again she was calling him by the name she had given him — *Sakewawin*. And then the tribal chant of Wapi and his people grew nearer and louder as they passed into the forest, and with a choking cry the Girl drew back from David and stood facing him.

"I — must hurry," she said, swiftly. "Listen! They are going! Hauck or Brokaw will go as far as the lake with Wapi, and the one who does not go will return *here*. See, *Sakewawin* — I have brought you a knife! When he comes — you must kill him!"

The chanting voices had passed. The paean was dying away in the direction of the forest.

He did not interrupt her. With hand clutched at her breast she went on.

"I waited — until all were out there. They kept me in my room and left Marcee — the old Indian woman — to watch me. When they were all out to see Wapi off, I struck her over the head with the end of Nisikoos' rifle. Maybe she is dead. Tara is out there. I know where to find him when it is dark. I will make up a pack and within an hour we must go. If Hauck comes to your room before then, or Brokaw, kill him with the knife, *Sakewawin*! If you don't — they will kill you!"

Her voice broke in a gasp that was like a sob. He struggled to rise; stood swaying before her, his legs unsteady as stilts under him.

"My gun, Marge — my pistol!" he demanded, trying to reach out his arms. "If I had them now. . . ."

"They must have taken them," she interrupted. "But I have Nisikoos' rifle, *Sakewawin*! Oh — I must hurry! They won't come to my room, and Marcee is perhaps dead. As soon as it is dark I will unlock your door. And if one of them comes before then, you must kill him! You must! You must!"

She backed to the door, and now she opened it, and was gone. A key clicked in the lock again, he heard her swift footsteps in the hall, and a second door opened and closed.

For a few minutes he stood without moving, a little dazed by the suddenness with which she had left him. She had not been in his room more than a minute or two. She had been terribly frightened, terribly afraid of discovery before her work was done. On the floor at his feet lay the knife. *That* was why she had come, *that* was what she had brought him! His blood began to tingle. He could feel it resuming its course through his numbed legs and arms, and he leaned over slowly, half afraid that he would lose his balance, and picked up the weapon. The chanting of Wapi and his people was only a distant murmur; through the high window came the sound of returning voices — voices of white men.

There swept through him the wild thrill of the thought that once more the fight was up to him. Marge O'Doone had done her part. She had struck down the Indian woman Hauck had placed over her as a guard — had escaped from her room, unbound him, and put a knife into his hands. The rest was *his* fight. How long before Brokaw or Hauck would come? Would they give him time to get the blood running through his body again? Time to gain strength to use his freedom — and the knife? He began walking slowly across the room, pumping his arms up and down. His strength returned quickly. He went to the pail of water and drank deeply with a consuming thirst. The water refreshed him, and he paced back and forth more and more swiftly, until he was breathing steadily and he could harden his muscles and knot his fists. He looked at the knife. It was a horrible necessity — the burying of that steel in a man's back, or his heart! Was there no other way, he wondered? He began searching the room. Why hadn't Marge brought him a club instead of a knife, or at least a club along with the knife? To club a man down, even when he was intent on murder, wasn't like letting out his life in a gush of blood.

His eyes rested on the table, and in a moment he had turned it over and was wrenching at one of the wooden legs. It broke off with a sharp snap, and he held in his hand a weapon possessing many advantages over the knife. The latter he thrust into his belt with the handle just back of his hip. Then he waited.

It was not for long. The western mountains had shut out the last reflections of the sun. Gloom was beginning to fill his room, and he numbered the minutes as he stood, with his ear close to the door, listening for a step, hopeful that it would be the Girl's and not Hauck's or Brokaw's. At last the step came, advancing from the end of the hall. It was a heavy step, and he drew a deep breath and gripped the club. His heart gave a sudden, mighty throb as the step stopped at his door. It was not pleasant to think of what he was about to do, and yet he realized, as he heard the key in the lock, that it was a grim and terrible necessity. He was thankful there was only one. He would not strike too hard — not in this cowardly way — from ambush. Just enough to do the business sufficiently well. It would be easy — quite. He raised his club in the thickening dusk, and held his breath.

The door opened, and Hauck entered, and stood with his back to David. Horrible! Strike a man like that — and with a club! If he could use his hands, choke him, give him at least a quarter chance. But it had to be done. It was a sickening thing. Hauck went down without a groan — so silently, so lifelessly that David thought he had killed him. He knelt beside him for a few seconds and made sure that his heart was beating before he rose to his feet. He looked out into the hall. The lamps had not been lighted — probably that was one of the old Indian woman's duties. From the big room came a sound of voices — and then, close to him, from the door across the way, there came a small trembling voice:

"Hurry, *Sakewawin*! Lock the door — and come!"

For another instant he dropped on his knees at Hauck's side. Yes it was there — in his pocket — a revolver! He possessed himself of the weapon with an exclamation of joy, locked the door, and ran across the hall. The Girl opened her door for him, and closed it behind him as he sprang into her room. The first object he noticed was the Indian woman. She was lying on a cot, and her black eyes were levelled at them like the eyes of a snake. She was trussed up so securely, and was gagged so thoroughly that he could not restrain a laugh as he bent over her.

"Splendid!" he cried softly. "You're a little brick, Marge — you surely are! And now — what?"

With his revolver in his hand, and the Girl trembling under his arm, he felt a ridiculous desire to shout out at the top of his voice to his enemies letting them know that he was again ready to fight. In the gloom the Girl's eyes shone like stars.

"Who — was it?" she whispered.

"Hauck."

"Then it was Brokaw who went with Wapi. Langdon and Henry went with him. It is less than two miles to the lake, and they will be returning soon. We must hurry! Look — it is growing dark!"

She ran from his arms to the window and he followed her.

"In — fifteen minutes — we will go, Sakewawin. Tara is out there in the edge of the spruce." Her hand pinched his arm. "Did you — kill him?" she breathed.

"No. I broke off a leg from the table and stunned him."

"I'm glad," she said, and snuggled close to him shiveringly. "I'm glad, *Sakewawin*."

In the darkness that was gathering about them it was impossible for him not to take her in his arms. He held her close, bowing his head so that for an instant her warm face touched his own; and in those moments while they waited for the gloom to thicken he told her in a low voice what he had learned from Brokaw. She grew tense against him as he continued, and when he assured her he no longer had a doubt her mother was alive, and that she was the woman he had met on the coach, a cry rose out of her breast. She was about to speak when loud footsteps in the hall made her catch her breath, and her fingers clung more tightly at his shoulders.

"It is time," she whispered. "We must go!"

She ran from him quickly and from under the cot where the Indian lay dragged forth a pack. He could not see plainly what she was doing now. In a moment she had put a rifle in his hands.

"It belonged to Nisikoos," she said. "There are six shots in it, and here are all the cartridges I have."

He took them in his hand and counted them as he dropped them into his pocket. There were eleven in all, including the six in the chamber. "Thirty-twos," he thought, as he seized them up with his fingers. "Good for partridges — and short range at men!" He said, aloud: "If we could get my rifle, Marge. . . ."

"They have taken it," she told him again. "But we shall not need it. *Sakewawin*," she added, as if his voice had revealed to her the thought in his mind; "I know of a mountain that is all rock — not so far off as the one Tara and I climbed — and if we can reach that they will not be able to trail us. If they should find us. . . ."

She was opening the window.

"What then?" he asked.

"Nisikoos once killed a bear with that gun," she replied.

The window was open, and she was waiting. They thrust out their heads and listened, and when he had assured himself that all was clear he dropped out the pack. He lifted Marge down then and followed her. As his feet struck the ground the slight shock sent a pain through his head that wrung a low cry from him, and for a moment he leaned with his back against the wall, almost overcome again by the sickening dizziness. It was not so dark that the Girl did not see the sudden change in him. Her eyes filled with alarm.

"A little dizzy," he explained, trying to smile at her. "They gave me a pretty hard crack on the head, Marge. This air will set me right — soon."

He picked up the pack and followed her. In the edge of the spruce a hundred yards from the Nest, Tara had been lying all the afternoon, nursing his wounds.

"I could see him from my window," whispered Marge.

She went straight to him and began talking to him in a low

voice. Out of the darkness behind Tara came a growl.

"Baree, by thunder!" muttered David in amazement.

"He's made up with the bear, Marge! What do you think of that?"

At the sound of his voice Baree came to him and flattened himself at his feet. David laid a hand on his head.

"Boy!" he whispered softly. "And they said you were an outlaw, and would join the wolves. . . ."

He saw the dark bulk of Tara rising out of the gloom, and the Girl was at his side.

"We are ready, *Sakewawin.*"

He spoke to her the thought that had been shaping itself in his mind.

"Why wouldn't it be better to join Wapi and his Indians?" he asked, remembering Brokaw's words.

"Because — they are afraid of Hauck," she replied quickly. "There is but one way, *Sakewawin* — to follow a narrow trail Tara and I have made, close to the foot of the range, until we come to the rock mountain. Shall we risk the bundle on Tara's back?"

"It is light. I will carry it."

"Then give me your hand, *Sakewawin.*"

There was again in her voice the joyous thrill of freedom and of confidence; he could hear for a moment the wild throb of her heart in its exultation at their escape, and with her warm little hand she gripped his fingers firmly and guided him into a sea of darkness. The forest shut them in. Not a ray fell upon them from out of the pale sky where the stars were beginning to glimmer faintly. Behind them he could hear the heavy, padded footfall of the big grizzly, and he knew that Baree was very near. After a little the Girl said, still in a whisper:

"Does your head hurt you now, *Sakewawin?*"

"A bit."

The trail was widening. It was quite smooth for a space, but black.

She pressed his fingers.

"I believe all you have told me," she said, as if making a confession. "After you came to me in the cage — and the fight — I believed. You must have loved me a great deal to risk all that for me."

"Yes, a great deal, my child," he answered.

Why did that dizziness persist in his head, he wondered? For a moment he felt as if he were falling.

"A very great deal," he added, trying to walk steadily at her side, his own voice sounding unreal and at a great distance from him. "You see — my child — I didn't have anything to love but your picture. . . ."

What a fool he was to try and make himself heard above the roaring in his head! His words seemed to him whispers coming across a great space. And the bundle on his shoulders was like a crushing weight bearing him down! The voice at his side was growing fainter. It was saying things which afterward he could not remember, but he knew that it was talking about the woman he had said was her mother, and that he was answering it while weights of lead were dragging at his feet. Then suddenly, he had stepped over the edge of the world and was floating in that vast, black chaos again. The voice did not leave him. He could hear it sobbing, entreating him, urging him to do something which he could not understand; and when at last he did begin to comprehend it he knew also that he was no longer walking with weights at his feet and a burden on his shoulders, but was on the ground. His head was on her breast, and she was no longer speaking to him, but was crying like a child with a heart utterly broken. The deathly sickness was gone as quickly as it had stricken him, and he struggled upward, with her arms helping him.

"You are hurt — hurt — " he heard her moaning. "If I can only get you on Tara, *Sakewawin*, on Tara's back — there — a step. . . ." and he knew that was what she had been saying over and over again, urging him to help himself if he could, so that she could get him to Tara. He reached out his hand and buried it in the thick hair of the grizzly, and he tried to speak laughingly so that she would not know his fears.

"One is often dizzy — like that — after a blow," he said, "I guess — I can walk now."

"No, no, you must ride Tara," she insisted. "You are hurt — and you must ride Tara, *Sakewawin*. You must!"

She was lifting at his arms with all her strength, her breath hot and panting in his face, and Tara stood without moving a muscle of his giant body, as if he, too, were urging upon him in this dumb manner the necessity of obeying his mistress. Even then David would have remonstrated but he felt once more that appalling sickness creeping over him, and he raised himself slowly astride the grizzly's broad back. The Girl picked up the bundle and rifle and Tara followed her through the darkness. To David the beast's great back seemed a wonderfully safe and comfortable place, and he leaned forward with his fingers clutched deeply in the long hair of the ruff about the bear's bulking shoulders.

The Girl called back to him softly:

"You are all right, *Sakewawin?*"

"Yes, it is so comfortable that I feel I may fall asleep," he replied.

Out in the starlight she would have seen his drooping head, and his words would have had a different meaning for her. He was fighting with himself desperately, and in his heart was a great fear. He must be badly hurt, he thought. There came to him a distorted but vivid vision of an Indian hurt in the head, whom he and Father Roland had tried to save. Without a surgeon it had been impossible. The Indian had died, and he had had those same spells of sickness, the sickness that was creeping over him again in spite of his efforts to fight it off. He had no very clear notion of the movement of Tara's body under him, but he knew that he was holding on grimly, and that every little while the Girl called back to him, and he replied. Then came the time when he failed to answer, and for a space the rocking motion under him ceased and the Girl's voice was very near to him. Afterward motion resumed. It seemed to him that he was travelling a great distance. Altogether too far without a halt for sleep, or at least a rest. He was conscious of a desire to voice protest — and all the time his fingers were clasped in Tara'a mane in a sort of death grip.

In her breast Marge's heart was beating like a hunted thing, and over and over again she sobbed out a broken prayer as she guided Tara and his burden through the night. From the forest into the starlit open; from the open into the thick gloom of forest again — into and out of starlight and darkness, following that trail down the valley. She was no longer thinking of the rock mountain, for it would be impossible now to climb over the range into the other valley. She was heading for a cabin. An old and abandoned cabin, where they could hide. She tried to tell David about it, many days after they had begun that journey it seemed to him.

"Only a little longer, *Sakewawin,*" she cried, with her arm about him and her lips close to his bent head. "Only a little longer! They will not think to search for us there, and you can sleep — sleep. . . ."

Her voice drifted away from him like a low murmur in the tree tops — and his fingers still clung in that death-grip in the mane at Tara's neck.

And still many other days later they came to the cabin. It was amazing to him that the Girl should say:

"We are only five miles from the Nest, *Sakewawin,* but they will not hunt for us here. They will think we have gone farther —

or over the mountains!"

She was putting cold water to his face, and now that there was no longer the rolling motion under him he was not quite so dizzy. She had unrolled the bundle and had spread out a blanket, and when he stretched himself out on this a sense of vast relief came over him. In his confused consciousness two or three things stood out with rather odd clearness before he closed his eyes, and the last was a vision of the Girl's face bending over him, and of her starry eyes looking down at him, and of her voice urging him gently:

"Try to sleep, *Sakewawin* — try to sleep. . . ."

It was many hours later when he awoke. Hands seemed to be dragging him forcibly out of a place in which he was very comfortable, and which he did not want to leave, and a voice was accompanying the hands with an annoying insistency — a voice which was growing more and more familiar to him as his sleeping senses were roused. He opened his eyes. It was day, and Marge was on her knees at his side, tugging at his breast with her hands and staring wildly into his face.

"Wake, *Sakewawin* — wake, wake!" he heard her crying. "Oh, my God, you must wake! *Sakewawin* — *Sakewawin* — they have found our trail — and I can see them coming up the valley!"

CHAPTER XXVI

Scarcely had David sensed the Girl's words of warning than he was on his feet. And now, when he saw her, he thanked God that his head was clear, and that he could fight. Even yesterday, when she had stood before the fighting bears, and he had fought Brokaw, she had not been whiter than she was now. Her face told him of their danger before he had seen it with his own eyes. It told him that their peril was appallingly near and there was no chance of escaping it. He saw for the first time that his bed on the ground had been close to the wall of an old cabin which was in a little dip in the sloping face of the mountain. Before he could take in more, or discover a visible sign of their enemies, Marge had caught his hand and was drawing him to the end of the shack. She did not speak as she pointed downward. In the edge of the valley, just beginning the ascent, were eight or ten men. He could not determine their exact number for as he looked they were already disappearing under the face of the lower dip in the mountain. They were not more than four or five hundred yards away. It would take them a matter of twenty minutes to make the ascent to the cabin.

He looked at Marge. Despairingly she pointed to the mountain behind them. For a quarter of a mile it was a sheer wall of red sandstone. Their one way of flight lay downward, practically into the faces of their enemies.

"I was going to rouse you before it was light, *Sakewawin*," she explained in a voice that was dead with hopelessness. "I kept awake for hours, and then I fell asleep. Baree awakened me, and now — it is too late."

"Yes, too late to *run*!" said David.

A flash of fire leaped into her eyes.

"You mean. . . ."

"We can fight!" he cried. "Good God, Marge — if only I had my own rifle now!" He thrust a hand into his pocket and drew forth the cartridges she had given him. "Thirty-twos! And only eleven of them! It's got to be a short range for us. We can't put up a running fight for they'd keep out of range of this little pea-shooter and fill me as full of holes as a sieve!"

She was tugging at his arm.

"The cabin, *Sakewawin*!" she exclaimed with sudden inspiration. "It has a strong bar at the door, and the clay has fallen in places from between the logs leaving openings through which you can shoot!"

He was examining Nisikoos' rifle.

"At 150 yards it should be good for a man," he said. "You get Tara and the pack inside, Marge. I'm going to try to get two or three of our friends as they come up over the knoll down there. They won't be looking for bullets this early in the game and I'll have them at a disadvantage. If I'm lucky enough to get Hauck and Brokaw. . . ."

His eyes had selected a big rock twenty yards from the cabin from which he could overlook the slope to the first dip below them, and as Marge darted from him to get Tara into the cabin he crouched behind the boulder and waited. He figured that it was not more than 150 yards to the point where their pursuers would first appear, and he made up his mind that he would wait until they were nearer than that before he opened fire. Not one of those eleven precious cartridges must be wasted, for he could count on Hauck's revolver only at close quarters. It was no longer a time for doubt or indecision. Brokaw and Hauck were deliberately pushing the fight to a finish, and not to beat them meant death for himself and a fate for the Girl which made him grip his rifle more tightly as he waited. He looked behind him and saw Marge leading Tara into the cabin. Baree had crept up beside him and lay flat on the ground close to the rock. A moment or two later the Girl reappeared and ran across the narrow open space to David, and crouched down close to him.

"You must go into the cabin, Marge," he remonstrated. "They will probably begin shooting. . . ."

"I'm going to stay with you, *Sakewawin*."

Her face was no longer white. A flush had risen into her cheeks, her eyes shone as she looked at him — and she smiled. A child! His heart rose chokingly in his throat. Her face was close to his, and she whispered:

"Last night I kissed you, *Sakewawin*. I thought you were dying. Before you, I have kissed Nisikoos. Never any one else."

Why did she say that, with that wonderful glow in her eyes? Couldn't be that she saw death climbing up the mountain? Was it because she wanted him to know — before that? A child!

She whispered again:

"And you — have never kissed me, *Sakewawin*. Why?"

Slowly he drew her to him, until her head lay against his breast, her shining eyes and parted lips turned up to him, and he kissed her on the mouth. A wild flood of colour rushed into her face and her arms crept up about his shoulders. The glory of her radiant hair covered his breast. He buried his face in it, and for a moment crushed her so close that she did not breathe. And then again he kissed her mouth, not once but a dozen times, and then held her back from him and looked into her face that was no longer the face of a child, but of a woman.

"Because. . . ." he began, and stopped.

Baree was growling. David peered down the slope.

"They are coming!" he said. "Marge, you must creep back to the cabin!"

"I am going to stay with you, *Sakewawin*. See, I will flatten myself out like this — with Baree."

She snuggled herself down against the rock and again David peered from his ambush. Their pursuers were well over the crest of the dip, and he counted nine. They were advancing in a group and he saw that both Hauck and Brokaw were in the rear and that they were using staffs in their toil upward, and did not carry rifles. The remaining seven were armed, and were headed by Langdon, who was fifteen or twenty yards in advance of his companions. David made up his mind quickly to take Langdon first, and to follow up with others who carried rifles. Hauck and Brokaw, unarmed with guns, were least dangerous just at present. He would get Brokaw with his fifth shot — the sixth if he made a miss with the fifth.

A thin strip of shale marked his 100-yard dead-line, and the instant Langdon set his foot on this David fired. He was scarcely conscious of the yell of defiance that rang from his lips as Langdon whirled in his tracks and pitched down among the men behind him. He rose up boldly from behind the rock and fired again. In that huddled and astonished mass he could not miss. A shriek came up to him. He fired a third time, and he heard a joyous cry of triumph beside him as their enemies rushed for safety toward the dip from which they had just climbed. A fourth shot, and he picked out Brokaw. Twice he missed! His gun was empty when Brokaw lunged out of view. Langdon remained an inanimate blotch on the strip of shale. A few steps below him was a second body. A third man was dragging himself on hands and knees over the crest of the *coulée*. Three — with six shots! And he had missed Brokaw! Inwardly David groaned as he caught the Girl by the arm and hurried with her into the cabin, followed by Baree.

They were not a moment too soon. From over the edge of the *coulée* came a fusillade of shots from the heavy-calibre weapons of the mountain men that sent out sparks of fire from the rock.

As he thrust the remaining five cartridges into the chamber of Nisikoos' rifle, David looked about the cabin. In one of the farther corners the huge grizzly sat on his quarters as motionless as if stuffed. In the centre of the single room was an old box stove partly fallen to pieces. That was all. Marge had dropped the sapling bar across the door, and stood with her back against it. There was no window, and the closing of the door had shut out most of the light. He could see that she was breathing quickly, and the wonderful light that had come into her eyes behind the rock was still glowing at him in the half gloom. It gave him fresh confidence to see her standing like that, looking at him in that way, telling him without words that a thing had come into her life which had lifted her above fear. He went to her and took her in his arms again, and again he kissed her sweet mouth, and felt her heart beating against him, and the warm thrill of her arms clinging to him.

A splintering crash sent him reeling back into the centre of the cabin with Marge in his arms. The crash had come simultaneously with the report of a rifle, and both saw where the bullet had passed through the door six inches above David's head, carrying a splinter as large as his arm with it. He had not thought of the door. It was the cabin's vulnerable point, and he sprang out of line with it as a second bullet crashed through and buried itself in the log wall at their backs. Baree growled. A low rumble rose in Tara's throat, but he did not move.

In each of the four log walls were the open chinks which Marge had told him about, and he sprang to one of these apertures that was wide enough to let the barrel of his rifle through and looked in the direction from which the two shots had come. He was in time to catch a movement among the rocks on the side of the mountain about two hundred yards away, and a third shot tore its way through the door, glanced from the steel top of the stove, and struck like a club two feet over Tara's back. There were two men up there among the rocks, and their first shots were followed by a steady bombardment that fairly riddled the door. David could see their heads and shoulders and the gleam and faint puffs of their rifles, but he held his fire. Where were the other four, he wondered? Without doubt Hauck and Brokaw were now armed with the rifles of the men who had fallen, so he had six to deal with. Cautiously he thrust the muzzle of his rifle through the crack, and watched his chance, aiming a foot and a half above the spot where a pair of shoulders and a head would appear in a moment. His chance came, and he fired. The head and shoulders disappeared, and exultantly he swung his rifle a little to the right and sent another shot as the second man exposed himself. He, too, disappeared, and David's heart was thumping wildly in the thought that his bullets had reached their marks when both heads appeared again and a hail of lead spattered against the cabin. The men among the rocks were no longer aiming at the door, but at the spot from which he had fired, and a bullet ripped through so close that a splinter stung his face, and he felt the quick warm flow of blood down his cheek. When the Girl saw it her face went as white as death.

"I can't get them with this rifle, Marge," he groaned. "It's wild — wild as a hawk! Good God! . . ."

A crash of fire had come from behind the cabin, and another bullet, finding one of the gaping cracks, passed between them with a sound like the buzz of a monster bee. With a sudden cry he caught her in his arms and held her tight, as if in his embrace he would shield her.

"Is it possible — they would kill *you* to get me?"

He loosed his hold of her, sprang to the broken stove, and began dragging it out of the line of fire that came through the door. The Girl saw his peril and sprang to help him. He had no time to urge her back. In ten seconds he had the stove close to the wall, and almost forcibly he made her crouch down behind it.

"If you expose yourself for one second I swear to Heaven I'll stand up there against the door until I'm shot!" he threatened. "I will, so help me God!"

His brain was afire. He was no longer cool or self-possessed. He was blind with a wild rage, with a mad desire to reach in some way, with his vengeance, the human beasts who were bent on his death even if it was to be gained at the sacrifice of the Girl. He rushed to the side of the cabin from which the fresh attack had come, and glared through one of the embrasures between the logs. He was close to Tara, and he heard the low, steady thunder that came out of the grizzly's chest. His enemies were near on this side. Their fire came from the rocks not more than a hundred yards away, and all at once, in the heat of the great passion that possessed him now, he became suddenly aware that they knew the only weapon he possessed was Nisikoos' little rifle — and Hauck's revolver. Probably they knew also how limited his ammunition was. And they were exposing themselves. Why should he save his last three shots? When they were gone and he no longer answered their fire they would rush the cabin, beat in the door, and then — the revolver! With that he would tear out their hearts as they entered. He saw Hauck, fired and missed. A man stood up within seventy yards of the cabin a moment later, firing as fast as he could pump the lever of his gun, and David drove one of Nisikoos' partridge-killers straight into his chest. He fired a second time at

Hauck — another miss! Then he flung the useless rifle to the floor as he sprang back to Marge.

"Got one. Five left. Now — damn 'em — let then come!"

He drew Hauck's revolver. A bullet flew through one of the cracks, and they heard the soft thud of it as it struck Tara. The growl in the grizzly's throat burst forth in a roar of thunder. The terrible sound shook the cabin, but Tara still made no movement, except now to swing his head with open, drooling jaws. In response to that cry of animal rage and pain a snarl had come from Baree. He had slunk close to Tara.

"Didn't hurt him much," said David, with the fingers of his free hand crumpling the Girl's hair. "They'll stop shooting in a minute or two, and then. . . ."

Straight into his eyes from that farther wall a splinter hurled itself at him with a hissing sound like the plunge of hot iron into water. He had a lightning impression of seeing the bullet as it tore through the clay between two of the logs; he knew that he was struck, and yet he felt no pain. His mind was acutely alive, yet he could not speak. His words had been cut off, his tongue was powerless — it was like a shock that had paralyzed him. Even the Girl did not know for a moment or two that he was hit. The thud of his revolver on the floor filled her eyes with the first horror of understanding, and she sprang to his side as he swayed like a drunken man toward Tara. He sank down on the floor a few feet from the grizzly, and he heard the Girl moaning over him and calling him by name. The numbness left him, slowly he raised a hand to his chin, filled with a terrible fear. It was there — his jaw, hard, unsmashed, but wet with blood. He thought the bullet had struck him there.

"A knockout," were the first words, spoken slowly and thickly, but with a great gasp of relief. "A splinter hit me on the jaw. . . . I'm all right. . . ."

He sat up dizzily, with the Girl's arm about him. In the three or four minutes of forgetfulness neither had noticed that the firing had ceased. Now there came a tremendous blow at the door. It shook the cabin. A second blow, a third — and the decaying saplings were crashing inward! David struggled to rise, fell back, and pointed to the revolver.

"Quick — the revolver!"

Marge sprang to it. The door crashed inward as she picked it up, and scarcely had she faced about when their enemies were rushing in, with Henry and Hauck in their lead, and Brokaw just behind them. With a last effort David fought to gain his feet. He heard a single shot from the revolver, and then, as he rose stagger-ingly, he saw Marge fighting in Brokaw's arms. Hauck came for him, the demon of murder in his face, and as they went down he heard scream after scream come from the Girl's lips, and in that scream the agonizing call of "*Tara! Tara! Tara!*" Over him he heard a sudden roar, the rush of a great body — and with that thunder of Tara's rage and vengeance there mingled a hideous, wolfish snarl from Baree. He could see nothing. Hauck's hands were at his throat.

But the screams continued, and above them came now the cries of men — cries of horror, of agony, of death; and as Hauck's fingers loosened at his neck he heard with the snarling and roar-ing and tumult the crushing of great jaws and the thud of bodies. Hauck was rising, his face blanched with a strange terror. He was half up when a gaunt, lithe body shot at him like a stone flung from a catapult and Baree's inch-long fangs sank into his thick throat and tore his head half from his body in one savage, snarling snap of the jaws. David raised himself and through the horror of what he saw the Girl ran to him — unharmed — and clasped her arms about him, her lips sobbing all the time — "*Tara — Tara — Tara. . . .*" He turned her face to his breast, and held it there. It was ghastly. Henry was dead. Hauck was dead. And Brokaw was dead — a thousand times dead — with the grizzly tearing his huge body into pieces.

Through that pit of death David stumbled with the Girl. The fresh air struck their faces. The sun of day fell upon them. The green grass and the flowers of the mountain were under their feet. They looked down the slope, and saw, disappearing over the crest of the *coulée*, two men who were running for their lives.

CHAPTER XXVII

It may have been five minutes that David held the Girl in his arms, staring down into the sunlit valley into which the last two of Hauck's men had fled, and during that time he did not speak, and he heard only her steady sobbing. He drew into his lungs deep breaths of the invigorating air, and he felt himself growing stronger as the Girl's body became heavier in his embrace, and her arms relaxed and slipped down from his shoulders. He raised her face. There were no tears in her eyes, but she was still moaning a little, and her lips were quivering like a crying child's. He bent his head and kissed them, and she caught her breath pantingly as she looked at him with eyes which were limpid pools of blue out of which her terror was slowly dying away. She whispered his name. In her look and in that whisper there was unutterable adoration. It was for *him* she had been afraid. She was looking at him now as one saved to her from the dead, and for a moment he strained her still closer, and as he crushed his face to hers he felt the warm, sweet caress of her lips, and the thrilling pressure of her hands, at his blood-stained cheeks. A sound from behind made him turn his head, and fifty feet away he saw the big grizzly ambling cumbrously from the cabin. They could hear him growling as he stood in the sunshine, his head swinging slowly from side to side like a huge pendulum — in his throat the last echoing of that ferocious rage and hate that had destroyed their enemies. And in the same moment Baree stood in the doorway, his lips drawn back and his fangs gleaming, as if he expected other enemies to face him.

Quickly David led Marge beyond the boulder from behind which he had opened the fight, and drew her down with him into a soft carpet of grass, thick with the blue of wild violets, with the big rock shutting out the cabin from their vision.

"Rest here, little comrade," he said, his voice low and trembling with his worship of her, his hands stroking back her wonderful hair. "I must return to the cabin. Then — we will go."

"Go!"

She repeated the word in the strangest, softest whisper he had ever heard, as if in it all at once she saw the sun and stars, the day and night, of her whole life. She looked from his face down into the valley, and into his face again.

"We — will go," she repeated, as he rose to his feet.

She shivered when he left her, shuddered with a terrible little cry which she tried to choke back even as she visioned the first glow of that wonderful new life that was dawning for her. David knew why. He left her without looking down into her eyes again, anxious to have these last terrible minutes over. At the open door of the cabin he hesitated, a little sick at what he knew he would see. And yet, after all, it was no worse than it should be; it was justice. He told himself this as he stepped inside.

He tried not to look too closely, but the sight, after a moment, fascinated him. If it had not been for the difference in their size he could not have told which was Hauck and which was Brokaw, for even on Hauck, Tara had vented his rage after Baree had killed him. Neither bore very much the semblance of a man just now — it seemed incredible that claw and fang could have worked such destruction, and he went suddenly back to the door to see that the Girl was not following him. Then he looked again. Henry lay at his feet across the fallen saplings of the battered door, his head twisted completely under him — or gone. It was Henry's rifle he picked up. He searched for cartridges then. It was a sickening task. He found nearly fifty of them on the three, and went out with the pack and the rifle. He put the pack over his shoulders before he returned to the rock, and paused only for a moment, when he rejoined the Girl. With her hand in his he struck down into the valley.

"A great justice has overtaken them," he said, and that was all he told her about the cabin, and she asked him no questions.

At the edge of the green meadows they stopped where a trickle of water from the mountain tops had formed a deep pool. David followed this trickle a little up the *coulée* it had worn in the course of ages, found a sheltered spot, and stripped himself. To the waist he was covered with the stain and grime of battle. In the open pool Marge bathed her face and arms, and then sat down to finish her toilet with David's comb and brush. When he returned to her she was a radiant glory, hidden to her waist in the gold and brown fires of her disentangled hair. It was wonderful. He stood a step off and looked at her, his heart filled with a wonderful joy, his lips silent. The thought surged upon him now in an overmastering moment of exultation that she belonged to him, not for today, or tomorrow, but for all time; that the mountains had given her to him; that among the flowers and the wild things that "great, good God," of whom Father Roland had spoken so often, had created her for him; and that she had been waiting for him here, pure as the wild violets under his feet. She did not see him for a space, and he watched her as she ran out her glowing tresses under the strokes of his brush.

And once — ages ago it seemed to him now — he had thought

that another woman was beautiful, and that another woman's glory was her hair! He felt his heart singing. She had not been like this. No. Worlds separated those two — that woman and this God-crowned little mountain flower who had come into his heart like the breath of a new life, opening for him new visions that reached even beyond the blue skies. And he wondered that she should love him. She looked up suddenly and saw him standing there. Love? Had he in all his life dreamed of the look that was in her face now? It made his heart choke him. He held open his arms, silently, as she rose to her feet, and she came to him in all that burnished glory of her unbound hair; and he held her close in his arms, kissing her soft lips, her flushed cheeks, her blue eyes, the warm sweetness of her hair. And her lips kissed him. He looked out over the valley. His eyes were open to its beauty, but he did not see; a vision was rising before him, and his soul was breathing a prayer of gratitude to the Missioner's God, to the God of the totem-worshippers over the ranges, to the God of all things. It may be that the Girl sensed his voiceless exaltation, for up through the soft billows of her hair that lay crumpled on his breast she whispered:

"You love me a great deal, my *Sakewawin*?"

"More than life," he replied.

Her voice roused him. For a few moments he had forgotten the cabin, had forgotten that Brokaw and Hauck had existed, and that they were now dead. He held her back from him, looking into her face out of which all fear and horror had gone in its great happiness; a face filled with the joyous colour sent surging there by the wild beating of her heart, eyes confessing their adoration without shame, without concealment, without a droop of the long lashes behind which they might have hidden. It was wonderful, that love shining straight out of their blue, marvellous depths!

"We must go now," he said, forcing himself to break the spell. "Two have escaped, Marge. It is possible, if there are others at the Nest. . . ."

His words brought her back to the thing they had passed through. She glanced in a startled way over the valley, then shook her head.

"There are two others," she said. "But they will not follow us, *Sakewawin*. If they should, we shall be over the mountain."

She braided her hair as he adjusted his pack. His heart was like a boy's. He laughed at her in joyous disapproval.

"I like to see it — unbound," he said. "It is beautiful. Glorious."

It seemed to him that all the blood in her body leaped into her face at his words.

"Then — I will leave it that way," she cried softly, her words trembling with happiness and her fingers working swiftly in the silken plaits of her braid. Unconfined, her hair shimmered about her again. And then, as they were about to set off, she ran up to him with a little cry, and without touching him with her hands raised her face to his.

"Kiss me," she said. "Kiss me, my *Sakewawin!*"

*   *   *   *   *

It was noon when they stood under the topmost crags of the southward range, and under them they saw once more the green valley, with its silvery stream, in which they had met that first day beside the great rock. It seemed to them both a long time ago, and the valley was like a friend smiling up at them its welcome and its gladness that they had at last returned. Its drone of running waters, the whispering music of the air, and the piping cries of the marmots sunning themselves far below, came up to them faintly as they rested, and as the Girl sat in the circle of David's arm, with her head against his breast, she pointed off through the blue haze miles to the eastward.

"Are we going that way?" she asked.

He had been thinking as they had climbed up the mountain. Off there, where she was pointing, were his friends, and hers; between them and that wandering tribe of the totem people on the Kwadocha there were no human beings. Nothing but the unbroken peace of the mountains, in which they were safe. He had ceased to fear their immensity — was no longer disturbed by the thought that in their vast and trackless solitude he might lose himself forever. After what had passed, their gleaming peaks were beckoning to him, and he was confident that he could find his way back to the Finley and down to Hudson's Hope. What a surprise it would be to Father Roland when they dropped in on him some day, he and Marge! His heart beat excitedly as he told her about it, described the great distance they must travel, and what a wonderful journey it would be, with that glorious country at the end of it. . . . "We'll find your mother, then," he whispered. They talked a great deal about her mother and Father Roland as they made their way down into the valley, and whenever they stopped to rest she had new questions to ask, and each time there was that trembling doubt in her voice. "I wonder whether it's *true*." And each time he assured her that it was.

"I have been thinking that it was Nisikoos who sent to her that picture you wanted to destroy," he said once. "Nisikoos must have known."

"Then why didn't she tell me?" she flashed.

"Because, it may be that she didn't want to lose you — and that she didn't send the picture until she knew that she was not going to live very long."

The girl's eyes darkened, and then — slowly — there came back the softer glow into them.

"I loved — Nisikoos," she said.

It was sunset when they began making their first camp in a cedar thicket, where David shot a porcupine for Tara and Baree. After their supper they sat for a while in the glow of the stars, and after that Marge snuggled down in her cedar bed and went to sleep. But before she closed her eyes she put her arms about his neck and kissed him good-night. For a long time after that he sat awake, thinking of the wonderful dream he had dreamed all his life, and which at last had come true.

*   *   *   *   *

Day after day they travelled steadily into the east and south. The mountains swallowed them, and their feet trod the grass of many strange valleys. Strange — and yet now and then David saw something he had seen once before, and he knew that he had not lost the trail. They travelled slowly, for there was no longer need of haste; and in that land of plenty there was more of pleasure than inconvenience in their foraging for what they ate. In her haste in making up the contents of the pack Marge had seized what first came to her hands in the way of provisions, and fortunately the main part of their stock was a 20-pound sack of oatmeal. Of this they made bannock and cakes. The country was full of game. In the valleys the black currants and wild raspberries were ripening lusciously, and now and then in the pools of the lower valleys David would shoot fish. Both Tara and Baree began to grow fat, and with quiet joy David noticed that each day added to the wonderful beauty and happiness in the Girl's face, and it seemed to him that her love was enveloping him more and more, and there never was a moment now that he could not see the glow of it in her eyes. It thrilled him that she did not want him out of her presence for more than a few minutes at a time. He loved to fondle her hair, and she had a sweet habit of running her fingers through his own, and telling him each time how she loved it because it was a little gray; and she had a still sweeter way of holding one of his hands in hers when she was sitting beside him, and pressing it now and then to her soft lips.

They had been ten days in the mountains when, one evening, sitting beside him in this way, she said, with that adorable and almost childish ingenuousness which he loved in her:

"It will be nice to have Father Roland marry us, *Sakewawin!*" And before he could answer, she added: "I will keep house for you two at the Château."

He had been thinking a great deal about it.

"But if your mother should live down there — among the cities?" he asked.

She shivered a little, and nestled to him.

"I wouldn't like it, *Sakewawin* — not for long. I love *this* — the forest, the mountains, the skies." And then, suddenly she caught herself, and added quickly: "But anywhere — *anywhere* — if you are there, *Sakewawin!*"

"I too, love the forests, the mountains, and the skies," he whispered. "We will have them with us always, little comrade."

It was the fourteenth day when they descended the eastern slopes of the Divide, and he knew that they were not far from the Kwadocha and the Finley. Their fifteenth night they camped where he and the Butterfly's lover had built a noonday fire; and this night, though it was warm and glorious with a full moon, the Girl was possessed of a desire to have a fire of their own, and she helped to add fuel to it until the flames leaped high up into the shadows of the spruce, and drove them far back with its heat. David was content to sit and smoke his pipe while he watched her flit here and there after still more fuel, now a shadow in the darkness, and then again in the full fireglow. After a time she grew tired and nestled down beside him, spreading her hair over his breast and about his face in the way she knew he loved, and for an hour after that they talked in whispering voices that trembled with their happiness. When at last she went to bed, and fell asleep, he walked a little way out into the clear moonlight and sat down to smoke and listen to the murmur of the valley, his heart too full for sleep. Suddenly he was startled by a voice.

"David!"

He sprang up. From the shadow of a dwarf spruce half a dozen paces from him had stepped the figure of a man. He stood with bared head, the light of the moon streaming down upon him, and out of David's breast rose a strange cry, as if it were a spirit he saw, and not a man.

"David!"

"My God — Father Roland!"

They sprang across the little space between them, and their

hands clasped. David could not speak. Before he found his voice, the Missioner was saying:

"I saw the fire, David, and I stole up quietly to see who it was. We are camped down there not more than a quarter of a mile. Come! I want you to see. . . ."

He stopped. He was excited. And to David his face seemed many years younger there in the moonlight, and he walked with the spring of youth as he caught his arm and started down the valley. A strange force held David silent, an indefinable feeling that something tremendous and unexpected was impending. He heard the other's quick breath, caught the glow in his eyes, and his heart was thrilled. They walked so swiftly that it seemed to him only a few moments when they came to a little clump of low trees, and into these Father Roland led David by the hand, treading lightly now.

In another moment they stood beside someone who was sleeping. Father Roland pointed down, and spoke no word.

It was a woman. The moonlight fell upon her, and shimmered in the thick masses of dark hair that streamed about her, concealing her face. David choked. It was his heart in his throat. He bent down. Gently he lifted the heavy tresses, and stared into the sleeping face that was under them — the face of the woman he had met that night on the Transcontinental!

Over him he heard a gentle whisper.

"My wife, David!"

He staggered back, and clutched Father Roland by the shoulders, and his voice was almost sobbing in its excitement as he cried, whisperingly:

"Then you — you are Michael O'Doone — the father of Marge — and Tavish — Tavish. . . ."

His voice broke. The Missioner's face had gone white. They went back into the moonlight again, so that they should not awaken the woman.

*   *   *   *   *

Out there, so close that they seemed to be in each other's arms, the stories were told, David's first — briefly, swiftly; and when Michael O'Doone learned that his daughter was in David's camp, he bowed his face in his hands and David heard him giving thanks to his God. And then he, also, told what had happened — briefly, too, for the minutes of this night were too precious to lose. In his madness Tavish had believed that his punishment was near — believed that the chance which had taken him so near to the home of the man whose life he had destroyed was his last great warning, and before killing himself he had written out fully his confession for Michael O'Doone, and had sworn to the innocence of the woman whom he had stolen away.

"And even as he was destroying himself, God's hand was guiding my Margaret to me," explained the Missioner. "All those years she had been seeking for me, and at last she learned at Nelson House about Father Roland, whose real name no man knew. And at almost that same time, at Le Pas, there came to her the photograph you found on the train, with a letter saying our little girl was alive at this place you call the Nest. Hauck's wife sent the letter and picture to the Royal Northwest Mounted Police, and it was sent from inspector to inspector, until it found her at Le Pas. She came to the Château. We were gone — with you. She followed, and we met as Metoosin and I were returning. We did not go back to the Château. We turned about and followed your trail, to seek our daughter. And now. . . ."

Out of the shadow of the trees there broke upon them suddenly the anxious voice of the woman.

"Napao! where are you?"

"Dear God, it is the old, sweet name she called me so many years ago," whispered Michael O'Doone. "She is awake. Come!"

David held him back a moment.

"I will go to Marge," he said quickly. "I will wake her. And you — bring her mother. Understand, dear Father? Bring her up there, where Marge is sleeping. . . ."

The voice came again:

"*Napao — Napao!*"

"I am coming; I am coming!" cried the Missioner.

He turned to David.

"Yes — I will bring her — up there — to your camp."

And as David hurried away, he heard the sweet voice saying:

"You must not leave me alone, *Napao* — never, never, never, so long as we live. . . ."

    *   *   *   *   *

On his knees, beside the Girl, David waited many minutes while he gained his breath. With his two hands he crumpled her hair; and then, after a little, he kissed her mouth, and then her eyes; and she moved, and he caught the sleepy whisper of his name.

"Wake," he cried softly. "Wake, little comrade!"

Her arms rose up out of her dream of him and encircled his neck.

"*Sakewawin*," she murmured. "Is it morning?"

He gathered her in his arms.

"Yes, a glorious day, little comrade. Wake!"

THE END

www.ingramcontent.com/pod-product-compliance
Lightning Source LLC
Chambersburg PA
CBHW030524020726
47494CB00004B/1219